INSANE JANE

A novel by John Garavaglia

Adapted from the graphic novel series created by
Darren G. Davis and written by Zachary Hunchar

Paperback: ISBN 978-1-912700-48-6
eBook: ISBN 978-1-912700-49-3

Book design by: Ian Sharman
Cover by: Hal Laren

www.markosia.com

First Edition

*Dreams save us. Dreams lift us up and transform us.
And on my soul, I swear until my dream of a world where
dignity, honor and justice becomes the reality we all share.
I'll never stop fighting. Ever.*

—Superman, *Action Comics #775* (2001)

ALSO BY JOHN GARAVAGLIA
AND PUBLISHED BY
MARKOSIA

DORIAN GRAY

SINBAD: ROGUE OF MARS

ALSO PUBLISHED BY
MARKOSIA

THE THRONE ETERNAL

ZAK RAVEN: CODE ALPHA

SWANSONG

WORDS ON A WALL

STORIES FROM THE CHICKEN SHED HOUSE

PROLOGUE

It was just another ordinary day for Jane Travers. She was on her way to work at the Beauty Today salon, where she had a ton of clients lined up at her chair. She was definitely looking forward to her lunch date with Pete Young, the handsome clerk who worked in the pet shop next to the salon. Nothing could ruin her day.

The world began to slow around her in a sensation that she knew all too well.

Her Calamity Sense was trying to warn her of something. Imminent danger, but from where?

And suddenly her vision felt as if it was everywhere at once, taking in people and objects all around and bounding off them with supernatural certainly, one by one, determining that his one posed no threat, that one posed any threat.

Jane jerked her head around, heard gasps of fright and astonishment from the people around them.

"What the...?" She stared, her mouth hanging open. From the steps of the bank across the street, a single figure had suddenly emerged—not the sort of person one normally saw on the streets of this fair city every day. There were some crazies here, but this one looked like he must have escaped from the nuthouse, or maybe a costume party.

He cursed at the SWAT team that was now pounding down the steps behind him in full riot gear. Whatever had happened in the bank, the man with the green cape had earned the sincere displeasure of law enforcement.

As the SWAT team members shouted warnings, they finally opened fire.

The costumed man suddenly jumped from the steps as if he meant to sprout wings and fly—it would hardly have been a surprise, considering what he'd done so far—but he did not fly. Instead, he sailed clear across the street, landing neatly in a crouch on the sidewalk, not far in front of Jane. The people in the nearest vicinity prompting scattered, though more surged up behind the cab, eager to catch sight of the commotion's source.

Jane recognized the man as the Exploding Ghost. A super-villain thought dead after his battle with the heroine the Avenging Star. His powers overloaded and caused an explosion at an abandoned warehouse on Canal Street. So it appeared that the rumors of his demise were greatly exaggerated. He'd probably used whatever energy he had to reconstitute himself, and had been keeping a low profile until now.

Most of the SWAT team ran across the street slowing up as they approached him, a handful of street cops now frantically setting up partitions to herd people away from the scene, and the man shot out some green, radiating energy from his palm. His hand erupted in a flash of neon green, so bright and searing that it irradiated the officer. Jane was nearly flash blinded. And she caught a quick impression of the officer being literally turned into an X-ray image of himself. Then Jane could no longer see him (or whatever was left of him), for the crowd was pressing around him. A beat later, she saw Dynamite Diana leap atop the shoulders of another officer, her knees flanking his head, and as she gave an abrupt twist, he, too, collapsed to the ground where Jane could no longer see what was happening.

Jane had somehow already stripped to her blue and white costume, and was just now placing her cowl over her head. "Time to go to work."

She took a flying leap toward the action, and suddenly, the crowd's attention was diverted away from the business with the SWAT team and the villains focused solely on Jane.

"Look!" Shrieked a little girl who stood nearby with her parents. She was blonde with her hair in two soft pigtails. "It's *The Avenging Star*!" The girl pointed eagerly up to another fire escape where the superhero was now perched, unwrapping a grappling hook from her side.

The crowd erupted into cheers and hollers of approval, though where it was because they recognized her from the news footage where she foiled that bombing at City Hall and brought Troublemakers, Incorporated to justice

The grappling hook struck out and neatly wrapped itself around the ankles of the Exploding Ghost, who began howling and clawing like a caged animal. The Avenging Star jerked the cable, hard, stringing the flaying psychopath upside down from the bottom rung of the fire escape. The Exploding Ghost contorted his body, bending at the waist so he could reach for the Avenging Star, slashing with glowing green hands. She drew back, still holding the grappling cable taut like a thick calf-roper, wiping blood from her cheek in a sudden, lightning-quick movement, she hauled off and socked Exploding Ghost right in the face, silencing his obscenities.

"Avenging Star!" The crowd was yelling, the people having picked up on what the little blonde girl had said. The same girl was still cheering for her hero, jumping up and down and clapping, pink ribbons bobbing in her hair.

"Hooray for the Avenging Star!" The crowd screamed, the shouts excited and many-voiced, "Go, Avenging Star!"

The Avenging Star stretched her lips into a crazed grin. Blood streamed out of her mouth like a grisly waterfall. "You're going to have to try harder than that, you fiend," she taunted, waving him over. "And here I thought the Exploding Ghost was the most lethal member of Team Boom-Boom."

The Exploding Ghost snarled at her, raising his fists in the air. "You'll beg for my mercy once you're bombarded with the concussive force of 28 Hiroshimas!"

The Avenging Star snorted, trying to keep a straight face. "Mister…you can't even blow up a balloon."

Like a lioness on the hunt, the Avenging Star pounced toward the over the overzealous super-villain and delivered a devastating haymaker in the face. Exploding Ghost didn't only see the super heroine's giant star on her uniform, but several others twinkling all around him. He doubled over and landed on the floor with a thud loud and hard enough to shake the room.

Out like a light.

The Avenging Star stood over her fallen enemy, triumphant. She was quite pleased with her work. But her smirk was replaced with a grimace. She inspected her fist and groaned.

"I think I chipped a nail." Then she turned her attention back to the unconscious body of the Exploding Ghost. "Maybe you'll stay dead this time, Ghost!"

Dynamite Diana didn't even stand a chance against the Avenging Star. She went down after a swift kick across the chin of the heroine's steel-toed boot. Diana could feel her teeth shattering upon impact. The Avenging Star just made her foe's dentist a very rich man.

"You need some churchin', Dynamite Diana," the Avenging Star quipped. "This is the only sole you've got!"

Man, I should start writing these down!

Diana spat out a red mist of blood, followed by a hailstorm of broken teeth. Each of them clattered onto the ground, scattering about like candy being thrown at a parade. She slovenly engaged into a defensive fighting stance. Before she could even raise her fists, the Avenging Star surprised her with a sucker-punch. She felt the sweet crack of bone on bone. Dynamite Diana found herself drifting amongst the stars and being sucked into a black hole.

"I see some rehab in your future," the Avenging Star said to her knocked-out adversary. "You're looking a little…punch-drunk."

Then she frowned.

"Are you even listening to me?" She asked, feeling annoyed by the villain's silent treatment. "I'm giving you gold and you're just being rude."

"Actually puns are just lazy writing, Avenging Star," said a voice behind her. She turned around to discover it was the Dictator—the leader of Team Boom-Boom. His eyes turned into a yellowish hue and grew brighter with radioactive energy. "Your continued meddling in our affairs impedes my ascendance to malignant ruler of the world."

"Whoa, slow down, Dictator," said the Avenging Star. "You're confusing Ghost."

The Exploding Ghost groggily woke up from his stupor. He noticed the police had already placed an inhibitor collar around his neck. He won't be able to use his powers to escape. He was so dazed he couldn't understand what his boss and the Avenging Star were saying.

"What?" He groaned before drifting back into unconsciousness.

The Avenging Star threw up her arms. "See?"

In a flash, the Avenging Star used all of her strength to pick up an U.S. Mailbox, and hurled it at the criminal mastermind. "Mail's arrived, Dictator! You've been thrown out of office."

The Dictator's eyes shot out a pair of beams that didn't only sever the mailbox in half, but also incinerated its contents. Numerous letters went up in flames. The steel of the mailbox became warped and started to melt into grey metallic goop.

"When will you learn that your behaviour is only appropriate in one place…a mental hospital?"

The Dictator threw a punch across her face. The Avenging Star quickly ducked and swept the villain's legs to send him falling down to the concrete. Pounding his fist in anger against the street, his eyes flashed green. He was going to shoot a hole through her forehead.

She anticipated this attack. The Avenging Star reached into her utility belt and pulled out a handheld mirror. She shoved it in front of her where the Dictator's eyebeams bounced off the reflected surface and ricocheted back to their owner. The Dictator felt the excruciating pain of his own lasers penetrating his brain tissue.

The Avenging Star produced a long steel cable and began to tie the villain up. He tried to swat her away. He lunged forward and opened his eyes.

His face was twisted in terror.

"My powers…" he gasped, "they're gone. My powers are gone!"

The Avenging Star smirked. "I knew you were going to try to fry me with your nuclear vision. So I came up with a plan to incapacitate the part of your brain where you housed your powers. It was my last resort."

"Curse you, Avenging Star!" The Dictator exclaimed, feeling his bonds tightening. "CURSE YOU!"

The Avenging Star delivered her neatly wrapped "package" to the waiting arms of the cops. A tall, thin-faced officer slapped a pair of cuffs on the unconscious Dynamite Diana while the Avenging Star unwrapped the cable from her ankles. She took another flying leap and disappeared into the crowd before the cops could so much as say, "Thank you."

* * *

"You have such a great imagination, Jane," Dr. Hammerschimdt said, smiling.

Jane sat across from her in her office. She wasn't out on the street anymore. She wasn't in her Avenging Star uniform. She was wearing a blue shirt with a pair of matching pants and white slippers. It was the standard uniform for the mental hospital's patients.

"No imagination really needed, Dr. Hammerschimdt," Jane chuckled. "That actually happened. Team Boom-Boom is all locked up in the super-villain prison famously known as The Pit. The citizens of this fair city can sleep soundly tonight."

Her friend laughed softly. "All in a day's work for the Avenging Star." Then her smile went into a dismal demeanor. "And what about the other villain, the Shadowy Man?"

Jane frowned and lowered her head. "He's the worst," there was pain in her voice. "He's the ultimate enemy."

Hammerschmidt knew this was going to happen. But she came prepared. "Oh, I have something for you," she said to Jane, handing her a fancy gift bag.

Jane smiled. "Aw," she said, taking the bag. "It's not even my birthday."

"I got this for you just because," the doctor replied. "Go ahead. Open it."

Jane opened the bag and spread the pastel tissue paper apart. Her face lit up when she peered to the bottom of the bag and pulled out its hidden contents.

There was a pack of 11x17 Bristol board, with a set of art pencils, Micron pens, and rulers. "What is all this?"

"Director Pavlich would like to understand you better," Hammerschmidt replied. "He's more of a visual person. And I think it would be fun if you write and draw your adventures. I've seen your drawings and they all look awesome. And since you love comics so much, I think it would make an interesting graphic novel."

Jane was going through all the art supplies in the gift bag. She marveled at the very sight of them. "The paper is from Blue Line Art. That's the stuff the pros use! There's also a T-square, French curves, and—Copic markers? No, no. This is too much." Jane sent the bag back to Hammerschmidt, but she refused.

"No, no, no. They are all yours. I'm looking forward on seeing what you can come up with."

To all who read this, these words are the truth. And it is the truth that shall free us. Once, long ago, I was like you.

Mortal. Weak. Useless.

But in time, things changed in my life. Bad things happened. As the proverb says, it didn't kill me. Therefore, it made me stronger. It made me a hero.

Forget what you think you know about superheroes. Because this is the real world, and in the real world there is no such thing as "mutant healing" or "spider-sense" to keep someone alive. In the real world, there's just a woman in a mask.

And that woman is I, Jane Travers.

I know I'm not much to look at, but I'd like to think of myself as a butterfly and I was at my caterpillar stage. Through the love and loss and hardships I faced during that dark time shaped me into the hero you are reading about right now.

I'm writing this as a declaration of intent so no one would be confused. You may have heard about me on TV or might have read about what I've done in the papers. There is more to the story than anybody realizes. And if I should fall in the line of duty, let this be my confession.

It has been an honor to serve.

--*Jane Travers*
The Avenging Star

BEFORE

CHAPTER ONE

There was no better place in the city to get primped and pampered than Beautiful You. That's where Jane Travers worked and where she'd spent a majority of her time when she was growing up.

The beauty shop was always buzzing with cackling women, many of who shared their most intimate secrets with their hairdressers as they cut and styled their hair. Stacy was a master at permanent and finger waves, but she was superior at keeping secrets (especially her own).

The shop's proprietor was Debra Reynolds, a young woman in her late twenties with dark curly hair. She was nice when she felt like it. And she was tough when she had to be.

The beauty shop had four orange Formica shampoo stations—complete with mirrors, porcelain sinks, and black vinyl chairs that swiveled back and forth, and also went up and down. As a child, Jane loved to climb in one of those chairs when everyone wasn't looking and spin as fast as she could until she got dizzy.

Posters of stylish women sporting the latest hairdos hung on the yellow stucco walls. Kendrick Lamar, Cardi B, and Camila Cabello played on Spotify in the background. The competing scent of permanent wave lotion and hairspray wafted throughout the salon.

The sunroom, which was also known as the dryer room, was located on the east end of the beauty salon. This roomed six orange hair dryer chairs. After Jane would wash and rinse her customers' hair, she'd take them to this room where they'd sit under the dryer for about 45 minutes and read the latest issue of *Cosmopolitan* or take a nap. Their heads bobbed up and down as they slept and their cheeks turned beet red from the warm air blowing out of the clear acrylic dryer hoods.

Jane and the other girls would gently take their elderly customers by the arm and escort them all the way from the dryer room to their styling chairs at the other side of the salon. Some of them were so frail they could barely walk without assistance. They held on to their arms and slowly shuffled across the room. Jane rarely saw any of the other beauty operators go to such great lengths to assist their customers the way she did. Her customers always appreciated her kind of attentiveness.

She learned patience from her mother, who was also a beautician. When Jane was eight, she was old enough to help her mother whenever she got busy. She'd sweep up the hair around her chair or greet her customers when they walked in the door.

"Go say hello to Mrs. So-and-So," her mother would say. Or, "Jane, please take the rollers out of my customer's hair."

Jane eagerly hopped up from her chair and did as she was told. She didn't mind touching the customers' heads. First, she removed the pink plastic picks from the rollers, and then she would carefully unroll the brush rollers and placed them in the wicker basket that sat on the customer's lap. Her mom occasionally glanced over from her styling chair across the room to make sure Jane kept each curl in tact. She smiled with approval.

As she removed the pretty rollers, the customers would often ask, "Do you want to be a beautician when you grow up, Janie?"

Before she could answer, her mom usually chimed in and said, "No, I want Jane to go to college and get a degree." She was adamant that Jane would get a good education so that she wouldn't have to stand on her feet all day long like her mother did.

Sometimes Jane would tell the customer what she really wanted to do with her life. "I want to be a superhero when I grow up," she said softly.

In her mind, she already had her whole career mapped out. She wanted to travel the world, wear capes and masks, appear on TV and magazines, and most of all, help people. She wanted to be like Adam West or Van Williams in those old reruns of *Batman* and *The Green Hornet*. Well, not like Van Williams, but more like his co-star Bruce Lee. He was the reason people actually watched the show. During that time he showed something that nobody had ever seen before: kung fu! Jane didn't want to be a beautician. Instead, she wanted to be famous.

While the other girls would go out for a smoke or have lunch with their boyfriends during their break, like a creature of habit, Jane Travers could be found indulging on two of her greatest loves: Powdered donuts and reading some of the comics on this week's pull list from Galaxy Comics.

Whenever she wasn't reading comics, she was busy making her very own. A spiral sketchbook was spread out in front of her. Sketches of her own original superheroes battling villains and monsters, and there were also some heroic versions of Jane herself that filled the pages. Colored pencils were scattered atop the table of a booth at the back of the salon.

She wasn't like the other girls who worked at Beauty Today. While everyone else was swapping beauty and fashion tips and gossip, Jane would go off on a tangent on how weird it was when Jake Gyllenhaal was set to replace Toby Maguire in the second Spider-Man movie—the best one in the entire series—due to the latter being injured while filming that forgettable racehorse movie. Fifteen years later he had landed the role of the villain in the Marvel Studios franchise. Instead of wearing designer clothes, Jane wore screen print tees that featured her favourite pop culture characters. Today she was rockin' with the 10th Muse, as a light dash of powdered sugar sprinkled down around the character's logo between bites.

At the moment, she was so entranced by the latest issue of *Hit-Girl*. No longer under the tutelage of her superhero father Big Daddy, the pintsized hero was taking her one-girl war against the criminal underworld on the road. Jane loved the direction where series creator Mark Millar is taking the character, and how she missed the artwork of comic great and frequent co-creator and collaborator John Romita, Jr. However, she liked the new guy's style. It was reminiscent to Japanese anime, and it really fits into Hit-Girl's fast-paced madcap world. Jane was so into this one action sequence where Hit-Girl was brutally slaughtering this group of Columbian drug lords; she couldn't hear what her boss Debra was saying.

"Jane? Jane? Jane!"

Jane snapped out of her reverie. Fresh out of the four-colored world where men and women wore resplendent costumes and performing daring, impossible feats, she crashed back into the real world where her no-nonsense boss shot her an annoyed look. Jane nearly choked on her donut in mid-bite and dropped the comic to the floor. She rose into attention, awaiting her orders like a grunt on the first day of boot camp.

"Jane," Debra said flatly, "not today. Mr. Johnson, our *top* client, is in need of a shave. Since Elizabeth is on vacation this week, and everyone else here is booked up and your break is nearly over. I need you to take care of him."

"Uh, yeah," Jane replied, wiping the traces of powdered sugar from her lips. "I got some time."

She shifted her gaze from her boss to the well-dressed man standing next to her. He looked impatient. The one thing Johnson didn't like the most is dawdling. He was due in the boardroom in an hour to talk about a possible business merger. And he needed time to mentally prepare for his presentation. Before every important meeting, he would go to Beauty Today for a close shave. Elizabeth was truly an artist when it comes to handling a straight razor. Many men feel that one of the biggest benefits of shaving with a straight razor is how incredibly manly it makes them feel. There's nothing like staring down death every time you need to shave, which is exactly what using a straight razor is. They didn't earn the nickname "cutthroat" razor for nothing. No other method even comes close to making a man feel like as much of a badass as using a straight razor.

"Just a shave, then?" Jane asked.

"Yes," Johnson said sternly, "just a shave. I have business meetings all this week. However, I trust no one but Elizabeth to cut my hair. I cannot afford even one nick." Then he narrowed his eyes and leered at her. Jane could feel this sense of dread shivering down her spine. "Don't screw this up."

Jane's upper lip quivered and she gulped loudly. Her stomach was in knots and it had absolutely nothing to do with all those doughnuts she had just eaten. "Uh, ye-yes sir," she stammered. "Right away, sir."

She led him to her chair and wrapped the gown over his suit. As she tied it around his neck, Debra whispered directly into her ear, like a ghost warning a trespasser in a haunted house. "Not. *One.* Nick. Got it?"

Jane couldn't breathe, or even let out a single word. All she could do was nod and watch Debra take her place at the counter, and survey the entire beauty salon like a hawk.

Jane gave Mr. Johnson the hot towel treatment to open up his pores, making his skin smooth and soft. She applied the lather onto his face with the brush. She was gentle, and the cream was cool and soothing to him. Now that prepping was done, it was time to bring out the razor. She placed the razor at the bottom of the strip and pushed it away from her, toward the top. Then she flipped it over so she could do the other side. She couldn't help to hum the melody of one of the songs from *Sweeny Todd*. Before she began, she thought that she and Mr. Johnson had gotten off on the wrong foot. And to alleviate the situation, she started off with a joke.

"Wanna know how I got these scars?" Jane asked in a dusty loner kind of voice, as she wielded the razor. She moved her face forward until it almost touched Johnson's. He backed away, feeling very uncomfortable. "My father was a drinker and a fiend. He'd beat Mommy right in front of me. One night, he goes off crazier than usual. Mommy gets the kitchen knife to defend herself. He doesn't like that. Not. One. Bit."

Before she could utter another word, Johnson said, "What do you think you're doing?"

Jane's crazed look faltered. She was confused. "Um, why so serious?"

"Because you're holding a razor near my face and regaling me with an anecdote from your messed up childhood."

She was floored. "No, no. Heath Ledger's famous line from *The Dark Knight*." Johnson was still drawing a blank.

"One of the greatest superhero movies ever made? He won Best Supporting Actor post-humorously?"

"Posthumously," corrected Johnson.

"Yeah, that's it. It made a ton of money at the box office?"

"Well, while you were out going to movies and reading comic books, I was busy getting my M.B.A. in business administration. Maybe if you had put more effort into your studies instead of retreating into an infantile mindscape, you wouldn't be working in a beauty parlor." He began to step out of his chair and tried to remove the gown. "If you're not going to take this seriously, I'm going to leave."

As he struggled with the collar, Jane looked over to the counter to see Debra glowering at her, bringing Jane back to the task at hand. Johnson was the salon's best customer. He could've gone to any upscale shop but he chose to frequent this one. When he first came there he gave a glowing review of Beauty Today online and recommended it to several of his business associates. So if they were to lose him as a client, then everyone else would follow suit. They couldn't afford to take such a hit.

"Wait, Mr. Johnson," pleaded Jane. "I know you're a very busy man, and I'm sorry to waste your time. But please, give me another chance. It'll be the quickest and smoothest shave you'll ever have. Just don't go."

Johnson seethed and looked at his watch. "You have five minutes."

Jane breathed a sigh of relief. "Oh, thank you, thank you, Mr. Johnson. I promise you won't regret it."

"See that I don't," he replied, taking his seat.

Jane smiled nervously and saw Debra mouthing silently to her, "Not. *One.* Nick." She wagged her finger back and forth on each word, like a metronome.

Jane's hand began to shake. She could barely keep the razor in place. She took a deep breath and steadied herself. This was do or die time. Not only was her job hanging in the balance but also the salon's clientele.

Johnson's eyes were closed, and away Jane went. They were short, rapid, downward strokes. Jane felt a sudden burst of confidence. No longer she was a scared little girl, but now she possessed the skills of a surgeon. With only one minute to spare, her customer's face was silky smooth.

"All done, Mr. Johnson," she said, handing him the mirror. "Would you like to take a look?"

Johnson took the hand mirror away from Jane. He raised it right in front of him and began to inspect all the angles. Jane was beside herself. She was as careful as she could be. She awaited his feedback. But all she heard where the inconsistent hums from each view of his face. To what seemed to be ten minutes to her, he finally placed the mirror down. He got up from the chair and looked her in the eye. Her heart stopped, thinking to herself, *this is it. There goes my job.*

Johnson reached into his pocket to take out his money clip. He went through this huge wad of cash and finally pulled out a ten-dollar bill.

"Well done," he said, giving Jane her tip. "And I thought Elizabeth was the only one here who knew how to handle a blade."

Jane smiled and accepted the money. "Thank you, Mr. Johnson! You have a good day, sir."

Johnson went over to the counter to pay the bill. Debra nodded in approval. As soon as he left the shop, Jane fell onto the chair, feeling relieved. Then she leaned back, a triumphant look on her face. Before she could get up, something caught her eye. It was the newspaper Johnson left behind. The front-page headline read a bank robbery had taken place yesterday. Jane's smile faded, as it was replaced with a frown. After reading those words in bold type she fell into deep thought. This was the third bank robbery this month. The police still had no leads.

Before she could read any further, Debra popped out of nowhere startling her.

"Jane, you've done such a great job," she said, putting her fears to rest. "You still need to work on your people skills, though. But that was the finest shave I have ever seen. Now back on your feet. Your next appointment will be here shortly."

Flustered, Jane got out of the chair. "Yes. Thank you, Debra."

The rest of the day went well for Jane. She did a couple of haircuts for little kids, and a perm for a little old lady. As she gathered her things she waved good-bye to her co-workers and began to make her way home.

Along the way was Pet Paradise. Usually, Jane would stop and look at the puppies in the front window. She thought it was cute to see them scurrying about and romping with their puppy brothers and sisters. Then she looked up to see a young man in his early twenties. He had dark hair and a very kind face. He was dressed in a blue polo shirt and slacks. Nothing fancy, but it was the standard attire for this particular pet store chain.

She smiled. The best thing about walking home from work every night was seeing Pete. She adored him. There was no question in her mind about that. He was, indeed, hard not to adore. With that luscious head of dark hair…with that exquisite mouth that could start as a pout that could crush your heart, then transform into a smile that could send it soaring into the stratosphere…with those piercing blue eyes that could look into your soul.

Aside from that, Pete Young was a fair package. Good lines to his face, the kind of clean-shaven, handsome features that may have started out slightly pretty but which, improved as he got older.

Every girl wanted him, and every guy wanted to be like him. Jane liked him as well. Who wouldn't? He seemed like a nice person. Not that she knew too much about that, as she had never really talked to him. As a matter of fact, not many people get to have more than a few words with him a day. Normally he would be on his own or with others.

Jane had a thing for Pete for a very long time. She thought about going inside to talk to him, and see if he would like to go out with her to dinner and a movie. Every time she saw him she could hear Terence Trent D'Arby's "Wishing Well" playing in her head.

Before she could reach for the door, she saw several beautiful women with their respectable pets lined up to the register. Each of them was more beautiful than the next, and they seemed to be much more interested in Pete than pet supplies.

Jane saw her own reflection from the store window. She lowered her head comparing and contrasting herself to the other girls.

Idiot, she chastised herself. *He wouldn't be interested in you. Not with women like them around him all the time.*

She helped herself to one last glance of Pete before she took off feeling defeated.

The worst thing she hated about her walk was dealing with that jerk who was always creeping on her. Some bad boy movie cliché with a black leather jacket and went by the street name Big T. She was hoping he wouldn't be there.

She didn't feel like putting up with his crap. But to his disappointment, there he was, leather jacket and all. It had shiny silver spikes on the shoulders and it gave him a more forbidding look. He was a tall man, with a tight, thin physique, resembling a 1970's punk rocker. His jeans, as worn as his boots, marked him as a nomadic wanderer in a low budget post-apocalyptic movie or a simple motorcycle bum. He was definitely blue collar for sure. His hair was dark, sweeping back from his forehead was formed into spikes and he never went anywhere without a big diamond stud in his ear. He even had a bit of a widow's peak sloping down from his brow. He looked like the bastard son of Dracula and Danny Zuko from *Grease.* His back was against the brick wall, trying to look cool. He thought he was rocking it hardcore, but he was just Dave Matthews. Maybe he won't see her.

"Hey there, pretty lady," he said to Jane.

Shit. He did.

"How are you feeling tonight? Hmm?" Jane ignored him. She didn't even look his way. She kept her eyes forward. "You *must* be feeling bad—not wanting to talk to *me.*"

Oh, great, she thought, giving a grimace of disgust. *Not this again. Why won't he stop bothering me?*

Big T reached into his pocket and pulled out a small bag. He offered her a smile. "I got something here that would make everything better."

Jane turned around and yelled, "Everyone knows drugs are bad for you! And only bad men would try to sell them!"

Big T stood there and took it all in. It didn't faze him. Really not at all. He watched as Jane turned away and stormed her way out of his sight. He couldn't help but smile.

After a long day at work, what Jane wanted to do more than spend time with the people she loved. She walked up to her porch and inserted her key into the lock. With a gentle turn she can hear it click open. When she peered into the living room all she can see is darkness. She reached for the light switch and scanned the room for her parents.

"Mom, Dad?" She called out. She waited for a response but she got nothing in return. She took a few steps into the room and headed for the stairs. "Anyone home?"

There was still no answer.

She ascended the stairs, coming to the conclusion they must be out with her uncle Charlie. She went into her room and leaped onto her bed belly first. The cluttered bedroom reflected the diversity of her interests. A sewing machine rested on her desk, designs for new costumes strewn against the floor nearby. Bookshelves gagged beneath the weight of dozens of interesting volumes on a wide variety of graphic novels and Japanese manga. Photographs of her in various costumes, posing with her favorite writers and artists at the conventions she had attended were magnetized to her mini-fridge. One such picture was with comic book great and living legend Jim Steranko—the man responsible for Nick Fury, Captain America, and the influence to Indiana Jones' iconic look. She was dressed as Agent Carter holding a replica of Captain America's shield in full glory with Mr. Steranko's signature intact.

Looking at the photo took Jane back to the day of the convention. She was absolutely in love with Peggy Carter and she watched the show live every Tuesday night when it was still running. She had wanted to get back into cosplay scene for a while and figured it was perfect to go as one of her favorite Marvel characters.

The dress was made from regal blue Kona Cotton, machine sewed from the simplicity 8050 pattern. The wrist cuffs weren't in the pattern, so she just transferred them over from a men's button-down shirt. She also got a wig, shoes, and the fedora was actually a replica of the one created for the series sold by Stetson. Jane thought the most challenging part was that it featured some new things she hadn't done in her sewing career before, but doing them had helped her improve her sewing so much.

People loved her costume. One of her favorite feelings was always having her character recognized at a con and being asked to take picture. She thought one of her favorite moments was going out onto the stage during the costume contest and hearing the audience cheer. It just felt so rewarding. The most surprising part was that the pictures of that cosplay exploded on Twitter. She still got notes for it constantly and people have been so nice on there. Someone even wanted to renew *Agent Carter* with her playing Peggy. Maybe it would happen one day…

The first time she cosplayed her, most people actually thought she was Carmen Sandiego. She went over to one of the vendors tables and bought the life-sized replica of Captain America's shield so she could carry it around the con. That was a huge help. When people saw her walking the show floor they instantly knew who she was. It was just funny on how one little (and expensive) prop could change everyone's perception of who she was. She sprang for the 75th anniversary metallic shield. That's how committed she was to her cosplay. Every little detail counted. No matter how extravagant. She hung that shield on the wall in front of her bed. She wanted it to be the first thing she saw every morning as a source of inspiration and a reminder of there is good in the world and it's worth fighting for.

Now bored out of her mind, she reached for her Atlas action figure. She waved it through the air and made flying noises.

"What should I do today, Atlas?" She asked the inanimate object.

In a deep, heroic voice she said, "'Maybe you can go to McGriffin's. I bet there will be some fun people there.'"

Jane smiled all over. "Why, I think you're right, Atlas. That's a swell idea."

She placed her Atlas figure down and went through her closet. She had to find the coolest outfit she owned. She had to find something that didn't have a cartoon character or a smartass saying on the front.

She had a good feeling about tonight.

CHAPTER TWO

A neon sign was flashing the bar's name. The "N" had been burned out. Someone had put a song on the jukebox, and Jane winced at the ironic appropriateness of it: "Gettin' Jiggy with it." There were sounds of laughter, people living their normal lives, eating, drinking, socializing, and hitting on each other.

She stood just outside the door for a long time, wrestling with the prospect of going in or staggering out. Finally it came down to a matter of time allotted. She'd came all this way, just so she could…what? Be too chicken to go in?

Taking a deep breath, she entered the establishment. She wondered if anyone was going to notice her. She didn't need to for long. As if she were a feared gunslinger in some film about the Old West, conversation died out almost instantly the moment she entered the dim lighting of the bar.

There were people standing about, talking, a few dancing, in addition to the folks at the tables who had been in the midst of conversations before Jane entered. She causally walked in and slowly drank it in. She approached the bar and threw down $10 to get the bartender's attention.

"Grey Goose martini, please," she cheerfully chirped.

He nodded in response and made her drink. She took a sip and smiled in satisfaction. She turned around to check out everything. She let out a loud laugh to see Debra and Stacey, along with Elizabeth who had just got back from her vacation. All of them were dolled up and discussing about Elizabeth's time in Florida.

Smiling, Jane made her way over to their booth. "Hi, girls!" She exclaimed, breaking up their conversation. "It's so nice to see you! Isn't this place great?"

Out of everyone in that booth, Debra was the most surprised of all. She nearly choked on her drink. "Hi, Jane," she said, feeling so awkward. "This is a surprise. I wouldn't expect to see you here."

"Oh, yeah, this is one of my *favorite* places to hang at," she said, sitting right next to Debra. She and the other girls scooted down to make room for her. "I was real bored tonight since my parents weren't home. So I was talking to a friend of mine and he suggested I go out and tear up the town. So I got all dressed up and went to my favorite place. Isn't this just the best?! All of us are here—it's like fate or something. So what are you gals doing? Drinks? Dancing? Dinner? The three R's? Hah! We should do this more often! I hardly know anything about all of you. We never have time to chat while at work. Always busy, busy, busy. Hee-hee!" She looked over to see the cute waiter with the bowtie. "Oh, waiter!"

She called, waving her glass. "I'd like another Grey Goose martini, s'il vous plait. That's French for 'right now.' Hah! J.K.!"

Debra feigned a smiled, while the other girls were wondering when Jane was going to finish.

She paused for a breath, and then went on. "I mean, do you have boyfriends, or is this why you come here? 'Cause this is a *great* place to meet guys. I see it happen all the time! Do you want to order some appetizers or something 'cause I'm hungry enough to eat a horse. Oh, speaking of horses—did you see that there is a horse show coming up this month? I luuuuuuuvve horses! Ever since I was a kid, I've wanted my own horse. What do you think about—?"

In order to stop this madness, Elizabeth went to her phone and opened her iTunes app and played the last song she listened to before coming over to McGriffin's. Not nearly halfway through Jane's one-woman show, "Pony" by Ginuwine began to play very loudly. Elizabeth quickly picked up her phone and "answered" it.

"Hey, what's up?" She greeted her imaginary caller. "Yeah. Yeah, yeah. Uh-huh. Yeah. Mmm-hmmm. No. Uh-huh. Right. Sure. Okay. We'll see you later." And then she "hung up." "Listen…um…Jenn. That was the call we were waiting for." Debra and Stacy both nodded eagerly, not wasting any time on gathering their purses. "We've got to run. We'll see you tomorrow."

Debra gave Jane a polite smile and waved before she left with the rest of the girls. Jane felt hurt that they didn't invite her along. But it stung even worse when two guys walked passed her and they were laughing about what happened. She even heard one of them calling her a loser. She didn't feel like she belonged there. She paid for her second drink and left, wondering why she kept on coming to places like this.

Contemplating whether or not she should go somewhere else or straight home, Jane saw two men running into the Mr. Mart convenience store just across from her. She quickly ducked behind a parked car and observed the two men drawing their guns, yelling at the clerk to empty the register.

She couldn't breathe. Her first instinct was to run away, but someone had to help that poor kid behind the counter. Jane fumbled clumsily for her phone. Her heart was racing trying to remember the number for 9-1-1. She kept her eye at the action across the street. She could see through the windows as one of the robbers held the clerk at gunpoint, while his partner was ransacking the grocery aisle, helping himself to a wide colorful variety of candy bars and cheap sunglasses.

Jane thought she hit the icon for the keypad, but accidently activated Snapchat. She frantically exited the app and finally called for help.

"Nine-one-one, what's your emergency?" Said the voice at the other end of the line.

Jane felt her heart stopped. She went deaf. All she could hear was a piercing buzzing sound that stabbed her brain. The robbers were now trashing the store. Knocking down shelves and throwing liquor bottles against the wall. They were having the time of their lives.

"Hello?" Called the operator. "Is anyone there?"

Jane snapped out of it. "Listen," she said, quivering, "I want to report a robbery that is happening right now!"

"Did you say a robbery, ma'am?"

"Yeah," Jane replied breathlessly. "YEAH! I'm at the corner of Broad and Patterson, just outside of McGriffin's. It's happening at the Mr. Mart!"

"Ma'am, can you tell me how many suspects are there, and are they armed?"

"There are only two guys," answered Jane, "and they've got guns, and—OMIGOD!"

One of the crooks pistol-whipped the clerk. He went down hard, knocking over the March of Dimes jar in the skirmish. Change and dollar bills exploded onto the floor. The thieves scattered all over picking up the fallen cash.

"Ma'am? Ma'am!" The operator alarmingly called out. "Is everything all right?"

Jane raised the phone to her ear. "No! They've just attacked the clerk...and they're stealing from the disabled kids!"

"Ma'am, I just notified a nearby patrol car. They'll be over there soon. I need you to go back into McGriffin's where you'll be safe."

Jane couldn't hear her. She was captivated by what was happening right in front of her. Then she heard the sound of sirens filling the air. She watched as the robbers stumbled off from the floor and the fear in their faces was forever imbedded into her memory. Red and blue lights bounced off the store windows' reflections, giving her a pseudo mask made of light.

"Ma'am, are you still there?"

"Yeah," Jane said to the receiver. Watching as the police surround the convenience store. "Right. Thanks!"

She was frozen in place. She watched as the brave police officers apprehended the thieves and escorted them to the back of their cruisers. The clerk was taken to the back of the ambulance where EMTS were giving him the once-over.

"I saved a life," Jane said softly.

A smile slowly stretched across her face. Her eyes lit up like a marquee promoting a hit Broadway play.

She was a hero.

A real, honest to goodness hero!

It was right then, she decided she wanted to be more than just an ordinary hairdresser. It was time for her to revisit her childhood career path.

She took out her sketchpad from her purse and flipped through its pages to find the rough sketches of little cartoon versions of her thwarting evil and protecting the weak and the downtrodden.

Jane Travers was the happiest person on the planet.

Jane swung the front door wide open, exclaiming, "Mom? Dad!"

Her uncle Charlie emerged from the kitchen with a warm cup of coffee in his hand. His eyes widened in surprise.

"Jane? Is everything all right?"

"Omigosh! You'll never believe it, Uncle Charlie!" She shrieked, embracing him. Taken by surprise he spilled his hot coffee all over his shirt. He wailed in pain while Jane still held him. "It's the most amazing thing! Ever! Oh! My! God! Holy cow! I can't believe it! It was incredible! Crazy! Wild! Jeez—can you imagine how great this is?!"

"Whoa, little niece," Charlie said, gently pulling her away. "Take a deep breath. Slooooowwww down, and start from the beginning. Where were you and what happened?"

Jane took her uncle's advice and took a deep breath. The next thing she said was a blur but Charlie got the gist of it.

"Okay, well, I was with some friends of mine from work. We were at McGriffin's. So, we were all getting ready to go to this other event. I was gonna follow them over, but I saw these guys robbing a store so I called the police and stopped the crime! I was just like Liberty Lady out there—a hero! A real, live hero!"

Charlie smiled and placed his hands on her shoulders. "Well, I have to say you did a great thing today, and I'm extremely proud of you. Much more than I already am. And friends, eh? I can't tell you how happy I am to hear that. Who are they?" Then he paused. "And—wait a second—you weren't drinking, right? You know you can't…"

"Oh, Uncle Charlie," she laughed, "you know I don't do that sort of thing. Jeez, we were just gonna go dancing. Those gals are great—Debra and Stacy and the gals. Why, I can't wait to do it again!"

Everyone in the world dreams of being a superhero!

It's our nature to wish we were better and to show the world that we would stop the bad guys, get all the glory and accolades just like in the comics. The only problem is this isn't the comic world where you either get bitten by radioactive insects or hit by gamma bombs to acquire supernatural powers.

Nope.

This is the <u>real</u> world. The world where all we can do is eat, sleep, dream and die. I always thought that's what my life would be like, until that night.

There was a cool breeze in the night air. It didn't affect Jane who was wearing her sweats and holding onto her tennis racket. She was still on an emotional high from what happened at the convenience store, and like a junkie she was ready for her next fix. Jane had been following the news about a string of attacks on young women at Bayview Park. The police had no leads and each victim gave a vague description of the attacker. None of the artist renderings were consistent. Knowing the authorities would frown upon vigilantism, Jane came up with a ruse for the police in case they question her about her involvement. And the best she could come up with was tennis lessons.

Now, all I have to do is wait here, she schemed, hiding behind the bushes. *There have been several assaults in this park.* She slowly poked her head through the foliage; her eyes were like a hawk's scanning its domain and ready to swoop in on the first sign of trouble. She clutched the tennis racket like a soldier with his rifle. *I figure I wait long enough; I can just use this racket to deal with anyone who makes trouble.*

Jane's eyes narrowed to slits as she watched from the bushes. Her senses were more keen than any hunting predator's. She could see clearly in almost total darkness, yet the sudden flash of the streetlights could strip her of that night vision in a flash.

Under the streetlight she saw a woman, not much younger than her, walking her poodle. She was plugged into her iPhone listening to the new Imagine Dragons album. The volume was unreasonably high. At this rate that girl would suffer partial hearing loss by the age of thirty.

Walking past her was some skeezy-looking dude in a long coat. He did a quick double take on the woman who walked past him.

"Hey," he said to the unsuspecting dog walker. She stopped and turned down her music so she could hear him better. "You know it's not safe to be her after dark?" He added, in a preachy tone of voice. "Bad things have been known to happen here."

The girl gently removed her ear buds. She felt something was squeezing her heart. "Bad stuff?" She gulped, feeling a little terrified. Then she dared to ask the big question: "What kind of...bad stuff?"

The man grinned and opened his jacket. "*This* kind of bad stuff," he answered, brandishing a very large knife.

In one swift move he reached out and grabbed her arm, pulling her forward. She froze, dropping the lease to her dog that started barking. He was strong. It was enough to leave an abrasion on the girl's wrist.

"No!" She cried, trying to break free. The more she struggled, the tighter his hold was on her. "Why are you doing this? Leave me alone! HELP!"

Jane couldn't stand idly by any longer. Now was the time for action.

The man pushed the girl to the ground. She landed on her palms and tried to get up. But she saw his shadow looming over her from the streetlight. She slowly turned her head to see her attacker raise the knife over his head, ready to plunge it into her.

"Scream all you want," he taunted. Her eyes were mesmerized by the glint o the blade. "No one is gonna help you."

Like a cobra striking its prey, Jane emerged from the bushes in top speed. She reeled the tennis racket back and followed through on her forehand swing.

"Kii-yaaa!!!" She shrilled, delivering one powerful blow to the back of the mugger's head.

The impact was enough to tumble him. He dropped his knife and tried to get up. But Jane wouldn't let him. She kept hitting him with the racket. Each blow was more powerful then the last. She went full John McEnroe on him. Between pants of breath she uttered every obscenity in the English language, with a little Klingon and Dothraki thrown into the mix.

When the mugger was down for the count, Jane was wiping sweat from her forehead with her sleeve. She looked around, dazed. The she turned her attention over to the shocked expression of the girl, cradling her dog. She was in a state of shock. She was frozen in her place. Her eyes were locked on Jane who had beaten a man almost to death with a tennis racket.

"Are…you…all right, ma'am?" Jane huffed.

The girl managed to blink and slowly nod, as her dog whimpered.

Jane's lips stretched into a smile and threw her arms in triumph! "YES!!!" She screamed to the dark sky, the racket flying through the air. "Saved a life!" She broke into a small victory dance that made the girl question her hero's sanity. Then Jane ended the routine with a dab.

Detective Joseph Roberts was on his way home after a hard day's work at the precinct. He thought he would make it home early and spend time with his wife Brenda and his infant son Bradley. He had been burning the candle at both ends trying to find some leads to the string of bank robberies that have been rocking the city. But to his utter disappointment none have surfaced, and he had feared the trail went cold.

He was only three minutes away from home until he got a call from the two-way announcing there was an attempted mugging in Bayview Park and a citizen's arrest had been made. He cursed under his breath and picked up the receiver.

"This is Roberts," he said grudgingly. "I'm nearby and on route."

This was rookie stuff. But he couldn't ignore something that was in his own backyard. As soon as he got to the park, he'd seen a parked squad car with its lights flashing and two uniformed officers doing their duty. One had a shifty-looking fella in cuffs, and his partner was checking on a young woman who was holding her pet poodle. She appeared to be unharmed and relieved that help was there. Roberts concluded she was the intended victim.

And then he saw the person who had made the citizen's arrest. She had the biggest smile he had ever seen on a person. The other thing he noticed was the tennis racket she causally held. Roberts felt dubious about this whole situation. He took another look at the perp who at this time was being read his Miranda rights and back at little Mary Sunshine. She really did a number on this guy. It looked like a whole street gang had beaten him to a bloody pulp. Roberts did a double take and then shrugged it off, as he took out his notepad and proceeded to interview her.

"All right, so to sum this up—you were on your way home from tennis lessons when you heard her scream," he stated, taking down Jane's story.

Two patrolmen led the mugger away in handcuffs. He needed help on walking to the back of the squad car. It looked like Jane had hit him a little too hard. He was staggering around like a drunk and he could barely see out of his left eye that was swelled shut. Jane turned her attention back to the detective who was still getting her story straight.

"You came running. Saw what was happening and hit the perpetrator with your racket. Is this correct?"

"Yes, detective," Jane replied. "Just like that."

Roberts turned to the side to see the victim relaying her story to the other officer. She and her dog were perfectly safe.

"Well," he said, looking amused, "it was a brave thing you did. But it was also dangerous. Now in the future if something like this happens, you'll call the police, right?"

Jane gave him a friendly smile. "Of course, Detective. I sure will."

"Good," he said, returning the smile, "because I wouldn't want you getting hurt by being a hero."

Yes! Jane celebrated in her privacy of her thoughts. *Validation!*

She had been officially recognized as a hero, and she may have made an ally against her war on crime in the process. This was a taste of things to come in her budding superhero career. She skipped the whole saving a cat out of a tree rite of passage into stopping a mugger.

How could her life change so much in one day? It was baptism by fire.

CHAPTER THREE

As soon as Jane woke up the next morning, she checked online to see if there was any news about the incident at the park. She wasn't disappointed when she saw that she was the talk of the town.

While she was glad to see the mugger was caught and arrested, it was unbelievable to hear everyone talking about the hero who stopped him. It put a big smile on her face to see her name and picture in the news headlines.

LOCAL HAIRDRESSER SAVES WOMAN FROM ASSAULT

"Jane?" Her father shouted from downstairs. "I need to go to work early today. Are you sure you're still up for going to the salon? It's O.K. if you want to take a personal day."

"No, I'm fine," she called back. There was no way she was going to miss out on the girls' reaction to this news at the salon. She was so excited, Jane nearly jumped out of bed to get dressed.

On her way to work, she brushed past people in the streets with the occasional few looking at the news on their smartphones. She would try to check to see if any of them were looking up news about her, but all she got were weird stares from people who didn't like her invading their personal space.

Before she knew it she was standing in front of the door of Beauty Today. She reached for the handle and with a deep breath she opened the door, entering the salon. A gaggle of voices greeted Jane as she stepped inside.

Then the sound of a single clap filled her ears. It was a slow clap. Then several people joined in, and everyone else started clapping and they all sped up the tempo followed by cheers. Jane turned around to see Debra holding a red velvet cake.

"Oh, Jane, we are so proud of you!" She praised. "Who would have known we had a hero working here?"

Jane looked around as all the girls at the salon were patting her on the back and saying kind sentiments. She wasn't expecting this at all. She had no idea the other girls felt this way about her. She felt a sense of pride among them, and the feeling of finally being accepted into the group. Debra gave her a genuine smile, not like that forced one she had at McGriffin's. This time she was happy to see Jane.

"Jane," she said, handing the cake over to her, "Mr. Johnson is here for a shave—and a haircut."

"Two bits!" Jane blurted out, which sent the salon into a raucous of laughter.

Debra chuckled. "Yes, yes. I've set you up for that one. Now, Mr. Johnson was quite happy to hear you could fit him in today. But don't take too long, because you've got quite a few appointments."

Jane greeted her toughest customer with a smile. Something was very different about him. He seemed a little less stick-up-your-assy.

"Um…so, gosh, Mr. Johnson," she began, feeling a little flustered. "I don't know what Elizabeth normally does for you."

"You do whatever you feel will look the best," he said, laughing. It was an odd thing. Not once since she was first hired at Beauty Today did she see Mr. Johnson like this. It was like he was replaced by a pod person, or by his Earth-2 doppelganger. Or the operation was a complete success and the surgeon finally removed the stick from up his ass. Jane wasn't one to look a gift horse in the mouth. "Just don't use a tennis racket," the buoyant businessman added.

Another round of laughter erupted in the salon. Even Jane found herself joining in on the fun. She placed the gown on Mr. Johnson and was about to go to work. When she reached for the scissors, she saw something walking past the front window.

It was Pete from the pet store.

Oh, gosh! Is that…is that Pete?!

He turned his head over to Jane. He flashed her a smile and waved to her.

He waved to me! I can't believe it! He knows who I am!

Maybe…maybe he even likes me. If he saw the same article in the paper…why, he may want to talk to me. Yeah—over dinner! Mmmm…dinner. Maybe we could go to that new French restaurant over by the highway. I've always wanted to go there. And we could get crepes. Do I look all right? Maybe he'll come in here. I hope I don't have powder sugar on my—

"Jane?" Said Debra, derailing her celebrity stylist's train of thought. "Is everything all right?"

Jane laughed nervously. "Um, no—just, just trying to decide what would look best on Mr. Johnson."

With a grin wider than the Chesire Cat's and determination in her eyes, she began planning.

I know what I need to do now.

Jane Travers was brimming with confidence. It was a pleasant feeling, one that she was unaccustomed to, given the usual assortment of people criticizing her, beating her down, or at least trying to. During work, she couldn't think of anything other than the idea of what it would be like to be a true, honest-to-goodness superhero. Being cheered by adoring fans, having fans mob her, and becoming a new inspiration for people everywhere. However, what the people should cheer had her stumped. She thought about finding a name would be the easiest part in the hero biz. Well…it wasn't. Peter Parker had a clue with the thing that gave him powers. Superman, just because he was…well, super!

Her?

Nothing seemed memorable or at least original.

It was the end of the workday and everyone congratulated Jane once again before heading out. Her tip jar was overflowed with singles and five-dollar bills. This was the most she had ever made on a single day since she started working at Beauty Today. Debra had been getting calls all day from people who would like to schedule hair appointments with the Hero of Bayview Park. By the rate things were going, Jane would be booked up for the next two years.

Jane was the last one to leave the salon and while she was walking down the block, she almost bumped into Pete who was locking up. She was startled and inched her way backward. Their eyes met, and there was a silence between them. Jane had been thinking about what she wanted to say to him all day. She thought about saying something classy and admirable, but that wasn't her style. She didn't want to overthink it and concluded she would just ask him out plain and simple.

Jane squared her shoulders, which struck herself as rather funny. Jane couldn't have looked more serious if she'd been preparing to enter a ring with a maddened bull, armed with only a dishtowel. She approached Pete, who saw her coming, turned and smiled that million-watt smile at her. He looked expectantly to her, and he waited for her to say something.

And waited.

And waited.

The moment went from energy-charged to awkward. Pete tilted his head slightly, expectantly, like a dog trying to pick up a high-pitched noise. Jane couldn't be sure, but she thought that something in Pete's expression just then seemed to be wavering. It was as if he wanted to hear what Jane had to say but couldn't bring himself to do so. Or perhaps there was even more to it than that.

Desperate to have matters progress, Pete said to Jane, "Hi. How ya doing?"

Jane smiled in return. Her jaw twitched once, twice more, which was good since it indicated that she was, in fact, alive. She seriously hoped she wasn't blushing as hard as she imagined. She probably looked like Bashful from *Snow White*. Okay, now she knew for sure she was blushing. It wasn't hard enough to try and form a coherent sentence without her thoughts getting jumbled around and shaking up her nerves.

Then she walked away quickly as she could. Pete looked at her quizzically as she scurried down the street.

Later that night, Jane was enjoying a classic episode of *Rick and Morty*. One hand she held a glass of Wild Cherry Pepsi and the other was dug into a bowl of popcorn. Every time she would hear someone say, "Pickle Rick" she would take a drink. Her parents stood by the kitchen, peering through the archway. A worried look appeared on their faces. They exchanged soulful glances and proceeded into the living room.

"Jane, honey," said her father. "Could you turn that off? Your mother and I want to talk you about something."

Savoring the sweet taste of cherry soda, she obliged. "Sure, Dad," she replied, following a hiccup. "What's up?"

Her mother took a seat next to her on the couch, while her father sat in his favorite armchair. Jane could tell something was up. The last time she had this uneasy feeling was when they had to tell her all about gerbil heaven. Her mother placed a comforting hand on her forearm, which didn't help at all. She prepared for the worst.

"Honey," her father began, leaning forward. His back ached with the sudden weight of the feelings he was going to unload onto her daughter. "You know your mother and I are very happy that you acted so brave." This brought a smile to Jane's face. She felt her fears were being put to the rest. "The world truly does need people who help other people."

"It's just that we're your parents and we worry about you," her mother chimed in. Her demeanor was much more serious than her husband's. "And though this was very courageous of you, it's just…well, it was very risky. You could have been hurt."

"But, Mom," Jane protested, "I had to do something. That lady was in danger. If I hadn't been coming home that way—from my tennis lessons—I don't know what would have happened!" She shot up from the couch and punched the sky. "You should have seen me! I was just like Judo Girl!"

"Jane, we understand that you helped that woman," said her father, trying to be extremely delicate to his very spirited daughter. "But what if you had been hurt? I don't think we could ever stand anything happening to our princess. *Please*. Don't do anything like this again."

Jane felt something pierce her heart. She expected this kind of deterrence from her mother, but not him too. Ever since she was a little girl her parents told her if she worked hard enough and believed in herself, she could be anything she wanted. She mentally came to the conclusion of the lesson was "dream big, but not too big." Her eyes welled up and her face burned. She covered her face and ran out of the living room in a bolt of light. Her parents heard the rapid stomps against the staircase, immediately followed by the loud slam of her bedroom door.

"I didn't know she was taking tennis lessons," said her mother.

"I thought the only kind of tennis she played was that video game, starring that mustachioed fella with the red cap."

Jane was in a rage of emotions. She had a clear understanding on how Bill Bixby must have felt every time he turned into the Hulk. It was bad enough everyone else thought she was a joke. But having no emotional support or even any spiritual guidance from her own parents about her new vocation, really hurt Jane. She opened her closet and tore through its contents.

"I'll show them," she grumbled, searching for her old convention costumes. "I'll show them all—Mom and Dad—and that lousy detective. I'll show them what I'm capable of." She pulled out her old Catwoman costume from *Batman Returns*, and parts of her female Captain America costume. She rushed over to the sewing machine on her desk and began to plot out the necessary alterations, while she still fumed about tonight's events. "I'll not just show them I can do this—I'll prove that I'm the greatest hero of all."

The Atlas action figure lied slantwise on the desk. It stared at the young intrepid hero with its frozen, heroic expression.

"What are you going to do, Jane?" Jane said in the superhero's overly masculine voice.

"Every great superhero needs a costume," she replied to the inanimate object, as she brought out her sketchpad, and quickly flipped into a blank page. "And I'm gonna make one!" She proudly proclaimed, gathering her pencils, Micron pens, and markers.

Jane sat hunched over her desk, working expertly on the design to her new costume. When designing and rendering a costume, the most important thing to consider is the totem to represent the costumed alter ego. While lightly sketching on her pad, Jane thought about Batman and his iconic symbol. The bat strikes fear into mortal hearts because of mystic associations that have persisted through the ages: Bats are bloodthirsty. Bats are vampires. Bats are creatures of darkness. In choosing the bat to his totem, Bruce Wayne could take full advantage of the unique attributes (flight, echolocation, etc.) as well as its ability to frighten. But not having access to that technology—even if it did exist—left Jane very limited.

She continued to check her research, making more notes upon notes, waiting for something to hit her.

Nothing did.

"Nothing," she muttered. "Nothing...*nothing*..."

Days of bottling up her escalating frustration exploded from her, and Jane slammed her desk with such ferocity that knocked several of he action figures to the floor. In total aggravation and despair, Jane's head thudded down onto the desk. The impact caused something to fell off the end of the desk and hit the floor with a crash.

Slowly Jane lifted her head. The world looked distorted to her, and she realized it was because she had managed to smash her face flat when she'd struck the desk.

She turned her gaze to the sky and prayed for inspiration. The light from the full moon filtered through the window in Jane's bedroom. She rubbed her eyes, unable to believe that they could feel any more tired than they did.

Then Jane saw it, in all its stunning simplicity.

A shooting star's bright tail curved over the full moon, like a silver brow above an unblinking eye.

Feverishly, Jane hurried to a cluttered bookshelf and rummaged through the spiral notebooks. She withdrew a large sketchpad and went to the table. Carefully, she leafed through the illustrated sheets of monsters, heroes, and costume designs until she found a blank page.

While taking a moment of thinking about her symbol, Jane settled on bright colors to distinguish herself from the bad guys. Not seeing herself as a dark avenger, she concluded she wanted to be a symbol for hope. It was so simple she scolded herself for not thinking of it sooner. She drew a star across her figure's chest. It had to big enough to establish familiarity.

She needed to be larger than life, not laughable.

The suit needs to be lightweight. Armor and anything clunky was either going to weigh her down or distract her. It has to be tight fitting, but not constrictive that would allow freedom of movement for acrobatic and fighting maneuvers. And use of colors that would camouflage easily because it could save her life. Only a virtually invulnerable hero, who operates in the daytime, would wear bright blue, red, and yellow. However, black and dark gray would allow her to blend into the shadows and more stealthily.

The color was a pretty easy choice, going with her favorite, blue. As for whether to have a cape or not, she thought *The Incredibles* had taught her capes might not be the best thing. She grabbed a sheet of paper and began drawing her idea. It took a few attempts and different styles to see which suited her vision best. Finally, she had one that struck out the most.

A mask is an absolute necessity in super heroics. *I gotta protect my identity, after all,* Jane mused, going over several types of masks. The domino would make her features too obvious, but the cowl, however, would afford her extra protection.

Now it was time for the gloves and boots. They aren't just bold fashion statements. The gloves would ensure that she would never leave behind fingerprints that would tip off the police to her identity as Jane Travers. The boots would be lightweight but reinforced with steel toes for delivering devastating kicks.

And what superhero costume is complete without an utility belt? A must-have for every crime fighter to keep most of the tools of the trade in there, although these are supplemented by tricks hidden throughout the costume. Jane would keep most of her vital utilities "close to the belt", where they are more reliably accessible and useful, especially when she finds herself trussed up by a foe.

Her utility belt is lightweight and streamlined. It featured a buckle with a quick-release hasp for easy removal; eight pouches to contain small tools and gadgets. A fanny pack would have been less time consuming and more cost effective. But Jane was not one to cut corners. Miniaturization was key. The belt shouldn't be bulky or carry weight that could hamper her actions. Jane procured the belt with the necessary equipment. A small digital camera to photograph crime scenes, zip ties for rounding up perps, a burner phone, and a med-kit.

Her robust figure was wrapped tightly inside a dark blue body suit designed for stealth. Piercing blue eyes gazed out from behind a cowl. She looked at herself in her full-length mirror. She seemed very pleased with the turnout. Even though she wasted a half hour on whether or not the ensemble should include a cape. Then she finally agreed to add that feature to the final costume—for tactical purposes, of course.

She climbed onto her windowsill and observed her neighborhood as if she gazing at the skyline of a thriving metropolis. She breathed in the night air when a sudden gust of wind raised the train of her cape.

She felt right at home.

"Though the world mocked Jane Travers," she dramatically narrated, "it would soon marvel at the awesome might of…the Avenging Star!"

CHAPTER FOUR

Batman protected the city of Gotham. Spider-Man swung through the concrete jungle of New York. Green Lantern had an entire sector to uphold law and order. But for the Avenging Star...she had Bayview Park.

No trace of Jane Travers could be found in this tight formfitting bodysuit she quickly put together. Except for a flow of red hair that railed down the back of the cowl. The only complaint about the suit was that it gave her a wedgie when she crouched from behind the bushes. She should have covered herself in baby powder so she can slide smoothly into her new uniform.

She returned to her hiding spot from the night before. On her previous excursions to the park, Jane had shown up under the cover of night, skulking around like a thief, clinging to the shadows. She totally found her niche. Jane kept a vigil watch throughout the park. Waiting for some evildoer to prey upon a hapless bystander that would force her to spring into action and making the Avenging Star's official debut. Tonight, either Jane Travers' life would end, or the Avenging Star's life would begin.

This will be perfect, Jane grinned with glee. *I can see everything from here. I'll be able to see all of the good citizens. And all of the villains—beware!*

The night was breezy and cool. She was warm enough in her costume, but the chill felt nice on her face. Every breath was exhilarating. She scanned the park, appreciating it for the first time since her previous excursion.

Jane waited with anticipation. She had the whole encounter planned out in her head. Some lost citizen would be out for a late night jog or some other mundane errand, until someone jumps out of the shadows threatening violence. That would Jane's cue to make her grand entrance—probably shouting some sort of battle cry, or something very witty and snappy to banter with the villain. They throw down and at end the Avenging Star would be deemed the victor and the front-page story of every major periodical in the country. Thus prompting her to become the city's guardian and deputized as an official law enforcer with the police department. Complete with her very own Avenging Star signal shining in the night sky.

Oh, and the parades! There will be a parade, showering the streets with confetti and glitter. As the grand marshal she will be marching through the street, kissing hands and shaking babies...

Wait! Is that right?

Oh, well, she'll have plenty of time to figure that out.

And it would all end with the mayor giving her the Key to the City, which she hoped it would also come with a 10% discount on food, movies, and sporting events.

It would be everything she had ever dreamed.

Awakening from her daydream of glitter and grandstanding, she returned to guard duty. With huge smile, she said to the unknown, "Try something, you dastardly villains."

So she waited.

And waited.

And waited.

And…waited.

Nobody ever told her that keeping a diligent watch could be so boring! Batman and Robin staked out the Penguin and his thugs on a nightly basis and there was never a dull moment. She came to the solid conclusion that the Dark Knight and the Boy Wonder only fought boredom between the panels. After several hours of nothing, Jane rolled down her glove so she could see her watch.

Cripes, she groaned. *It's late and I've got work tomorrow.* She let out a very long and agonizing yawn that showed all her teeth. She stretched her arms out in an impressive wingspan and felt all of her muscles were being pulled apart. *I don't know how Captain Thunder can stay awake when he's on patrol.*

She looked both ways, doing one last check if anybody was lurking around. She changed back into her street clothes and groggily walked home. Along the way there, she prayed there would be more action tomorrow. She needed something to prove herself. She needed to prevent some catastrophic event to prove her worth as a hero.

It was another typical day at Beauty Today. Prom season was around the corner. That was when the salon made its real money. By next weekend, nearly every high school student in the city would come over to get primped and pampered for a night they would never forget. And given the publicity of Jane's heroic exploits they would make double what they had made the year before.

While Debra was already counting the money, she saw Jane sluggishly entered the salon. She appeared slovenly and haggard. Dark circles formed underneath her eyes. They were glassy and bloodshot. She usually moved with a spring in her step, but today she was just dragging. And it even looked like her clothes weighed a ton. That uneasy sight turned everyone's heads in the salon. Worrisome looks appeared on all the stylists' faces.

Sleep. That's what Jane Travers wanted more than anything in the world. She felt exhausted even though the day was barely hours old. She knew it was going to be a difficult and long day. But no matter how much she prepared herself for it, it couldn't begin to approach the reality of what she faced.

"Whoa, sister," said Debra, taking a good long look at her. "You must have been out partying till just about ten minutes ago. It's a good thing your schedule is open till this afternoon."

Jane wanted say some sort of witty retort, or even in this case something a little risqué. But she found it hard to open her mouth to speak, and trying to think of something was like driving a stake into her brain. She paused in front of a mirror and studied her reflection. The hollow shadows around her deep-set eyes gave her sculpted features of a skull-like cast. Then she looked over to her chair and found the morning paper.

Her eyes flared up when she read the headline:

CRIME WAVE!
ANOTHER BANK ROBBERY YESTERDAY
STILL NO CLUES ON THE PERPETATRATORS

Then she saw her opportunity. There was mystery here. Something very important, something that would even threaten the safety of the city,

Something a hero would investigate.

This would be a great start to her superhero career.

She grabbed the newspaper and ran out of the salon, causing mass confusion in her wake. "Uh, if that's the case, then I'm gonna go home and take a nap," she said to Debra, as she quickly dodged Stacy on the way out. "Yeah, yeah. I'm *real* tired. I'll be back later!"

Jane hated surveillance. It was so boring. Hell, it practically redefined the word. "Boring", adjective, tiresome. See also: Surveillance."

She was camped out behind the wheel of her green sedan—aptly named "The Star Mobile"—that was parked across the street from the bank. Donuts and coffee rested upon the dashboard, vital necessities for the long hours ahead. The hot and muggy weather made her wish she could run the car's air conditioner for a while. Perspiration glued her Avenging Star costume to her back. Her mask rested upon her lap. She rolled down the window to let in a little fresh air.

Stakeouts were hard on the body too. Sitting in the same place, focusing on the same thing for five, six, maybe even *eight* hours at a time definitely gave you a whole new appreciation for over-the-counter painkillers. She brought out a bottle of generic aspirin from the glove compartment and poured a couple tablets into her palm. She washed the pills down with a mouthful of cold coffee.

In theory, surveillance could not be performed alone, at least not well, sighing wearily; she pulled out a notepad off the dashboard and scribbled a terse notation to the effect that was absolutely nothing to report. She glanced over the previous entries of earlier that morning.

9:00 AM: Nothing

10:00 AM: Nothing

11:00 AM: Nothing

Noon: Man and woman get into a screaming match over the President. Total shocker.

1:00 PM: Nothing

2:00 PM Nothing

Abundant doodles attested to her continuing boredom. She found herself wishing the couple would come back just to break the monotony.

I'm going stir-crazy in here, she took a bite of the sugary powdered donut.

Distracted, she stared out the window at the bank across the street. She glanced at her watch. She scanned the street impatiently.

Minutes dragged on endlessly until, *Finally,* a four-door sedan rounded the corner.

"Come on, come on…"

The sedan had dark-tinted windows and out-of-state license plates sped between two school buses and jerked to a stop at an intersection. The front passenger door opened, and a tall man climbed into the vehicle. He was a large, muscular man with a boxer's build; his nose had been broken too many times to count. Once inside, he pulled a ski mask from his pocket, pulled it on, and turned to face the other two masked men.

"Crackle, Pop. Let's do this," he said, cocking his gun.

"This is it!" Jane cried excitedly. She quickly donned her cowl and adjusted the eyepieces. "This is the real thing!" She swung the door open and performed her first superhero pose. "Time to be a hero!"

She shook when she heard a pair of gunshots in the air.

"No!" She exclaimed, making a beeline across the street to the bank. "Those were gunshots. I've got to hurry!"

* * *

The man in the passenger backseat named Pop, looked up from loading a compact submachine gun.

Back at the street, the driver guided the car to a parking spot in front of the bank. He kept the engine running while his comrades exited the vehicle and went into the bank. Snap, Crackle, and Pop carried assault rifles; they carried several empty duffel bags as well. Once inside, Snap charged into the lobby and pulled out the sub-machine gun and opened fire on the monitors, which exploded in a shower of sparks and shattered plastic.

A different kind of chaos erupted. Horrified customers hit the floor or else raced for the exits, only to find their way blocked by yet more gunmen. There were shouts from the tellers, a warning cry from a bank executive. Pop hit the security guard on the head with the butt of his weapon, while Crackle closed the door and lowered the blinds and he joined his compatriots, hording the hostages into the center of the room. Smoke and the smell of gunpowder filled the air. Desperate tellers pleaded for their lives.

Snap, who appeared larger and better built than the other two, strode onto the floor like a conqueror. Muscles bulged beneath his black leather jacket. It fit as snugly as a second skin. He had the build of a bouncer or a professional wrestler, and held his head high.

Getting a sensational thrill from driving the fear from others, he raised his gun and fired a burst into the ceiling.

He fired another burst and yelled, "Everybody down on the floor—**NOW!**

"Feel free to file a complaint with your customer service agent when we're finished," added Pop, watching all the customers and employees alike dropped to their hands and knees, then to their bellies. "In the meantime, everybody just be cool."

Then one of the tellers managed to press the silent-alarm button as she went down.

"Remain calm and you may survive this," Snap addressed the frightened customers. "Lay down on your stomachs. Put your hands out where they can be seen. Do *not* look directly at us."

Inside the lobby, people were nervously shuffling into line. Some were translating the robbers' comments for those who did not understand English. Women were removing their earrings and other jewelry with shaking hands. Men were taking off their watches and pulling wallets out of their pockets. One by one, the bank customers stepped forward and dropped their valuables into Crackle's satchel.

The tellers were already in the bank trying to open the main vault, which looked like it belonged on the hub of a submarine. Sometimes the combos for the door worked, sometimes they didn't. It depended if anyone had the magic touch that day or not.

This day, the tellers did not have the magic touch.

The young teller sat in a chair in front of the submarine door, biting the sheet of codes between her teeth while trying to get combos to work. Fortunately, she had a spare teller box with money in a smaller vault in the back room.

"Get that vault open right now!" Thundered Snap, as he brandished his submachine gun at the teller's face.

She struggled to breathe. "P-please, it's my first day. Just wait—"

"In every minute that vault is not open I'm going to waste a hostage, and I'm going to make *you* choose!"

The crowd shared a collection of gasps and screams. Small children were crying as their parents held them close, shielding their eyes from the carnage.

"We don't want to hurt you so don't struggle," Snap strongly advised. "This money is insured by the government, anyway. If there are no heroes, then there will be no casualties."

"Well, I'm not planning on being a casualty," a bold voice called out from the other side of the building.

Everyone turned their heads to discover a woman in a formfitting, dark blue unitard with a long flowing cape. Her head was encased in a cowl that covered her eyes but left her mouth and chin exposed. She wore large white star that was emblazoned across her chest like it were a code of arms.

"But I am going to stop you!" She further declared, placing her hands on her hips in a manner that was in total authority.

The robbers stopped what they were doing and stared at this crazy woman. Even Snap who was the tough guy in the group was always calm in a crisis, was at a loss for words. When he did managed to speak, he stammered, "Who...er, *what* are you?"

"I am the Avenging Star," Jane answered with great showmanship. Her whole attitude changed in an instant. She dropped the coy, girlish act and took on a cockier, more confident posture. "And you are all under arrest! Put your guns down and surrender. Don't make me have to resort to violence!"

The group exchanged puzzled looks, while the robbers once again tried to make eye contact with the Avenging Star. She held her focus on Snap.

He paused for a moment, and took all this in. Then he broke into laughter. Crackle and Pop joined in as well. Snap laughed so hard there were tears in his eyes.

"A superhero, eh?" He examined the strange girl. He looked over to the hostages who were just as clueless as him. They cowered when he waved his gun in the air. "Seriously, is this someone's birthday or something? Better yet, some sort of bachelor party gag?"

Pop zipped up the duffel bag, not before pulling out several crisp dollar bills. "Over here, honey!" He carried out, waving the money. "I got something for you. My safe word is blueberry pancakes."

Snap shot him a look. "You wanna take it down a notch, Pop? And that's coming out of your share."

Ignoring the sexist taunts from her blue collared adversaries, she addressed the hostages. "Have no fear, citizens. I will save you."

She was still oozing with confidence. She felt like she could take on the whole world. Nothing could stop her now.

Except for a similar face that stood out in the crowd that broke her concentration. "Pete?"

Why is he here?! I have to be perfect…for him!

Why, I can't let my future husband come to any harm. Relax and remember: what would Judo Girl do?

Jane landed on her feet, crouching. Then she stood slowly and faced the bank robbers. She looked tall and strong and fearless, and her cape flowed in the breeze of central air.

"Put down the gun," she said. Her voice was deep and commanding.

Snap sneered, "Bite me."

Jane marched up to Snap and went for his gun. "I'll just take that."

She struggled to pry the sub-machine gun from him, but he was just too strong. With one good yank, he toppled Jane. Before she could react, he smacked her across the forehead with the gun. She dropped to the floor in a heap. Her head felt like it was caving in and she could see blood leaking onto the floor in front of her.

Jane lifted her head, on the verge of passing out. Her blurry eyes widened.

Seeing stars, she groaned, "Wait…that wasn't supposed to happen."

Her vision went blurry as she held her head in her hands. Blood starting to drip down her arms. She was too afraid to close her eyes, thinking that she might go unconscious.

She tried to get up, but found herself being pushed against the floor with a barrel of a gun being pressed against the back of her head.

"This dumbass chick thinks she's a hero—costume and all," said Pop. "What kind of powers do you have—the ability to eat lead? Don't you know there ain't no such thing as superheroes? You're nuts, lady."

Snap was doing what he did best—supervising. He had been planning this heist for a very long time and he wasn't going to have some geek ruin everything. An example must be made.

"Pop," he called over to his partner. "Take the mask off. It's a little distracting."

To her utter shock, Pop yanked off her mask. The robbers hadn't given the slightest thought as to what this chick really looked like, but they were all surprised to se just how young she was.

The mask was gone.

The Avenging Star was gone.

Jane Travers took her place. But to everyone else in the bank, she was nobody. Except for Pete, who felt his jaw hit the floor.

"What the hell?" He whispered in awe.

Her secret identity has been exposed. It was out there for the whole world to see. Not only did the bad guys know her face, but she also had made Pete a target. And worst of all, she ruined her big chance on being a real hero.

"Well, I've got bad news for you, 'heroine'," said Snap, walking to her with his gun held high. "You've just screwed up our timetable for this robbery. We should have had more time to get the money so it's going to cost you. It's going to cost you your life." He nodded over to Pop, who had been ready to make his bones ever since he joined this gang. "Kill her."

CHAPTER FIVE

Out of all the three robbers, the one known only as Crackle was the brains of the outfit. His real name was Finley Rogers. Everyone else called him Fin. He and his brother Snap, or Calvin when he's off the clock had been robbing banks for quite a while and they knew every trick in the book. They learned the art of bank robbery from their father who led a secret double life. When he wanted accomplices, he turned to the two people he trusted most in the world: his kids. One might say it was a family business.

Their grandfather was a loan officer at First Federal Savings and Loan. After their mother passed away their father, Alfred, went into a downward spiral. He began to drink heavily and fell behind on house payments. The whole family had to move into the grandparents' house after the bank foreclosed on them. Alfred went through a couple of jobs, but none of them seemed to stick. Times got tough when his car was repossessed.

During that time, he began thinking about how to make extra money. He remembered one day his father had come home and said First Federal had been robbed. When he asked why no one had stopped the thief, his father replied that the tellers were trained to comply with robbers—because the money was insured and the bank would get it back.

One morning, after dropping off the kids at school, he drove to a branch of his dad's old bank. He strode in wearing a ball cap, black sweats, a white painter's mask, and sunglasses. He was carrying a trash bag and an antique pistol that was unloaded. He went up to a window, demanded the teller's money, and ordered her not to add bait bills or dye packs. She dumped around $2,500 into his bag. He walked back to his truck, drove around for a while to see if he was being followed, and went home.

A couple of days later, the local paper published a grainy black-and-white frame from a video showing the robber. Alfred's own mother said the man looked a little like him and he just laughed.

Alfred did his next heist a year later after falling behind on bills, and he got $1,500 from another small bank. Then he landed a full-time job with an engineering company earning $25 an hour. Still, once a year he'd pulled off a robbery, bringing in $5,000 and $10,000.

He didn't feel like a criminal. He didn't load his pistol. He knew he wasn't going to shoot anybody. And he kept telling himself that whatever money he got was insured, so who was really being hurt?

Fin and Calvin never once suspected that their father had a secret life. Quickly before Alfred knew it, he was already planning another robbery.

Alfred knew that if he had accomplices, he could get cash from several tellers' drawers and perhaps even get to the bank's vault. But there was no one he could trust to stay quiet—except his two sons. Then he considered bringing them into the fold.

He thought long and hard about it. As long as they did what he said, they wouldn't get caught. And he would use the money to start a small business they could run.

He approached his sons and said he had a second job as a part-time bank robber. The way they looked at him, they knew he wasn't kidding.

Alfred said he would be the "muscle", leading the way in and scaring the employees and customers, and Calvin would be the "bag man", ordering tellers to put money into his bag. They'd wear disguises, go to the bank early in the morning before there were many customers, and be out within three minutes. Alfred told Calvin they would easily grab $40,000 or more.

On the morning of the robbery, Calvin was scared. Alfred did the robbery by himself, getting a few thousand dollars, and came home before lunch.

Fin joined them, and it wasn't long before he began talking to his father about a bank robbery. He wanted money for college.

Alfred picked out a nearby Comerica. He began walking past it in the mornings with the family's black Lab, Lucy, to see when it would get busy, and he had Calvin go in to learn the layout of the lobby. But they needed a getaway driver—and there was only one person who came to mind. Fin accepted.

In the house, Calvin and his dad practiced bursting into a bank and yelling at everyone to get their hands up. They planned the robbery for September 17th, when Fin had a day off from Best Buy. The night before, Alfred had the kids steal license plates from a car at another complex and put them over the Nissan's plates.

The robbery went off as planned. Outside, Fin gave them updates over the walkie-talkie. At the three-minute mark, Calvin and his dad managed to unlock the back door, and they jumped into the Nissan. Fin drove to another neighborhood, and Calvin and his Alfred threw their disguises, pistols, stolen plates, and gloves into a Dumpster. In their house they stared wide-eyed at the money, close to $70,000—a stunning haul from a small branch bank.

Alfred was awakened by his alarm clock, and then took a shower, dried off, got dressed, and walked into the living room. Calvin and fin were waiting for him on the couch.

"You ready, boys?" He asked.

The boys both nodded in unison. The family headed out the door and walked toward Alfred's 2003 Nissan. He was big, six foot four and 240 pounds, and he squeezed himself into the passenger seat. Calvin, who at the time, was six-two and 200 pounds, crammed into the backseat.

Fin started the car, and five minutes later, he pulled into a shopping center and parked about 50 yards from Comerica Bank. Alfred grabbed a black garbage bag from the floorboard and took out two pairs of white painter's coveralls, two painter's masks, two pairs of latex gloves, and two Airsoft pistols, which looked like real guns but shoot plastic pellets. He and Calvin put on their disguises in the Nissan. Alfred clipped a walkie-talkie to his coveralls and handed another to Fin.

It was nine-thirty. They sat for the next 30 minutes, until Alfred said it was time to make their move. Fin dropped them off a few stores from the bank and drove to the alley behind it. Minutes later, his dad's voice crackled through his walkie-talkie.

"We're going in," Alfred said.

The family was as unlikely a set of robbers as one could imagine. They had no pressing financial issues and no obvious personal problems. Alfred, who was a widower and worked as an engineer made pretty good money. Fin was a member of Geek Squad at Best Buy, and Calvin was going to enlist in the Marines.

Around the town they were regarded as "regular, everyday people." Yet when it came to robbing banks, they were very bold, very daring, and very risky. They were lucky they didn't get caught up in a shoot-out.

They pulled off the two robberies: the first being the Comerica heist and the second being the robbery of a credit union, two months later. They were getting ready for a third when Alfred collapsed on a heart attack. He died three days later.

Soon after Calvin shipped off to the Marines, leaving Fin by himself. Fin being the smart one of the family decided he could pull a heist all by himself. All he needed to do was plan accordingly and consider every possible outcome.

Fin took a page out of his father's book on the first heist. He walked into a bank and waited in line just like any customer. When the next teller was available, he simply walked up to the young woman behind the counter and handed her an envelope with a handwritten message. Thinking he was requesting for a withdrawal, she took out the necessary slip but before she could hand it over to him she finally read the envelope.

It was instructions…to give him all their $50s and $100s.

No mask, no gun, no threat. The teller did what he asked because that was what she was supposed to do.

Fin just told her what she wanted, and she complied. This was how it worked in America because the amount of money a bank gives up usually five or seven thousand dollars a year per bank robbery was infinitely less than the amount of business they'd lose if all hell broke loose in a bank full of customers.

He was never even armed. Except for a hammer he had strapped to his leg under his pants just below his knee in case he needed to break out of a locked door or something, but he never used a gun or anything like that.

He would rob banks around 3:00 p.m., when the cops were changing shifts. Afterwards, he would go out, usually at Applebee's or somewhere else. Each robbery would make him around $5,000, and he had a specific reasoning for asking for $50s and $100s. All of the marked bills, dye packs, and tracking stuff were in the twenty-dollar bills, so he definitely didn't want those. And all the singles, fives, and tens were even a small denomination that they wouldn't add up to much anyway. It wasn't worth the extra time for them to get *everything* out of their drawer.

Also if someone else noticed the teller clearing out the drawer, it might look weird and trigger some sort of response. Getting out a bunch of $50s and $100s, however, seemed to be the quickest way and drew no attention from other tellers.

A bank robbery, often portrayed very glamorously in the movies, is not a lucrative career. Most robberies result in a relatively small amount of money leaving the distribution. Banks are much more careful these days about keeping vaults stacked full of money (again, it's not like the movies). They knew that keeping too much cash around was an unwise idea for a variety of reasons.

Before he even went through with the robbery, he cased the bank five months earlier. He studied mostly the things that people did to get caught, and he just tried to plan around those things. It was hard to know how people got away since these details rarely make it to the news, but studying how people get caught was absolutely helpful in knowing what to avoid.

Once he did his first bank job, very little planning was needed for subsequent banks. He never really scoped out a particularly location other than to make sure there was parking that was out of view from the bank.

Fin was the smart one of the family, and he devised his own unique way on knocking over a bank. For this robbery he would need a police scanner, a Netflix subscription, a rebreather, hypochlorite bleach, a rubber bullet (just in case), acetone, tattoo stencils, gloves, and a license plate block-out kit.

Fin picked a smaller, single building bank in a smaller town, preferably in a hot state. He had gotten a safety deposit box at the bank and kept the key.

First part of the plan was to create chloroform using the hypochlorite bleach and acetone, mix the two ingredients slowly and distill it for human use using sulfuric acid. Then he set up an escape route in case something goes wrong. Fin had found the fastest route to a busy highway using Google Maps. His getaway vehicle will be a Chevrolet Silverado pickup. He applied the license plate blockout kit on both plates. Before he left for the bank he had Netflix running on his computer streaming a movie, one that he knew and one that was at least two hours long, and this two-hour long movie will play until 8:00 a.m.

Next would be the actual robbery. He went to the bank on a Tuesday at around 8:00 a.m., and made sure the AC was on. He boiled chloroform in a plastic bag tied to the AC unit using a magnifying glass to heat it up because chloroform evaporates very easily. Next he would apply his tattoo stencils to around his neck area and neck and apply a rebreather. He would walk into the bank wearing sunglasses, and a hoodie to block his face and hopefully everyone inside of this bank will be unconscious from the chloroform. He would try to flash his fake tattoos as much as possible to the security cameras without being obvious and calmly jump over the center to where the bank tellers were sitting, and grabbed as much individual tens, hundreds, and twenties as possible to avoid dye packs. Oh, those stupid dye packs. He would leave his scanner in the bank and get out of there at precisely 8:10.

Fin's goal was $5,000 and he would stash all the money inside of his safety deposit box, and walk outside of the bank. Then he would get into his Silverado, drove to the highway he had plotted on Google Maps, and intentionally get a ticket. He would use peppermint oil or another irritant to make his eyes bloodshot so he could appear high, and let the officer search his car. This would be his alibi in case he would become a suspect.

After receiving the ticket he went home, relaxed, and waited until the robbery appeared on the news. If he had done everything right he should have gotten away with it.

His brother Calvin, who had been discharged from the Marines was holding down two jobs as a construction worker by day and as a bouncer at a nightclub at night. Despite the money he brought in and also Fin's job as a Geek Squad representative at Best Buy; it wasn't enough to make ends meet. Missing the good old days with their dad, they decided to pick up where they left off years ago. They needed a third person for their team so they had settled on recruiting their childhood friend Nathan. Fin came up with the schemes and Calvin graduated from bagman to the muscle of the group.

The gang made their way across the country. Their strategies changed, and so had their names. In Chicago, they were known as Larry, Moe, and Curly. In Kansas City, they were Yippy, Yappy, and Yahooey. And now they were in the guise of beloved breakfast cereal icons Snap, Crackle and Pop.

As of late, Nathan has been the most unreliable. When he was first brought in, it was everything he could have hoped for. He never once had suspected the

Rogers brothers of being bank robbers. He was going through a rough patch himself with zero job prospects. Fin and Calvin taught him the tools of the trade and what they did with the spoils. Instead of stashing the money and saving, Nathan wanted to live the life of a rock star. He drank more than half that money away, while everything else went to girls and up his nose. They were about to cut him out, but Nathan begged to stay on and promised he would clean up his act. The booze and the drugs were one thing, but the main problem with Nathan was the way he escalated things. He had become an action junkie. After one heist was over, he kept pushing the brothers to pull of another as soon as possible. He was no longer a friend or a teammate. He had become a liability. The brothers were still on the fence about whether or not to beat their friend out of the gang, but they gave him one last chance.

Through an underworld connection Fin and Calvin hired a wheelman to help them with their robberies. The cardinal rule of hiring outside help was not to reveal any personal information that would incriminate everyone in the event of apprehension.

They had been hitting all the banks in the city, and decided to hit one more before moving onto another state. At the hideout, Fin logged onto his Netflix account and started to stream *Black Panther* before stepping into the car with Calvin and Nathan, and their getaway driver.

Fin glanced at his brother from the backseat. Dressed in a black sweater and cargo pants, Snap looked like the cool, highly skilled professional he was. As their getaway driver rolled up the street, Calvin's deep-set blue eyes constantly scanned the street—windows, roofs, pedestrians, vendors—everything. His mind and body were on hyper-alert.

As the driver slowed down, Fin started handing out their matching ski masks and announced to the group, "All right, let's review code names."

"Snap," said Calvin, methodically checking his nine-millimeter pistol before slipping it into his shoulder holster and taking his mask.

"Crackle," said Fin, pulling the black balaclava over his head.

Nathan dozed off since they left the hideout. Fin gave him a nudge to the ribs. Nathan jolted awake, exclaiming, "Pop!"

While Nathan got into character, Snap opened the door and hit the ground running. "Let's do this," he ordered his team.

Pop left the sedan and covered Snap's back as he trotted to the bank and opened the door. Crackle got out and covered the street, leaving the driver with the engine running.

And now there they were, pulling off their last heist in the city, until some chick in a Zorro outfit came flying through the door. It was like something out of a movie, and this was the part where the hero would beat up all the bad guys and save the day.

But unfortunately, this wasn't that kind of movie.

Jane should have been terrified. These men were killers and all had survived the ordeals that had been visited on Jane and the outnumbered her. They were armed, and her only weapon was her body.

"I'm sorry, 'Avenging Star', that you have to die," stated Snap, feigning sympathy. "It's nothing personal. It's just business."

Pop held Jane at gunpoint. He pulled back the hammer and grinned. "How lucky for you that I love my work."

Underneath his mask, Snap hid a confused expression. *When did Nathan start doing this tough guy shit? He seems to be enjoying this a little too much.*

Now she was more than scared. She was terrified! All the courage she had before was gone. These guys were out of control, and they would probably kill her if she tried to fight back. The fear emitting from the crowd didn't help either.

Jane couldn't help but laugh. The robbers looked at each other, confused.

"What's so funny, kid?" Asked Snap, feeling uneasy. "You're going to die and you're just laughing?"

"Oh, you poor, deluded fools," she said, smiling. "Surrender now, and you won't get hurt."

"Can you believe this chick?" Crackle asked his fellow bank robbers.

Pete almost answered him. *Yes, she is a little crazy. No, she's freakin' nuts!*

"I don't like it," Pop added, lowering his pistol. "You think she's suicidal? If she's doing all this superhero stuff so she could get someone to punch her ticket, I'm not interested. On the platform of assisted euthanasia, I am totally against it."

"This is getting weird for me, too," Snap chimed in. "I mean, look at the size of that star on her shirt. It might as well be a bull's eye. This didn't seem fun anymore. It is just sad. I say we refer her to a good counselor and be on our way."

While the robbers where discussing on what to do with Jane, Pete was able to go unnoticed. He saw it all from his place among his fellow hostages. Already terrified, he numbly watched Jane prepare herself for battle. He saw her lift her head, scanning the bank, her expression radiant with some strange energy. Then she did something that speared him with raw horror.

Jane leaned forward and pressed her forehead against the gun's barrel.

It's the weird girl from the salon, he shockingly discovered. *Is she trying to get us killed? I can't let them kill her—even if she is weird and always staring at me.*

Pete raised himself up and bull rushed the huge robber.

Let's hope all those years of wrestling have paid off!

Snap felt the floor disappear beneath him. He lost his balance and collided with Pop. The slender thief banged his head against the glass at the teller's booth and immediately went down. Crackle couldn't believe what he had just seen.

"What the—?!"

With Pop distracted, Jane leaned in and sucker-punched Snap. The huge bank robber toppled like an avalanche, sending him to the floor. His assault rifle scattered across the tiles away from his reach. Pop tried to hammer Jane like a tent pole with the handle of his pistol but caught his arm in mid swing.

"Yeeeahhh!" She shouted, wrestling him for the gun. "Here comes justice!"

Pop, who had yet to utter anything more coherent than a grunt, let out an agonizing moan.

Pop looked up at Jane, one of the veins in his massive forehead throbbing. "You find yourself amusing, you little bitch?"

"Well, I generally don't fly in the face of public opinion."

"You'll be laughing out of the other side of your—"

The rest of Pop's sentence was cut off by a well-placed punch delivered by Pete.

Quickly leaping up, she did the bravest and dumbest thing of her life…she grabbed the gun. She pointed it up toward the ceiling as she fired two shots.

BANG! BANG!

Pop got an arm free and gave Jane a good dig to the face.

She couldn't back down now. She kicked out his knees and he crashed down onto them.

He punched her in the stomach, and she fell to her knees as well.

Pop regained his footing and aimed his gun at her head. "Listen, this has been fun and all, but do you give up?"

"Give up?" Jane spat blood. "Never."

Even as she said the words, she knew they sounded foolish. She didn't know the extent of her power yet; this was the first time she'd really been in a fight. But she knew she could hold her own against any normal enemy. Then she did something very unexpected.

She punched him in the family jewels.

The momentum was not only enough for Pop to drop his gun but to also send him to ground as well. He curled up on the floor in the fetal position holding his fellas. His ski mask was soaked with tears and sweat. Crackle couldn't believe his own eyes. After months of planning, it all went down to the tubes because of some crazy chick and her overprotective boyfriend?

Crackle lifted his pant leg, and swiftly pulled apart the adhesive tape off his leg so he could get to the hammer he carried with him in case of emergencies. He didn't need to use it until now. He let out a loud yelp as the tape pulled out some hair and skin. He gripped the handle tightly and charged right at Jane, giving out a primal war cry. He was like a bull that just saw red.

"You ruined everything!" He yelled, raising the ball-peen hammer into the air.

All Jane could see was that hammer coming straight at her. Before she could even react, Pete jumped onto her attacker's back, putting his arms around his neck.

"Awwk!" Crackle croaked as Pete sprang off him, dropping the hammer in the process. Pete flipped the malicious mastermind over his shoulder.

Jane watched Pete take down the remaining robber. She was fascinated by his crime fighting skills. He was a hero in the making.

He's wonderful! Jane smiled with admiration. *I wonder if he'd team up with me…*

CHAPTER SIX

Down on the streets, police wagons lined up. SWAT teams waited coolly, used to the long hours of negotiation that might be necessary before they were ordered into sudden action. Detective Joseph Roberts stood at a street corner, waiting. He's been chewing on his third toothpick of the day. As the seasoned detective plucked it out of his mouth and tossed it aside, he took the time to observe the media circus that occupied Main Street. It really irked him to see numerous news reporters trying to get closer to the crime scene. They were all pushing and shoving each other behind the long yellow tape. It took several officers to break up the unruly crowd.

Roberts shifted his gaze over to the costumed young lady involved in the robbery. She sat on the tailgate of the ambulance while a paramedic tried to look over her. But she waved him away in defiance. She got a little ill-tempered when he tried to remove her mask. For some reason she looked familiar to Roberts. He knew her from somewhere but he just couldn't place her, as he ambled along the bank's steps. A rumpled tan trench coat was draped over his muscular frame. His weathered features wore a chronically sour expression.

On the sidewalk, soft-news reporters were speaking on camera, smugly aware that, for once, they were at the forefront of a breaking story. Roberts heard them as background commentary. He had walked beside the uniforms to take statements of the bank's customers and employees, as forensics gathered the evidence. The reporters spotted him and surged forward. A correspondent for the *Evening Star* shoved a microphone into Roberts' face and shouted a question he hardly heard. He shoved it back with an abrupt, "No comment," and raced after Pete.

An ambulance screamed up to the curb. Squad cars turned onto the street, their red, white, and blue lights flashing, reflections bouncing off the building's facades.

She was crazy…that was all she could say about herself. One could say she was brave and noble, but she was crazy and stupid. But she had to do it.

Jane had known that there was press all over the place. Certainly she'd seen scenes like this in movies and TV shows. But she had never experienced anything like this in real life, with reporters jockeying for position, shouting from all around, taking pictures from every direction.

"Miss," the paramedic said to her, snapping her back into reality. "We really do need to check you out. Witnesses say you may have been hurt when the robbers struck you."

"Really, I feel fine," she assured him. "Just a few bumps and…oh, my!"

She felt a quick surge of relief as Pete stepped out of the crowd. Jane looked at him long and hard. She thought more of this man than she had of anyone for a long time, she needed someone to unburden herself and Pete might even be able to help.

"There's Pete, talking to that officer. I hope my partner hasn't been traumatized by this public service! I could never forgive myself if anything happened to his dreamy face. Strong muscles. Beautiful smile. Strong voice. Penetrating eyes. Huh? Wait—is that the detective who questioned me in the park? I wonder what they're talking about?

The paramedic looked confused. "Miss? What are you talking about? *Who* is talking?"

Jane quickly turned her gaze away from the man of her dreams to the bewildered emergency response worker. Her cheeks flushed red with embarrassment.

"Uhhh…no one," she replied. "I must be in worse shape than I thought."

Before the paramedic could answer, an officer's badge caught his eye. "Excuse me, sir," said the head detective. "The lady and I need to speak. In private."

Jane didn't like the sound of that last sentence. The detective spoke in a tone similar to her father whenever she had done something wrong or misbehaved. She's about to get a lecture about leaving this sort of thing to the police.

"Detective," she said, standing in attention, "just the person I needed to see. No thanks is necessary. I only request a meeting with the commissioner. I have several designs for a possible searchlight he can shine in the sky in case of—"

"I don't want to hear it," Roberts said sternly. This took Jane back. This wasn't the response she was expecting. "Before we begin, will you please take that mask off? It's hard for me to take you seriously in that goofy getup."

Jane was aghast. How could he ask that? They only just met.

"You…you wouldn't take the mask off the Lone R—" She stammered.

"The mask," he demanded. "*Now.*"

Jane hesitantly complied. She slowly pulled back her cowl, as her auburn hair cascaded down past her shoulders. The detective's prying eyes grew wide. She felt naked and exposed for the whole world to see. She felt the insecurities envelope her and she just wanted to disappear.

Roberts took a breath. "Yes, I remember you," he said finally. Jane turned her head to the side, not making eye contact with him. "From the park, last weekend. Jane, right? I also remember what we talked about. We talked about the dangers of trying to be a hero. Clearly, you didn't listen to me. So I'll repeat myself for the last time. This ends now!" His tone was unmistakable. His relief had turned back to contempt. "What you're doing isn't a game! This is extremely dangerous!

People could have been killed in there! *You* could have been killed in there if it wasn't for that guy!"

"He's my partner!" Jane blurted. "You should have seen us in there! As a team, we were unstoppable! We totally had the situation under control—like clockwork."

The detective couldn't believe what he had just heard. The anger on his face was replaced by bewilderment. She hadn't gone off the reservation—she was opening her own damn casino!

"Jane, all of the witnesses said that had he not acted, you would be dead. He was worried about you. He doesn't even know who you are."

Jane didn't know what he was talking about. He absolutely knew nothing about their relationship. Who does he think he was on telling her what she could and could not do?

Roberts' sharp features became steely. His voice was calm, but his jaw shook with anger. He swallowed hard. After all these years on the force, he'd learned to distinguish the idle wacko threats from the real thing. Jane might be crazy, but she was on the level crazy. Roberts had absolutely no doubt that she meant business. He was ready to bet his detective's gold shield on that.

Jane shook her head. "I'm joining up," she went on, supremely confident.

Roberts was having none of it. "You're totally out of control. You're going to get yourself killed!"

"I'm going to be your partner," the girl assured him. "Whenever the call comes, I'll know. Whenever you go out at night, I'll be watching. And where's trouble, I'll be right there fighting alongside you. How are you going to stop me?"

Roberts gaze held Jane's. "I can stop you," he said simply, and Jane knew it was true. Angrily, she turned away and stormed through the crowd. Roberts stared after her, rubbed his eyes, and sighed.

Somehow his words seemed to shake Jane, as she tried to grasp what her onetime calling meant.

"I…" he hesitated, trying to break this delicately to her. "There is a counselor on the scene I'd like for you to talk with."

"Of course, he knows who I am," Jane insisted. "He's…he's just, just trying to protect our secret identities! You don't know what you're talking about!"

She could feel her hands shaking. There was a lump in her throat that was making hard for her to breathe. She could feel her eyes welling up.

"I need to…" she struggled. "I need to get out of here!"

She shoved past him and ran fast as she could through the crow of onlookers and uniformed officials. Detective Roberts' pleas fell upon deaf ears.

"Jane, wait!" He called out. "You need help!"

Through some bizarre turn of thought that probably made sense to Jane Travers, but certainly no one else, she thought the admonishment as some sort of challenge.

As soon as Jane returned home, her family was waiting for her. Her mother and father were sitting on the couch, while her uncle was leaning against the wall that separated the foyer and the family room. The tension was so thick Jane could cut through it with a knife. Jane had watched a lot of *A & E* to know an intervention when she saw one.

"What's this?" She asked her family.

Her mother gave her a smile and gestured sweetly over to the middle seat of the couch. "Honey, why don't you come over and have a seat."

Jane stepped back, she was close to the door. "I can't, Mom. I gotta—"

Uncle Charlie was blocking her way. He looked down on her with a steely gaze. She got a strange vibe coming from him.

"Jane," he said in a tone that was totally alien to her. It was rather stern and serious. "Sit down."

Not testing her uncle, she joined her parents over at the couch. She knew what all of this was about. The news about the bank robbery was all over town. Even her involvement was publicized. Now she had to sit there, and listen to her parents yell at her for doing something crazy and stupid. But instead, they decided to take a different approach.

"Sweetie," her mother said in a very nurturing voice. "We're all worried about you. This is not like you at all. The police said that you were nearly killed at the bank. And if it weren't for that man who stopped them…"

"Pete and I *both* stopped them," Jane told them. She was excited to tell them about her adventure. "We're a fantastic duo!"

Her father bit his lip. "Detective Roberts said—"

"He talked to you?!" Jane interrupted. She felt a little unhinged. "Who does he think he is? He has no right talking to you!"

"Yes, he did," her father boldly clarified. "And he's very worried about you. He looked over to his wife and Charlie. "*We're* very worried about you. We think you need some rest and quiet."

Jane lowered her head, feeling frustrated, feeling ashamed, feeling angry that she had gotten was more frustration and conflict. First her family criticizes her on her new career path. Now she herself was criticizing her values and methods on being a hero. A little more treatment like this and she'd be ready to throw herself off the roof.

"No," Jane said softly. "No!" Her outburst sent everyone back. This wasn't like her at all. "I will not! I'm doing good here! People need my help! And I'm not going to stop trying to help!" She got out of her seat and ran up the stairs. "I don't need your help! I don't even need *Pete's* help! I don't need anybody!" Then she slammed her bedroom door.

At the salon, the moment she walked along the reception desk, the atmosphere was tense—Ang Lee's *Hulk* tense. Jane could feel the eyes burning into the back of her workplace as she walked past each of the girls. It made her feel uneasy. She had gotten used to being ignored or forgotten, to the point where she was often mistaken for a new stylist because some people wouldn't even recognize her. To have that kind of attention now made her feel uneasy just for existing.

Debra was surprised to see Jane. She put a hand on her shoulder. Her eyes were filled with sympathy. "Jane, sweetie," she soothed gently. "We didn't expect to see you today. Here…let's go talk in the back."

Jane followed her into the supply closet. Jane noticed they're already gotten their new shipment on several hair care products, and she just had to leap in to look at each and every one, much to Debra's chagrin.

"Oh, I see the hair product re-supply just came in!" Jane said with glee. "I didn't even know Jason came by this week. How is he? He's such a sweetie! I mean, a total hunk! Oh, do I have any clients today? I'm sorry I wasn't here earlier." She looked over to the shelf and picked up a box filled with bottles of shampoo. "I hope Mr. Johnson is all right slumming it with Elizabeth. I totally threw the alarm to the other side of the room. If there are no clients, I'll be more than happy to unpack all of this stuff! I wonder if we got all the product I requested…"

Debra held her head and sighed exasperatingly. "Look, Jane," she said patiently, "we heard about what happened yesterday. We're all very worried."

Jane felt a little alarmed. "Oh, yeah. Well, I'm feeling okay today and I'm ready to work, so why don't I just get started on this. It'll be good to refocus and get my sea legs back and…"

Before she could utter another word, Debra grabbed her by the shoulders and leered at her. Jane was frightened.

"Jane, *STOP!*" Debra yelled at her. She had yelled at Debra a couple of times but not like this. "You need time off—right *now*. Go home. Get some rest!"

Jane broke away from her. "I don't need rest," she said, shouldering her satchel. "I'm fine! I feel great! Why can't you just let me be?!"

"But—" Debra tried to say. It was too late. Jane had already turned and burst out of the supply closet door.

"I don't need rest!" Jane shouted at Debra.

Debra went after her, ignoring her employees who stood to the side, shaking their heads. "Jane, wait! Stop!" She called out. But Jane became a hurricane around everyone around her. They all steered clear from her path.

She ignored the looks from the other stylists as she made her way to the door. She didn't notice that not all of them were mocking her little scene. Some of the male customers' eyes followed her nicely filled jeans.

"I've got to get out of here," she seethed. "I need to figure stuff out." Along the way she was getting scrutinized looks from both staff and customers alike. She exchanged smiles to everyone she passed. "I'll see you all later! Bye! Bye-bye!"

When she bolted out the door, she almost crashed into Pete. Like a deer frozen in headlights she raised her eyes to see his bewildered face.

"Uh, Jane. Are you all right? I didn't expect to see you there."

"Hi, Pete," said Jane, feeling surprised to see him. She must look like a mess after that argument with Debra. She assumed Pete thought she might have gotten in trouble with the police about her involvement at the bank. She guessed being knocked out earned some sympathy points. "Um, how are you today?"

He seemed hesitant to answer. "I'm, I'm okay. How are you? I was worried about you."

Her eyes lit up. "You…you were worried about me? Really?" It was nice of him to be concerned about her safety.

He really does care about me!

"Yeah," Pete continued. "Detective Roberts said you'd tried to stop *other* crimes before…"

"No," Jane interrupted. "I successfully stopped many crimes before this one." She felt quite proud of herself. "This was just my—our highest profile case! Didn't we do great?"

His kind smile turned into a frown. Suddenly he became serious—deadly serious.

"No, we *didn't* do good," he sternly replied. It was like talking to a child who didn't know better. "You nearly got all of us killed! There were three of them—with guns! People almost died!"

Given Pete's change in attitude, it didn't waver Jane's confidence. She smiled to him.

"No one died, silly," she casually commented. "We stopped them. Wait—now that I think about it, there was a fourth one—a driver! He got away. Pete we need to find him—he needs to be stopped. He might try to rob more banks. He might try to break his buddies out of jail. He could be after us right now—having sworn an oath to destroy us! We need to get out of here! There is no telling what he may be up to. There may have been more of them. They might be preparing to strike now."

She was talking more to herself than to Pete. Without any more patience he placed his hands upon her shoulders and began to shake her. She wasn't listening to reason. She was far more out of it than he thought.

"Jane! Jane! Jane! Stop babbling. Jesus Christ, this isn't a comic book. This is real life! I just run a pet store. You work as a hair stylist. We are *not* superheroes!" He berated her.

She nodded reflexively, at which point Pete was positive she wasn't listening. "Excellent!" She cheered. "You're doing a great job," he whispered. "No one will ever connect us to our secret identities. This is just the beginning of our rise to becoming heroes!"

"Jesus! People are right about you!" Pete decided he had heard enough. Jane's insipid blathering wasn't even worth replying to. Turning away from her, he headed toward the exit. "You're not well. Look, just keep away from me. Don't even come near me! If I see you anywhere near the pet store I'm calling the cops."

"Good one, Pete," she said, trying her best not to cry. "That'll convince them. So, I'll talk to you soon, right?"

A curt "not interested" was his response.

Jane was undeterred.

"Not interested!" Pete said again, forcefully and loud enough for the others to hear. He briskly walked back to the pet store and slammed the door shut.

Then he was gone, leaving Jane glaring balefully after him. "You were supposed to understand." Her eyes darkened with growing obsession. "I'll *make* you understand."

If Pete had been able to hear the quiet nuance in those words, he might have thought again.

CHAPTER SEVEN

The fire had bridged two tenements in downtown. From a rooftop near the fire—but not too far, he learned that lesson—the lone figure watched the firefighters and waited for the first of them to enter one of the buildings. He shouldn't have indulged into this temptation—it's what got him caught the last time—but if he were any good at resisting temptation, he wouldn't be where he was. Not that he regretted being where he was, although the road had been painful at times.

He had lost his train of thought as the first of the deck guns started up and steam exploded from the burning upper floors of the southern building. It was burning faster than the one to the north, and the boys were also laying water curtains down the alleys on either side of the fire. The grinning arsonist started to wonder when they were going to go surround-and-down; that wasn't what he wanted. From a pocket of his long overcoat he took out a transmitter. He'd give them a couple of minutes, and if they didn't go interior by then, he was going to change the rules of engagement. The timing of the whole enterprise was important. If the firemen didn't cooperate and the Avenging Star doesn't show up, he was going to have a little problem on his hands.

Checking his watch, he saw three companies of firefighters had opted for the surround-and-down approach. Worse yet, it appeared to be working.

Cowards, he thought. *Why not just wait for it to rain?*

Surround-and-down was the suburban strip-mall approach. Urban firefighters were supposed to go interior, supposed to be killing each other to get the middle, to make it stop.

So: he flicked a switch on the transmitter, and a despairing scream peeked out of a broken window on the fourth floor of the northern building.

"Help me!"

That did the trick.

The felonious voyeur watched with a professional's eye as an interior team deployed. He waited for the six of them to get inside the building, and then he started counting, figuring twenty seconds for each floor in full gear. One of the aerials backed closer to the northern building and raised its ladder between the structure and a close string of electrical lines, before it came to rest against the wall below the broken window, one of the firemen was half way up it.

Brave souls, the arsonist thought. *Such brave souls.*

When his count reached eighty, he toggled another switch on the transmitter, and every window on the third floor blew out in a magnificent halo of flame. The force of the explosion flung the man off the ladder; trailing smoke, he tumbled in a long arc and landed flat on his back in the middle of Cassady Street. A pair of paramedics was converging on the spot before he hit the ground.

Two more men were already on their way up the ladder, and the deck guns swiveled around toward the northern building, pouring water in the windows facing the street. Already there was water coming out the front door of the building, but while water was the best way to ensure that you killed a fire, it was also the slowest, and it only works if you can put enough of it on a fire to get the fire to waste all its energy vaporing water instead of carbonizing tenants.

This is what you get, you courageous self-righteous bastards, he thought. *Did you think you could just humiliate me, turn me into a scapegoat? Did you think you could just call me crazy, and that would be the end of it?*

Two more aerials were maneuvering into position, from companies in adjacent districts. Here's where the timing gets tricky. If he had planned right and caught a break, it'll take the rescue teams long enough to get to the trapped men that certain person will hear of the crisis and respond. If he had it, then at least he had gotten to the first part of his revenge. Either way, it was a pretty good day—but he wanted the Avenging Star. He wondered if any of them had spotted the speaker setup, he thought. Might be a more interesting game if they figured out that they're being haunted.

The man gestured proudly at the carnage. He chuckled gleefully as he casually walked away from its fiery splendor.

"Aw, kiddo," said Charlie, comforting his heartbroken niece. He handed Jane another tissue. "I hate seeing you like this. You've got to let me help you."

"It's…" sniffled Jane, wiping away tears. "It's just like how I feel! I want to help people. *I am* helping people! It's just so hard. They're always laughing and pointing at me. It was going to be so perfect—me and Pete!"

"That's the guy from the bank that…helped you, right?" Asked Charlie. Jane nodded in response. "He seemed like a nice guy."

"Oh, he's wonderful!" She swooned. "He's going to be my partner—I just know it! Maybe he'll even want to be more than that. I just have to prove I'm worthwhile."

Charlie smiled. "Well, if he's worth anything, he'll definitely know how great you are. You've got unlimited potential. If you just stay focused, you can do anything." Then he eased up on the emotional support. "By the way, have you been taking your meds?"

"Oh, right," she groaned. "I forgot all about the drugs. They make me feel good. I need to go and get them. Thanks, Uncle Charlie."

Then she had an idea that went against her principles, but in order to compete against the criminal element she had to be on an even playing field. And with shame and regret, she had to turn in her D.A.R.E. program completion certificate.

There were times when Thomas Gierko could still find it hard to believe, but for nearly a decade, he made his living as a drug dealer. Meth, cocaine, ecstasy, pot, GHB, Special K; you name it, he had it, and sold it.

Meth was a distant second to coke when he began but by the end it was by far his most popular product, accounting for half of his sales and two-thirds of his profits. It also became his personal drug of choice, and for eight years he smoked it every day. It was because of meth that he went to prison and it took prison for him to finally quit meth.

Gierko, known by his street name Big T, had a very impressive clientele and was pulling in six figures a year. All of that was tax-free. He was a one-man operation: the CEO, sales staff, shipping department and bookkeeper all rallied into one. He carried two cell phones at all times. One of them was a burner that he used for his drug orders, and the other for everything else, which wasn't much. Big T never lurked around schools and playgrounds to peddle dope to America's youth. Most of his customers were hard working, productive members of society. The kind of people anyone would never suspect—and rather not know—are habitual drug users. Among them, a half dozen doctors, several lawyers, two research scientists, and even a police dispatcher.

But there would be a downside. He was racing toward the poorhouse at breakneck speed. His real job couldn't be blamed. When he lost his job, he was forced to consider the unthinkable for the first time: dealing drugs on a fulltime basis. But even if he could overcome the stigma of such an occupation, and handle the risks involved, he didn't have enough customers and his debts were mounting even faster. He applied for a few jobs but they didn't pan out. His self-esteem hit an all-time low. With a mindset that he had little to lose, he plunged into dealing with the same vigor and work ethic he had displayed in every job he'd ever held.

At first he was deathly afraid he wouldn't make enough to survive; so he did anything he could to increase sales. He grounded the cocaine so his customers wouldn't have to. He delivered anywhere, anytime. He gave out free drugs for new customer referrals. He even took checks. By the end of the first month, he was able to let out a sigh of relief. He had made a profit in excess of $5,000 and it seemed like he was going to make it after all…as long as he didn't get caught.

By the end of his third "fiscal year", meth sales had driven his monthly profit to an average of more than $18,000. Then, in a single moment of betrayal, his world turned upside down. Several years ago, his oldest and best customer was arrested selling coke that Big T had sold to him. Thinking he could save his own neck, he set T up to take the fall. He was initially charged with intent to distribute and spent three days in jail before making bail. He spent the next three years on the outside, fighting his case. The district attorney conceded upfront that the vehicle stop, T's detainment, the search of his vehicle and the seizure of evidence had been illegal, and seven of the 11 counts were quickly dismissed. But after 69 court appearances and $120,000 spent in his defense, he lost anyway.

Of course, T was guilty all along. He ended up serving almost 10 months in state prison and he was just starting his ninth month on parole since his release. And what about all the money he made? T didn't have much to show for it, that's for sure. He never bought any big-ticket items and whatever money the government didn't seize as ill-gotten gains ended up going to his lawyers. He was more in debt now than when he started dealing fulltime.

T was at his usual spot, with his back against a brick wall and he was either talking to one of his customers or his supplier on his burner phone. He didn't even notice Jane approaching him cautiously. She was well aware he was in the middle of a very important business call.

She took this time to assess her surroundings—the dark, crumbling street with a few abandoned cars parked on it, a Dumpster coated in layers of graffiti, two street lights, neither which were lit.

"Look, man," Big T said to the other end of the line. Looked like he had gotten a compliant which was a rarity in his line of work. But Big T was very professional about it. "All I'm sayin' is that if a vampire got bitten by a werewolf, he would still have problems during the daytime."

He turned to see Jane standing there. He blinked in surprise. Flummoxed, his reaction was priceless. She smiled sheepishly and waved politely at him. His eyes narrowed. She was the last person he'd expect to see.

"Hold on," he said to his irate customer. "Lemme holla atcha back." He hung up the phone and gave Jane a mean look. "Watchoo want now? Here to give me another hard time?"

Jane raised her hands in defense. "Whoa, whoa," she said, trying to calm him down. "I come in peace. Look, I'm sorry about before. It was very rude of me. I'm sorry, okay?"

T was ready to let her have it, but then he recognized her. "Hey," he said, reaching into her jacket pocket and pulling out a rolled up newspaper. "You're that crazy-ass chick in the paper, ain't ja?" He did a quick double take of her and the picture on the front page. It was a candid shot of Jane in her Avenging Star costume except her mask was missing and she was talking to Detective Roberts. A photographer must have somehow gotten through the police line and snapped the pic. T smiled all over. "Yeah, yeah! You were at the bank." Then he frowned. "You ain't here to bust me, are you?"

"No, no," Jane replied. "Given the fact that bustin' makes me feel good, but I'm actually here in a much different matter. I…well…I need your help. *I* like to help people, but I'm not good at it. Helping makes me feel good, and I *want* to feel good. My uncle reminded me about drugs, and…" She paused and took a breath. The next thing she said went so fast it almost Big T off his feet. He felt like a speeding train hit him. "You know, like the Mega-Brainster! He takes brain pills and gets *real* superpowers! He can do things with his brain—things nobody else can! That's what I need!"

Big T grinned. He liked the way this chick thinks. He stroked his chin in deep thought. "Yeah, okay…I think I got just watchoo need, kid. Just watchoo need!"

Jane returned home to an empty house. She felt relieved that she didn't need to explain the big, brown bag full of illegal drugs she was carrying in her hand. She couldn't handle two interventions in the same week. She was now free to try the new stuff out, away from judging eyes.

Jane walked into the kitchen to pour herself a glass of water. By the sink there was the wastebasket and it was overflowing with trash.

"Jesus…" She groaned with disgust. "Does anybody here know how to empty a trash can?"

She bent over to lift up the liner, but she became confused when she saw her Avenging Star costume balled up into the heap.

"What the…?" She said, picking up her soiled costume from the garbage. "How on earth did *this* get here?"

She raised it up to eye level and saw there were traces of tapioca across the front and some leftover Chinese food as well.

Guess I must have left it here, she mused.

"It's a good thing I needed a drink for my…" Then she noticed something else under her costume, something that couldn't be ignored.

What's that?

It was a discarded copy of the day's newspaper. The front page had a huge photo of a nightclub fire from the night before. There was an arsonist on the loose and he's been torching clubs for quite some time now.

"Holy cow!" Jane heard herself say out loud. *I've been to that club. In fact, I've been to all of the clubs mentioned. Is someone targeting the clubs I go to?*

That must be it!

Someone is hunting me!

Jane struggled to get the container open, but the damned childproof cap wasn't cooperating with her. After some "careful" persuasion the cap popped open. She poured two pills into her hand and ingested them. Then washed it down with a glass of water.

"I've got my very own arch-villain!" She squealed, slamming the glass down on the counter. *Who is he? Is he going to strike again?* Then it dawned on her. *McGriffin's! Of course!*

She picked up her costume and prepared to change into her costume. Then she stopped.

I can't go in my costume. The police are probably looking for me after what happened at the bank. I'll just go in my civilian clothes.

That's it! I'll go undercover. I'll have the element of surprise on my side.

She set the wet newspaper down on the counter. Ink bled from the headline on page one. Without thinking twice she dashed out of the house. Maybe catching the arsonist would bring her back to the good graces of the media and the public.

McGriffin's was unusually packed for a Thursday night. Tony, who was tending bar, didn't complained when he was hard at work on accommodating all of his customers' requests. The smile on his face was genuine. He wished he worked more shifts like this. With the rate the tips are rolling in he might be able to make half of his half of the rent this month.

But his smile vanished like a ball from a cannon when he recognized the young lady who just walked through the door. She had been all over the news. The blood drained from his face.

"Look, lady," he said, shaking. "I don't want any trouble."

Jane shot Tony a smile. "Which is why I'm here," she said in bold confidence. "Have no fear, citizen—*I'm* on the case! Diet soda, please!"

The bewildered bartender looked at her with such scrutiny. Not wanting any trouble he took out a glass and filled it with ice and squirted her a Diet Pepsi from the tap. He handed it to her, his hand still shaking from fear. The ice in the glass rattled in an unsteady rhythm. She gently took it from her and smiled.

"Gotta watch the figure," she said, winking at him.

As she walked through the floor, she noticed some people were watching her. She turned to see two men looking at her. They both looked nervous.

Hey, it's those guys who laughed at me before! She immediately identified the two.

Her smiling face turned into a scowl. "Whadda ya lookin' at, punks?" She growled. "I got my eyes on you!"

The two men got out of their seats and left the bar in such haste. Tony watched them leave and shifted his gaze back to Jane. She was amazed how a girl would strike fear into the hearts of two frat boy types.

Jane grinned. "Yeah, you better run."

Then something came over her. She felt a little dizzy and her legs became limp like linguini.

I feel so weird, she thought. *Are the drugs starting to work? Maybe I've got some sort of Calamity Sense?*

Through the haze she saw Debra sitting all by herself at a booth with a drink right in front of her, drumming her fingers against the table. Jane wondered if she should go on over and say "hi." Then she noticed something was a little off. Debra was usually with the girls. Jane thought she many need some company. It would also be a good idea to clear the air on what happened at the salon earlier.

Before Jane could put one foot over the other, she saw someone else approaching Debra. Through the fog in her eyes, Jane was fully able to make out the other person.

Hey, there's Pete! She smiled. *What's he doing here? Jeeze, I hope I look all right! If I'd known he'd be here, I'd—*

Her train of thought was suddenly derailed, and she saw the penny on the tracks. Debra raised her eyes and smiled a welcome. Jane watched in slow motion when she saw Pete kissing Debra hello.

Jane couldn't breathe. Her skull was on fire. Her brain was scorching from the anguish of witnessing the man she loved in the throes of another woman. Her eyes were stinging.

"Traitor!" Jane snapped at her onetime partner, who was in the arms of another woman.

She dropped her drink and ran out of the club.

CHAPTER EIGHT

Jane was choking on her sobs. "He…he…I can't believe he would do this to me!" She wailed. "After all we've been through! After all we've shared—only to find comfort in the arms of that…that…<u>SLUT</u>!"

She was beyond furious. Debra was supposed to be her friend and she stole her dream man away from her. There was no way Pete would have done this to Jane. How would he be…be…canoodling with Debra? She is so-o-o old! She had to be at least twenty-eight. She must have brainwashed him or used some sort of hypnosis to make him her slave.

Yes! That's what happened!

Jane balled up her fist; her nails were digging into her palm. *Why, I should go right back in there and…* Then she heard something in the alley. She snapped to attention.

"What was that noise?"

She gingerly crept through the alley and peered around the corner to see a man with a gas can spraying something against the wall.

What's that guy doing? She silently observed. Then something filled her nostrils. *Is that gasoline I smell?*

No way! The drugs worked!

I <u>do</u> have Calamity Senses!

She ducked into an alley ahead of her where the man was throwing gasoline on the club's walls. She looked around the alley and found a plank of wood. She picked it up and gripped it tightly, waiting for the man to turn his back on her.

No impressionable fans to worry about, she thought, sneaking up on him. *So I'll just use this 2x4 to knock some sense into this base villain.*

The man placed the gas down and pulled out a box of matches. It'll be a hot time in the old town tonight. Before he could strike a match. Something struck his head and he folded like a napkin.

Jane held the 2x4 aloft and stood like a valiant knight who just slew a dragon. "One more blow against the forces of evil!" She boldly declared.

She found some rope and tied up the arsonist and left a note for the police.

This guy is the Nightclub Arsonist!
Courtesy of your pleasant, local
Avenging Star!

* * *

"Aww, sis—don't cry," Charlie said to his sister Michelle, who was worried about her daughter who hadn't returned home from work and there's an arsonist on the loose. "She'll turn up. She always does."

"This is different, Charlie," spoke John Travers with conviction in his voice. "*She's* different this time. You all saw it. I think she may have gone too far over the edge—and I'm afraid for her."

"She seemed lucid when I talked to her earlier," said Michelle, with fright. "But then she had some idea and took off. I don't know where, though."

John held his sobbing wife gently in his arms, let her rest her head on his shoulder. With one hand, he gently stroked her hair. With the other, he held Michelle tightly to him, to prevent her from collapsing.

"Shhhh," he whispered in her ear.

Behind her, Charlie stood impassively, whatever grief he was feeling tucked away some place deep inside him.

Charlie put on his coat and headed toward the door. "Try calling the police again and see if Roberts has heard anything," he instructed them. "I'm gonna try and find her."

"You have to find her, Charlie," she pleaded. "I'm worried something terrible has happened."

Big T wrapped up his phone call to his supplier. "Yo, fool—I'll holla back," he said, when he saw Jane running toward him. "What's up, my sweet thang?" He said with a smile. "So didja feel *goooood* last night?"

Jane couldn't contain her excitement. "Oh. My. God. That stuff worked great! I need more. And, and, and..."

"And...what?" He asked so curiously.

"And I wanted to see if you had something...*more* powerful," she inquired. "That stuff worked well, but I need something more. Something that will give me the edge I need. Something with oomph!"

"Oomph, huh?" Big T said, he smiled like a shark. "I think I've just the thing for you," he added, lifting up the trunk of his car. His leather jacket rode up his back when he bent over to get some of his merchandise.

Jane could see the handle of his gun he tucked into the back of his pants. A feeling of dread crept over her. She started to reconsider what she was doing. He found what he was looking for and handed a bag over to Jane, and quickly took her money.

"You gotta go easy on it, though," he strongly advised. "'Cause it has some serious kick to it..."

* * *

Jane arrived home, with her brown bag of contraband goodies in hand. She looked around the dark parlor, searching for any signs of life.

"Mom? Dad?" She called out. "Anybody home?" She peered around the corner.

She felt a presence. Something unfamiliar. She shrugged it off, blaming it on the paranoia with holding a bag full of drugs in her hand.

This would be the second time she would use drugs and she didn't want her parents to walk in on her while she's doing them. So on the way home she stopped at the dollar store and bought some chips, candy, and other stuff to make it look like she had bought some groceries.

She set the bag down on the floor and did another check. "Is someone here? Hello?"

There was still no answer. Thinking she was alone she reached into the bag and took out a bottle of water and a container of whatever it was Big T sold her. As she prepared to pop the pill she came to the realization that she forgot about Uncle Charlie. She called out his name and there was no answer. After a moment, she proceeded to take the pill and washed it down with some bottled mountain spring water.

Then she heard the floorboards creak. She choked on her water and placed her hand over her mouth to muffle her gagging. The sound came closer and closer. Moving on instinct, Jane hid the drugs underneath the kitchen sink. Then she saw something lingering around the archway.

"Who's there?" She called over into the darkness.

The figure took shape. It was a tall, slender, figure standing in the shadows.

He's a long silhouette of a man wearing a fedora hat and a long overcoat that stretched from his neck down to his ankles. Dark eyes gleamed above an intimidating black mask that concealed his entire face. The mask, made of a silk-like material exaggerated his distinguishing features. It gave his a face a vaguely demonic appearance. No sign of fear showed in the man's piercing eyes. He spoke calmly, and with complete assurance.

"Oh, you know who I am…Avenging Star," the man said, sending a chill down Jane's spine. He spoke in a low, sinister tone that demanded to be taken seriously. "You know exactly who I am."

"Who are you?" Jane stammered. A chill ran down Jane's spine. Her mouth went dry, and suddenly her palms were sweaty. She could feel fear grabbing at her stomach. Her secret identity's been exposed. That meant her family was a target. And Pete! If this strange man knew who she was, then it was quite obvious he knew Pete was her partner. "What are you doing here? What have you done to my parents?"

The living shadow cracked a smile. Jane felt a chill run through her. It was that grin. She could see it all in that smile. It was gleeful, not forced. People driven by life's circumstances into crime, they had a tight-lipped grimace about them that was disturbing and sad. This was different, a look she had seen rarely but still all too many times in her life. It was the look of anticipation, of sadism. He was a grim man. But unlike true predators, who don't just survive but thrive on pain and death, they were different.

Predators smile.

"For your first question—well, we're recent acquaintances. I am a very powerful man. You may call me…the Shadowy Man. As for your second question—you prevented my associates from completing their task at the bank."

The truth hit Jane like a ton of bricks. All the crime in town was connected to this Shadowy Man character, and now he's here to exact his vengeance upon her. This frightened Jane, but she tried not to show it. It was important to remain in control of the interrogation.

"You ruined a very deliberate plan," he continued. His eyes were emitting a fiery glow. A show of how powerful he was. "So I've come to exact my revenge—a pound of flesh, so to speak. *Your* flesh, I shall feast on. Your blood will flow like a river."

"I-I stopped those guys in the bank!" She warned him. "*Three* of them! You're no match for me—surrender!" The girl's utter confidence was unnerving.

The Shadowy Man chuckled. "Such bravado. Even if you're…exaggerating what really happened, mmm? I seem to recall there were two of you. Pete is not here to help you. In fact, he'll never be able to help you again!"

"You monster!" Jane yelled, her hand forming into a fist. "If you've so much as laid a hand on him, I'll…"

"Focus, Avenging Star," the Shadowy Man interrupted. "I did not touch him. Something did, though. As for your final questions, well, you should ask them… once you've joined them!"

As the Shadowy Man drew his gun, Jane felt the panic rise inside her again. She turned away, fighting back tears. This time, she really was helpless.

She saw the gun twitch and in the same instant she heard a sound like two boards being slapped together.

He raised his arm, pointed his gun at Jane's chest, and fired.

Crack! Boom!

Being able to sense the gunshots ahead of time, she ducked and took cover. She let out a small shriek when the bullet that was meant for her, obliterating her mother's valuable, Waterford crystal vase.

Fear was taking over Jane. She felt defenseless. Missing that bullet was dumb luck. And luck isn't really a superpower.

Well, maybe for Domino. But this was real life for crissakes, not a freakin' comic book! Or in this case the highest grossing R-rated movie in the history of Thursday night previews.

The gun twitched again in the Shadowy Man's hand. Soon there would be another slapping board sound.

A bead of sweat dripped down from her brow to the very tip of her nose. Jane crossed her eyes to see that single rivulet evaporate right in front of her. Her eyes grew large with wonder watching her own perspiration turn into steam. Suddenly her fear was replaced by something...fiery.

She noticed a strange glow surrounding her hand. It was being encased with this strange mystic energy. She only seen something like this in those old comic books her uncle Charlie gave her when she was a little girl. Especially from this one title from *Marvel—The Immortal Iron Fist*. This supernatural aura was deemed the Kirby Crackle by the fans.

The Shadowy Man lowered his gun and gazed at her, confused. For a brief moment Jane could see what the villain looked like through the darkness. Then she felt her hand was going to explode.

"Hey," the Shadowy man said, shielding his eyes from the blinding light. "Do you need a minute?"

"I don't know," Jane said. "I...I feel..."

Energy flowed out from her in waves. Jane straightened up and clenched her fists. "...I feel *strange*."

Suddenly, a jabbing pain shot through her hand. Jane stared down at her hand, glowing bright. Whatever this strange new energy was, it was clearly powerful. Jane's fists were clenched tight, energy flowing out from them in waves.

She felt invigorated—thrusting-dynamic. Her eyes gleamed with a sudden lust for power, as she briefly realized what was happening to her.

"M-my hands..." she panted, frightened by the strange surge of energy. "Feels like...*this*!"

She threw a punch right in front of her, while using her other hand to steady the fiery fist. Mystic blasts volleyed over the Shadowy Man who gracefully dodged each and every one of them.

The new drugs must have been kicking in. Jane smiled wildly and took aim. "<u>WARNING</u>: side effects may <u>KICK-ASS</u>!"

Hostile energy-blasts suddenly ricocheted off the walls. He was like the final boss in *Space Invaders*, crafty and sneaky. He made a dash to the door and offered Jane a smile.

Then the energy passed, ebbing away like a receding wave.

"An admirable attempt, my dear," he said, patronizing his new archenemy. He waved to her before he made his hasty retreat. "Ta-ta for now."

The shadowy figure moved swiftly out the door, with Jane racing after him. A heartbeat later, the shadow was gone. And so was the figure.

"Darn it!" She disdainfully exclaimed. "He got away!"

She looked back, astonished. The drugs she had bought from Big T gave her the powers she needed to hold her own against an A-list villain like the Shadowy Man. Impossible—all of it was. Than she realized that Big T is selling superpowers to people on the street. After she gets done with this Shadowy Man character, she has to go over and shut down Big T's illegal operation.

Out of the corner of her eye, she saw something leading into the kitchen. It looked like someone had spilt red wine on the floor. At first she thought her mother might have gotten a little carried away from her last book club meeting, but the next one wasn't until next Thursday.

She carefully approached the stain for further investigation. As she got closer, she came to the assumption that it was wine being soaked into the carpet. Her breath was taken away and she heard the loud pounding of her heart speeding up.

She froze at the threshold, and sprawled right before her were the bodies of the two people she loved most in the world.

"No!!!" Her voice was halfway between a strangled scream and a plaintive gasp.

The crumpled bodies on the floor confirmed her fears. Jane rushed to her dead parents' side, knelt down with an anguish cry.

"Mom! Dad!"

The pool of blood that surrounded them, that was already seeping into the carpet in the living room. Jane felt tears trickle down her cheeks, still flushed from the glory of preventing the fire at McGriffins' from earlier. It meant nothing, nothing at all. She'd trade her entire future if only this terrible thing could be taken back.

Her parents lay upon the bloodstained floor of the kitchen. A crimson river streamed beneath them.

They're both dead, Jane realized, the horror spilling through her belly like rancid oil. *The Shadowy Man killed my parents.*

Jane stood for a long moment, almost paralyzed. She struggled to collect her thoughts to make sense of what she had just seen. Time seemed to stop for a moment in that cozy kitchen.

She dropped to her knees, and took them into her arms.

They felt so small, so light, like nothing at all.

But they had been her entire world.

Why had it taken her so long to see that? Why had she wasted so much time, fighting other people's battles, and let the days, months, and years pass by apart from them? Years she could never have back now.

Her mother's hair had fallen down over her face. Jane brushed it back and touched her cheek.

The voices in her head were too much to bear.

She could hear her mother. "We're all worried about you."

Then she could hear her father. "We're very worried about you. We think you need some rest and quiet."

Their voices overlapped, encouraging her to embrace her destiny.

"You know your mother and I are very happy that you acted so brave."

"The world truly does need people who help other people."

She heard another voice then, behind those voices, a voice that grew louder and louder until it was the only thing she could hear. This voice spoke no words, though—it simply made a single, continuous guttural sound. A scream.

It was her, Jane Travers realized. She was screaming.

Her mother and father were dead, and she was screaming because it was her fault.

"I'm sorry! I failed you!" She sobbed. "I swear I won't fail you again. I will not stop until I avenge your deaths and bring those responsible to justice!"

She raised her fist into the air, taking a vow to fight for those who can't fight for themselves.

"So swears the Avenging Star!"

CHAPTER NINE

Jane sat among the bloodstained kitchen tiles. Something began to swell within her. She had no idea what it was, just that it was somehow connected to her parents and that she had to keep it in check...*had* to. She sat, and waited, and felt herself becoming numb all over, inside and out, except for that swelling thing in her chest.

Jane needed something. Anything. An edge. The Shadowy Man was poised to strike, and she was woefully unprepared. And it had cost her.

Her parents were dead.

Pete and Debra were dead.

She wasn't powerful enough. She couldn't save them. She swore a oath from her parents' blood to do anything and everything she could to prevent any more deaths. In the end, she still failed the ones she cared about the most.

Through the wreckage of what was once her living room, Jane could hear the evening news on the TV. The glow from the screen lit up the dark room.

"And now, to our top story," said the dapper anchorman. "The manhunt continues tonight after a string of arsons have cause incalculable damage. We now go live to Aleta Mentira, who is covering the police press conference. Aleta?"

The screen cut to a young field reporter. She had only been at the station for almost a year and fresh out of broadcasting school, and she's handling everything like a pro. Serious when she needed to be serious, and lighthearted when it was appropriate.

"Thank you, Gary," Aleta responded. "The situation here can only be described as bedlam. Police are searching for clues as to the identity, or identities, of whoever is responsible for the continuing city destruction."

Jane raised her head and turned her attention away from her slain parents and looked at the screen. She felt something was calling her. She couldn't draw away from it. She was a moth drawn to the flame and she never blinked.

"Numerous deaths have been attributed to the series of arsons," Aleta continued, until she saw something from the corner of her eye. "And...oh, wait—it looks like police chief Charles Cutroroa is about to address us!"

The station cut to a live feed of Chief Cutroroa coming up to the podium. The various microphones of each news affiliate in the city surrounded his face.

"Thank you for coming, ladies and gentlemen," he began. "This is what we know—in the past week, seven suspicious fires have been set in varying neighborhoods, the latest being at McGriffin's Bar & Grille."

Jane finally blinked.

"Wha…what about McGriffin's?" She asked, awakening from her trance.

"So far, fourteen bodies have been found in the wreckage and the coroner's office is trying to identify the deceased."

The camera cut to Aleta Mentira. "Chief? Aleta Mentira, Channel 13 News. Is this latest arson related to the other fires? If so, fourteen deaths brings the death toll to forty-two."

Jane swallowed hard. She didn't like the way this was going. She shuddered at the memory of the nightclub fire, and at the very mention of her stalker. The Shadowy Man had become synonymous with atrocities, at last in this part of the world.

"Oh, my God!" Jane gasped. "Forty-two people are dead?" This realization terrified her to the core. "This has the Shadowy Man's fingerprints all over it. That monster!"

"The fire from the nightclub spread to a second building and jumped floors in the first, trapping occupants between floors. An all-out rescue effort succeeded in rescuing all but Debra Reynolds, 28, and Peter Young, 24, whose bodies were only recovered after the fire was brought under control in the early hours of this morning. The names of the injured were not released, and doctors at Central Hospital were not available for comment. The fire department refused to comment on the possibility of arson, pending the results of their investigation."

The camera pulled back to reveal a throng of reporters attending the press conference. Wooden police barriers held back a crowd of civilian spectators, many of who clutched flowers or homemade signs of support. An impromptu shrine, piled high with stuffed animals and floral tributes had been erected in front of the remains of the torched building.

Jane couldn't believe her ears. Pete and Debra were *dead*? The shocking news dispelled all thought of her own lingering unease. And now somebody killed them? Jane's blood ran cold. What the hell was the world coming to?

Jane Travers had put the Avenging Star behind her, she'd thought. But she realized now that the Avenging Star was not behind but within her, deep inside her heart and soul. She wandered if an x-ray might show that beast's presence, a tumor laying dormant, worthy from the right moment to take complete control of her life.

Jane glimpsed at her parents one more time. She knew what she had to do. The police weren't trained for this. They had never handled a threat like the Shadowy Man. She picked up her discarded costume from the trash, washed it and began to take up the mantle of the Avenging Star once again.

As she was prepping for her search for the Shadowy Man, she could still hear faint traces of the news.

"Well, we're still examining the crime scene," Chief Cutroroa continued. "I called this press conference so we could provide what we do know. The lead investigator, Detective Joseph Roberts, will brief you now…"

And everything else was background noise.

Forget Roberts! She ordered herself. *Forget everything! Concentrate on the mission!*

In the vast, brightly lit room on the second floor of the Travers home, Jane was transforming herself. She was in a hurry. She put on the flexible tunic, the tights, the boots, the silk cowl, and the cape. She thrust her hands into the gloves and buckled the wide, compartmented belt around her waist.

The moment she slid the cowl over her long auburn hair, Jane Travers vanished. The only one in the room was the Avenging Star. And she was about to begin her hunt.

Now in her somewhat freshly clean costume, Jane crept out of the window and perched on the ledge as if she were one of the gargoyles on all churches around the world warding off monsters and demons alike. She breathed a steady sigh and took the night in.

Before she headed out to begin her search, she thought of her parents and the promise she made to them about not doing this kind of thing. She knew she was breaking it, but she had to do this, for Pete, Debra…and even for herself. As much as her uncle Charlie tried to convince her earlier that it wasn't her fault, and she really wanted to believe him. The guilt was still eating away at Jane. If she didn't stop the Shadowy Man tonight, and someone close would get hurt, or even killed, she would never be able to forgive herself.

She finally figured out what she had to do in order to combat the forces of evil and preserve the name of justice.

"I need to become a warrior!"

Charlie wasn't going to come home until he found his niece. He had seen this before when he worked social services and handled runaway cases. Never had he thought that something like this would happen to a member of his own family. He went to all the places Jane frequented—the hobby store, Yarn Barn, and Galaxy Comics. Even the storeowner was surprised something was wrong when Jane didn't pick up the latest issue of *Atlas*. But to Charlie's disappointment, he was greeted with the same response.

No one had seen her.

Then he decided to go to her workplace and ask her friends at the salon. When he walked to the door he saw the sign read "closed." Charlie checked his watch, seeing that closing time wasn't for another 45 minutes. He peered through the window to see two people were inside talking. One was a young woman with short blonde hair, and she was talking to a man in a trench coat. Charlie gently tapped on the glass, getting their attention.

The blonde came over and gingerly opened the door. She looked like she had been crying. She had been trying so hard to put on a brave face.

"I'm sorry," she said, "but we're closed for today because of the tragedy."

"Oh, I'm not here for a haircut," Charlie replied. "I'm looking for my niece, Jane."

Her eyes widened. "You're Jane's uncle? Oh, no, she's not here."

The man in the trench coat gave Charlie a once over. Something piqued his interest.

"I haven't seen her since, um, I think two days ago," the blonde added. "The morning after the bank robbery. She was talking to..." Then she broke down crying, covering her face. "Oh, God. Debra."

She excused herself and went to the restroom. The man approached Charlie. He looked concerned. He took the toothpick out of his mouth and introduced himself. "Hello, I'm Detective Roberts," he said, flashing his badge. "Did you just say you're related to Jane?"

"Yes," Charlie answered, "I'm her uncle. Her parents and I are worried since she didn't come home last night. I thought I would check here to see if her friends knew anything."

"Now may not be the best time," said Roberts. "It turns out the owner was killed in the fire at McGriffin's last night—as well as that kid who worked next door. A Peter Young. I...well, so far, there's no indication Jane was one of the bodies. We should still hope for the best."

This didn't put Charlie's fears to rest. He needed something concrete. Well-wishing and the power of prayer wasn't going to be enough for this old sailor.

"Well, then if she's not here, Detective, where is my niece? And is she in any kind of danger?"

Jane swiftly blocked a punch from her attacker.

She let out a loud grunt as she absorbed the impact in her right palm. She was afraid her "iron fist" would flare up again and accidently kill her opponent. She still hadn't figured out how it happened or if it was only a one-time thing.

This is a lot harder than it looks. She quickly dodged a roundhouse kick to the face. Just barely missing the tip of her nose.

I figured I'd pick this up in no time, she thought, *me being a superhero and all.*

Then she got the wind knocked out of her with a surprise attack that sent her to the ground.

Boy, it hurts getting dropped on my butt!

Her karate sensei offered his hand to her.

"You are distracted, child," he said sternly, helping her back to her feet. "You must focus. With true focus, anything can be accomplished."

Jane returned back to her fighting stance. Ready for the next round.

She thought of what her teacher just said. Oh, if he really knew. She was already focused. She had stopped super-villains and foiled crimes.

And with a simple flick of his finger, Jane was on the mat again.

"You've lost your balance and completely left yourself open for attack," he pointed out. He narrowed his eyes and decided to be real with her. "I've decided. You are not ready for this. You lack disciple. You have much maturing and growing to do before you may return."

Jane couldn't believe what he was saying. "But, I don't understand. Look how much I've picked up in the last half hour! I've improved so much since I first walked in!"

"You have learned how to do the mechanical aspects of each form, but you do not understand why you do it," her sensei replied. "Your mind is in turmoil. You look for solutions everywhere but where they lay. In here," he said pointing to her head. "And, in your heart. Until they are whole, you can never understand how to master wushu. And there is no point in even beginning. Good-bye."

Dejected, Jane gathered her things. She could've argued with him for a long time. But the point was moot. He had made his decision. And the most important rule in martial arts is to honor your sensei. And she had to painfully respect his wishes. Then she considered on finding a dojo that offered Krav Maga training.

Charlie returned home, hoping her niece was there safe and sound. Or even made some sort of contact with her folks.

"Hello?" He called out when he walked in. "It's Charlie! Is anyone here?" He didn't her anything. "Hello?" He called again, but there was still no reply. "Jane! Are you here?"

He looked down on the carpet and saw a huge stain. Charlie further investigated the insidious crimson pattern. It quickly absorbed into the carpet, and it appeared to be there for a while.

Charlie cautiously walked through the living room and saw both his sister and her husband lying on the kitchen's tiled floor.

Dead.

He opened his mouth to get his sister's attention…

With mounting fear, alarm bells exploding in his head, Charlie ran into the kitchen. He could taste the bile rising from the pit of his stomach. His throat burned by its acid. And then it got up into his eyes as if they were starting to melt. He lowered his face to his hands.

He rushed over to the phone and frantically dialed for help.

"Hello, 911?!" He gasped greedily for air. "I need an ambulance here, immediately! My sister and brother-in-law are..." He wanted to finish that sentence, but he couldn't face the cruel reality. "Oh, God!" He exclaimed, trying to look away from the grisly sight. "There's blood everywhere!"

Charlie Huntington howled in rage, fear, and despair.

CHAPTER TEN

When Jane came home, the blaring lights of emergency vehicles blinded her. She was even surprised when she discovered a news crew was there. The yellow crime-scene tape was already strung up, with the three patrol cars angled in with their lights flashing. Jane wanted to get in for a closer look, but she realized she was still in her Avenging Star costume. So she hid in the bushes and silently observed.

I guess someone must have called the police, she thought. *I'm sure my energy blasts made a lot of noise.*

Then she saw two figures walking out of the house. Her eyes became large when she identified the grieving man.

Oh, God, she whimpered. *Uncle Charlie must have found them! He looks terrible!*

She thought about stepping out of the bushes to comfort him, until she saw him being escorted by Detective Roberts. She was already on his bad side with what happened at the bank. And he had sternly warned her about putting on the mask and cape again. If he saw her, she would be arrested on sight.

But she was a witness to the crime. That meant the police would want to question her about the murders. However, that would take up too much time. She had to find the Shadowy Man and stop him.

"To the Star Mobile!" She exclaimed in a hushed whisper.

Detective Roberts swiveled his head to the bushes. For a moment he thought he heard someone talking. He shrugged it off, thinking it was just his imagination.

"You really should do what the paramedics suggested," he said to Charlie. "You're in shock and you should sit down."

"You're goddamned right I'm in shock!" Yelled Charlie. "I just found my sister on the kitchen floor in a pool of blood—and her husband's body lying *next* to her!"

In retrospect, maybe it was dumb thing to say. Roberts followed with, "I couldn't even begin to imagine how it feels like to lose two of your closet family like that. At least you may still have Jane."

Then Charlie remembered Jane!

What was he going to tell her? How could he bring himself to tell his niece that two of the most important people in her life were dead?

"Well, where is she then?" He spat at Roberts. "Why hasn't she been found yet?"

Roberts took a beat. He wouldn't want to press this agitated man any further.

"Well, new information has been brought to my attention," he replied, laying a comforting hand on Charlie's shoulder. "We're doing everything we can, sir."

"We've got to find her!" Charlie wasn't pleading. He was commanding the head detective. "She might be in danger!"

"You're right about the danger," Roberts concurred. "We do need to find her. You really should let us handle this. You're in no condition to be looking for her."

Jane Travers was not looking her best.

After nearly two weeks of costumed adventuring, her Avenging Star suit was torn and filthy. A split lip testified to her rough treatment at the hands of that man mountain Snap at the bank. Scabs and bruises, many of them left over from her losing battle with the Shadowy Man, formed a black-and-blue mosaic over her battered flesh. Her long red hair was matted and badly in need of a shampoo.

A constant lunatic rhythm echoed through Jane's brain, a rhythm produced to avoid thinking about *him*, the Shadowy Man. That was unhealthy. She wondered how the Shadowy Man broke into her house. The door wasn't broken, the windows weren't jimmied, and she couldn't find any signs of vandalism. She snapped herself to attention, refusing to let her mind drift into limbo while she was on the hunt. In her line of work, it took little to turn predator into prey.

On the drive downtown, she had looked only at the road. Her gaze never shifted down the reflection of streetlights and neon bar signs. What would she say if a cop stopped her, she'd wondered. What could she say?

As she sat in the car, she reached into the passenger seat and picked up her blue mask. The empty eye slits stared at her with ominous intent, or so she imagined. The entire ensemble was forbidding, despite the brightness of colors. It was a work she ought to be proud of, and might have been if it weren't associated with so many terrible things.

But it was the costume of a failure, and Jane Travers felt far worse when it came time to put it on. As she slipped on the mask, her face disappeared beneath another. Her identity was buried under the steel gaze of the Avenging Star.

Over at the Gas 'N Sip, Jane was met with another problem. The infamous Star Mobile had run out of gas. She punched the steering wheel and muttered, "I bet the Green Dragon never has this problem!"

She exited the vehicle and went to the pump. As she took out her credit card, she had a thought.

"Yeah! That's what I need—the Dragon Racer!" She dreamt as she swiped the card in the scanner. "I could find the Shadowy Man in no time with that. Think of the crimes I could stop if I had that car! Oh, sure, the Star Mobile has its uses and—"

Then she saw something beyond the pale near the gas station's entrance. The car parked just in front of the door looked like the one used at the bank robbery.

No!

It was the *same* one!

"Holy grilled cheese and tomato soup lunch!" She exclaimed in overdramatic superhero fashion. "That's the getaway car from the bank!"

Then she thought if that car was there then her enemy must be nearby. Then she saw a shadowy figure inside the store, and it was holding a gun to the kid behind the cash register.

"Yes!" Jane said in triumph, running towards the store. "This is my chance to prove what kind of a hero I am! It's time to end this!"

Ken Park yawned loudly. It had been a very slow night. Weeknights at the Gas 'N Sip were always pretty slow, but it felt like they hadn't had a customer for hours. He leaned his elbows on the counter, his head bent over a wrestling magazine that he was idly flipping through, scanning over the pictures rather than actually reading the articles. A few hours earlier him and his best friend Frank Thomas, had played a game of "rock-paper-scissors" to see who would be stuck in the store for the night since it was only the two of them working tonight. Ken had lost.

Working the night shift at a convenient store wasn't exactly every man's dream come true. It was a crap job with lousy pay and a hell of a lot of risks attached to the name badge. Beggars can't be choosers and all.

The only good thing that came out of it, really, was the fact that Ken had always enjoyed the act of people watching and as a clerk in a convenient store it was normal that the weirdest assembly of people that anyone could possibly think of. Ranging from middle-aged truckers looking for a brief relief from their hours long drives across the country to drunken frat-boys wanting to restock their supply on booze, the variety in the Gas 'N Sip customers was as diverse as it probably got.

As Ken heard the motion sensor by the door chimed, he glanced up at the clock on the wall. There were only six minutes left before he had to close up and he hoped that whoever was coming in wasn't going to take long. He didn't want to stay at work any later then he had to, he was itching to get out and do something. He figured Frank would be in any minute to help him close up and clock out.

Ken glanced over to the footage from the cameras over the gas pumps. There was one person that really took the cake on the diverse assortment of weirdoes in Gas 'N Sip history. There was a girl dressed in a mask and cape who was about ready to gas up her car. *This is a first,* he thought, turning his attention away from his recent customer. *Is she on her way to a costume party, or something?*

He shifted his focus over to see who had entered the store. It wasn't someone he recognized, but that wasn't terribly unusual or cause for alarm. The man was probably a few years older than his brother Jacob. He had an old pair of blue jeans that were beaten up and worn and a baggy brown coat zipped up to just under his chin. He looked a little rough, but that was pretty normal for this side of town and he wasn't concerned.

The man wandered in but didn't immediately head for the counter. Ken sighed, seeing that the guy was taking his sweet time. He watched as the man poked around the magazine rack for a few minutes.

"Is there something I can help you with?" Ken finally spoke up. "We're about to close."

The man grunted but turned and headed for the counter without picking up a magazine. Ken recognized the signs of what was about to happen just before it did. He realized that he really should have seen it coming the moment the guy walked in the door and started wandering around the store, but he just hadn't been paying enough attention and at this point he had no time to react. Why did he have to spend so much time watching that weird chick on the monitor?

He was staring down the barrel of a handgun that was pointed directly at his face. He felt his stomach drop down to somewhere around his feet. He had been in a lot of rough situations before, but in his twenty-three years of life he had never had a gun pointed at him like this. Ken realized that with twitch of this guy's index finger he could be dead in an instant, the thought terrified him. He very slowly raised his hands up off the counter with his palms out defensively to show that he would cooperate as he kept his face as blank as possible in an attempt to hide his fear.

"Money," the man spat. "Empty the register. Now."

He just nodded, not trusting his own voice not to betray how afraid he really was. He would give this guy anything he wanted at this point just to have this over with and behind him. He turned very slowly and reached for the register, not wanting to make any sudden moves.

"Hurry!" The man hissed.

Before Jane could open the door, the robber shot the clerk. The young man took a bullet in the shoulder, recoiling in pain.

"No-o-o-o-o!!!" Jane screamed. She was too late. She wasn't fast enough to save him.

The robber ran outside, pushing the door with such great force. There was just enough of it to smack Jane in the face and send her tumbling ass over teakettle.

The impact was enough for Jane to see stars. She was disoriented for a moment. She thought she heard the clerk from inside say something like, "I wasn't supposed to be here today!"

When she regained her bearings, she saw the car peeling out of the parking lot and sped through the street.

"No!" She yelled, pounding on the pavement. "No! No! No! He's not getting away again!"

A moment later Jane reached the sedan and yanked the door handle.

Locked.

Roaring, Jane bashed her fist against the window. The driver glanced back and for a second their eyes met.

Burning rubber, the sedan screeched away. Instinctively, Jane ran after it. In desperation, she leaped headfirst onto the car's trunk, fingertips clawing metal.

The driver braked hard, and Jane's face smacked the rear windshield. Howling with fury she came tumbling toward the pavement, twisting and turning.

As she painfully pulled herself up, she raced to the Star Mobile and jumped into the driver's seat. She started the ignition and was ready to floor it. Jane thought this called for some awesome chase music. She was between Saliva's "Click, Click, Boom" and Limp Bizket's "Rollin'." But decided to go with Hoobastank's "Crawlin' in the Dark."

Her foot pressed pedal to metal, and the not-so-mighty machine shot forward, ready to speed toward the twinkling lights of the city. But instead of being the best hits of the early 21st century, she heard the engine sputter.

"What the frack?" She cursed, trying to get the car to work. She looked down and suddenly realized she didn't put any gas in the tank.

"Dammit!" She yelled, her jaw dropping as if at some horrific realization. She leaned forward, and then banged her head against the steering wheel in self-inflicted punishment. "Dammit, dammit, dammit!"

Despite this minor…setback, Jane remained committed to her goal of saving humanity from itself, but her latest efforts were meeting with mixed results.

Being limited to these man-made devices for a locomotion was far too limiting! She needed to be faster—like the Accelerator! Nothing would stop her! She would be the fastest mortal alive, and able to dodge raindrops and much quicker than a beam of light. Even speedier than a forgotten dream!

"If I could just be like her," Jane said wistfully. "I could be everywhere at once! I just need…wait!" Then she got an idea. It was as if a bolt of lightning struck her. "There was a disaster that gave her the super speed! It was just chemicals!"

With the speed of more than the causal mall walker, Jane found herself at Beauty Today. With all the times she has forgotten her key. With no other option, she picked up a trashcan and threw it straight at the huge picture window.

"Do the right thing!" She shouted, followed by the sound of glass shattering.

She jumped into the salon and made a hasty retreat to the supply closet. She remembered they had just gotten a shipment of new hair care products that contain the exact chemicals she needed to perform her desperate experiment.

The comic never revealed what was mixed together that granted the Accelerator her tremendous powers. But Jane thought she had been awful lucky this far and would bet that luck will hold up even now.

Jane took the supplies to the sink and began mixing several chemicals together from the beakers that came with them.

"Let's see…" She began, pouring one solution to the next. "Benzalkonium Chloride, Dimethicone, Diazolidinyl Urea, Quarternium-22…I wish I knew what most of these things are." Then the solution began to bubble. A smile danced across her face. "There! That's got to be it."

She removed her mask and let her hair down. She had carefully prepared this formula. With all the things she had done to enhance herself, she just needed to know this would be the final piece that will allow her to be the greatest hero of all time.

She held the beaker over her head and began to pour the beaker full of mixed chemicals onto her scalp. She wondered if the effects of the mixture would be immediate. She was looking forward on getting superpowers. She needed an edge so she could battle the evil that was the Shadowy Man.

She could feel the solution running down on the left side of her face. She began to feel something. She laughed in wonder and felt the strange sensation growing stronger and stronger.

Strange, Jane thought. *I don't feel faster. It's all concentrated on my head. Is my face supposed to be burning like that?*

CHAPTER ELEVEN

Charlie was driving through town until he saw Jane's beauty shop and slammed on the brakes when he saw the broken window. He swerved out of the street, exited the vehicle and ran into the salon. He stopped; glass crunched under his feet. Before he could call Detective Roberts, he heard a bloodcurdling scream. The sound of sheer torture frightened him. Then he stopped in his tracks.

The scream was quiet—so faint that Charlie could barely make it out. But it felt deep and resonant, and it penetrated right into his skull. It sounded like someone—a woman—howling in agony.

Charlie whirled around, trying to locate the source of the scream. It seemed to be coming from inside the salon. He grabbed hold of the door handle. Then he stopped and turned to look back at the archway.

I should call the police, he thought. *That woman in there might need some medical attention.*

Then he heard the scream again. It was louder this time, and higher-pitched. *Someone,* he realized, *is in a lot of pain.*

He reached into his pocket to fish out his phone. He thought of the woman. Was she in trouble on the other side of the door?

Maybe I should just see if anyone needs help, he thought.

Another shout of pain and suffering pierced through his brain. Each scream intensified each moment. It was a deep, soul-chilling sound. Charlie recognized it immediately as the scream he'd heard outside.

"Jane?" He said softly. He peered through the broken glass and called out once again. "Jane?"

"Aarrgh!" Screamed the girl. She was curled up in a ball, holding her face in pain. "Oh, God!" She cried out again.

Charlie burst into the shop and ran toward the supply closet where his niece was sprawled out on the floor. Charlie's jaw dropped. "What the…?" The left side of her face was covered in chemical burns and her eye was red. What he couldn't understand was why she was in a superhero costume. "Good lord!" He blurted out, trying to help Jane up. "Jane, what happened? You're burning up!"

"Get away!" She screamed, covering her face. "I forgot the lightning bolt! How could I forget about the damned lightning bolt?!"

Charlie didn't know what the hell she was talking about. He considered it as delirium from the shock of experiencing such trauma. "Sweetheart, what's wrong?" Charlie said, his face inches from Jane's.

Jane was gasping, unable to catch her breath, and she could not answer her uncle.

"Stupid, stupid, stupid!" She repeated over and over again in an ungodly shriek. She felt like hitting herself against a brick wall for her ignorance and also to experience something else from this awful burning.

Why did I think that would work? It wasn't going to work!

"Jane, we've got to get you to a hospital," said Charlie, pulling out his cell phone. "I'm calling 911."

"No!" She contested, slapping the phone away from her uncle's hands. The phone flew into the air and landed a couple of feet away from them. The screen cracked as soon as it hit the hardwood floor of the salon. "I'm not going back there! I need to finish this. I need power to defeat my enemies."

Charlie looked at her as if she were a crazy person. None of what she was saying made sense to him. He was afraid.

"Enemies? What enemies? What the hell are you talking about?"

Jane's eyes narrowed. She was getting impatient. She didn't have time to explain, and she was tired on repeating herself to everyone who didn't understand. The burns on her face looked infected. It was as it had a mind of its own, as it looked like it was spreading across her face.

"The enemies!" She shouted very angrily. "The ones responsible for all the tragedies that have befallen me! The ones responsible for all the destruction, the deaths! I've been trying to fight him! *Him! The Shadowy Man!*"

She ranted and raved, shocking her poor, confused uncle.

"Jane! Jane!" He protested, breaking off from her. He went over to the sink and began pouring water into small glass. "Jane, sweetie," he said gently. "We need to get those chemicals off your face. Let's use this water to wash it off and then…"

"No! No!" She shrilled, pushing Charlie away. The old man tumbled and landed on the floor. "I need this!" She yelled, towering over him. "I need the powers it will give me! I just need to mix it again. I need to get the right combination. And the freaking lightning bolt that acts as the catalyst. A little discomfort is nothing compared to the power to stop evil. The power to save lives, Uncle Charlie! To heal and to bring villains to justice!"

Hoping her uncle would understand her vision of a perfect world; she looked at him with kind eyes. Him, however, didn't reciprocate. After hearing everything she had just said terrified him.

"You're crazy," he gasped, shaking his head in disbelief as he struggled to clear his vision. Jane's smile faltered. Her heart was breaking. "You're crazy!" He got up as fast as he could and began to make a break for it.

"Uncle Charlie?" Jane said, trying to get him back. "Wait! Wait! Don't leave me here! I can't do this alone!"

"Help!" Charlie called out. "Help!"

Jane rushed after him. "Don't leave me! Help me!"

Jane chased him across the block of stores until he turned a corner and slipped into an alley. Charlie looked back in shock and amazement. Jane was behind him, closing in fast. Thinking there was no place left for him to run she slipped right in. Coming to the conclusion Charlie would be trapped in the alley she as going to gently coax him back to her side.

Jane caught a glimpse of movement far down the sidewalk, and saw the Shadowy Man disappear round a corner.

What is he doing here? She thought, giving chase round the same corner. *I gotta get to Uncle Charlie before that freak does!*

When she finally reached the alley she looked up to see the Shadowy Man standing before her. Her brand-new arch nemesis appeared just as he had the last time Jane had seen him. Glowing fiery eyes regarded Jane with wry amusement.

A powerful hand grabbed onto Charlie's neck, lifting him from the floor. Charlie's feet dangled in the air as he found himself face-to-face with the Shadowy Man. The demonic entity slammed Charlie up against a graffiti-covered brick wall. The old man squirmed helplessly, unable to get away.

His eyes bulged in terror. He trembled uncontrollably.

"The Shadowy Man!" She heard her voice crack, and hated herself for it. She stiffened as an icy wind of fear blew right through her soul, chilling her to the bone. "What are you doing with my uncle?"

"Hello there, Avenging Star," he said patronizingly. "Isn't it obvious what I'm doing, hmmm? Why, all I'm doing is tying up the last loose end. Of completely and utterly destroying your miserable existence."

That's it, Jane thought. *Just keep the wacko talking until I'm in position.*

"Who are you, Shadowy Man? Why did this all have to happen?"

The villain deliberately ignored her. He turned his attention back to his captive. Charlie struggled to get away, but the Shadowy Man tightened his grip on him. Then he began to pull back his fist.

Jane shot both of her fists right in front of her. "No! Don't hurt him!"

Her fists were glowing with strange blue energy. Similar to the iron fist she had generated since she first encountered the Shadowy Man. But now her fists were glowing blue, not red. And they still emitted the strange Kirby crackle.

Jane gritted her teeth. *Guess this is it,* she thought. *Do you really want to be a hero?* Swallowing in fear, she nodded. She clenched her teeth willing the mystic energy to rise up inside her.

The Shadowy Man squinted against the blinding light. It was clear to him that Jane's power was growing. The energy seemed to have merged with her. Now she was as bright as a star.

Jane had almost become accustomed to this new energy. She was always half aware of it, like a fast heartbeat or an aching limb. Most of the time it pumped out a low, steady level, flaring up only when she needed to fight someone or punch through a wall.

Jane groaned. She tried to focus her power, to direct it at her opponent—but she couldn't concentrate. Her head felt like somebody had just fought a battle inside it.

The twin blasts struck the Shadowy Man. The light was piercing through the darkness like he was bleeding. It was enough force for him to let Charlie go.

Struggling to get back to his feet, he pulled the collar of his trench coat up to his face. He gave Jane a mean glare.

"That was a mistake," he warned her. "Another time, Avenging Star. Another time, another dance. We shall meet again soon, and the outcome will be different." Then he gave her an evil smile. "But for now, I leave you with this parting gift."

The Shadowy Man stood and shifted his gaze to Charlie, who was trying to steady himself against the brick wall. Charlie saw the Shadowy Man's flare up like a pair of faintly lit cigarettes. Then the light began burned brighter and brighter. Jane watched helplessly as the Shadowy Man used his optic blasts to kill her beloved uncle right in front of her.

Good God! Jane thought. She stared at the Shadowy Man in horror. *What kind of monster is this?!* The masked killer turned toward Jane. Then he nodded in her direction.

Charlie was staring down at a red splotch on his white shirt that spread from a small black hole. He crumpled, as though all his bones had dissolved at once.

Jane gave out a shriek that would shatter glass. She rushed over to him, as the Shadowy Man used her grief to ensure his escape. Before he disappeared into the night, he waved goodbye and smiled that terrible smile.

A predator's smile.

She had failed Charlie as she failed both her parents. If only she were fast enough or strong enough she could have saved him. Now she has to live with that guilt for the rest of her life.

"Uncle Charlie," Jane sobbed, "get up. Please, get up!" Her droopy shoulders shook with sorrow.

For a long time, Jane stared at her uncle's face. She heard a groan and bent down so that her face was close to his.

Jane clapped her hand over her mouth.

The cleansing fire in her eyes dimmed slightly as she bent to lift the smoking corpse from the ground. No heartbeat could be heard within the limp and lifeless form as Jane cradled the body in her arms. Sorrow showed upon her soft features as she realized that she had lost another person she had loved.

The rise and fall of a chest was her own. The breath she felt on her face was her own. She would never feel his heartbeat again.

Uncle Charlie was dead.

"Uncle Charlie!" She cried out in despair. She cradled the dead man's upper torso in her arms. His blood splattered on her costume. "Shadowy Man!"

Tears cascaded down her cheeks and rolled onto her costume. Sorrow clouded her vision and thoughts. She could only see him. Only hear his voice. Every memory she saw was of him.

Jane cradled Charlie's smoldering remains in her arms. It was hard to believe that he was really gone, but the evidence was impossible to deny. As Jane thought of her family's murderer, and a new profound anger grew within her.

Now truly alone, she had nothing else left to lose. It was dark for Jane. Her family was gone. Her friends were getting picked off, left and right. More friends were in danger but the pieces were falling into place. The villains had finally slipped up. His identity discovered. It was time for her to bring the monster to justice.

Victory would be hers!

She held her uncle in her arms. Blood from his cracked skull stained the brick wall.

"Don't leave me, Uncle Charlie!" She pleaded. Tears were cooling and stinging her facial burns at the same time.

CHAPTER TWELVE

It's said that children often resemble their grandparents more than their parents. Jane, uniquely, took after her mother's brother. For as long as she could remember, she and Charlie had been soul mates. Born to two joyless people plagued by depression and personal demons too dark to shake, Jane came alive only when Charlie visited her world. He had been well aware of the troubled nature of his sister's household and had shown special interest in his niece. Jane's parents were not bad people. They did not abuse her. They saw to her physical needs and her schooling, but they had no business being parents. They were desperately unhappy people too crippled by their own emotional turmoil to ever properly nurture their precocious only daughter. No doubt Jane would have slipped down some drain they were circling had it not been for her uncle's instincts and intelligence.

Charlie took to Jane, however, out of something more than familial concern. There was a tie between the two, an intangible shared quality that drew them together as co-conspirators within a larger family from which they stood apart. Their personalities, their enthusiasm for life, their senses of humor and attraction to adventure, were one and the same and not shared by the greater Travers family. They were born best friends, despite the age difference, and that was all there was to it as far as they were concerned.

Charlie and Jane spent time together whenever possible. He introduced her to museums and comic books and baseball games and The Beatles and Mexican food. He shared her enthusiasm for things both great and small. She was the child he never had and he was the father she needed. They filled a void in each other that the rest of their family could never supply.

Of course, the young Jane had never thought of her and Charlie's mutual attraction in terms that specific. All Jane knew was that Charlie was the greatest, coolest person in the world, the sunshine in an otherwise gray existence.

Why does it keep happening? Why did the Shadowy Man want to bring this kind of pain into her life? It wasn't like people hated her. She had lots of friends, kids from school, neighbors, and there were also the people where she worked.

Well. Stacy didn't always seem to be nice to her. Jane figured it was okay, though. On account they were both professionals.

So whom did that leave?

Then something popped into her head. *That guy at the salon,* she thought. *Mr. Johnson. Why, he specifically wanted _me_ to cut his hair. It must have been to get close to me.* Everything was falling into place. All the puzzles were laid out before her. Even that weird-looking piece was the one she needed to complete the whole picture. *Maybe he can read minds or see what your weaknesses are! This explains everything. He's the one responsible for all of this. All this time, right there—under my nose! How could I have been so blind?*

"Well, my eyes are wide open now," she said out loud, cradling her poor uncle. "And I know how to find him."

She ran back to the salon and entered through her makeshift entrance. The jagged shards of glass crunched underneath her steel-toed boots. She marched up to the reception desk and shuffled through the client list.

"Johnson's contact info has to be here somewhere," she said, rapidly searching the desk. She had found the "J" section of the records, and began to go through each and every one of them. "Let's see…High, Huston, Jacobs, Jamison…Johnson! Here we go." She took a moment and red his information very carefully. "Hmmm, he lives downtown near the harbor."

She looked over the contact list for every employee at the salon. And something caught her eye.

"Hey; wait a second," she said, picking up the list for a closet look. "He doesn't live that far from Stacy. And I bet my mint copy of *Batman: Damned #1* that he's going to go after her next."

Jane had an obligation to check on Stacy. Even though they weren't in the best of terms, but Stacy had found herself on the Shadowy Man's hit list. And if Jane were the superhero she claimed to be, then she wouldn't dare let her own feelings interfere on protecting the life of an innocent. No matter how mean and rude Stacy had been to her since Jane had started working at Beauty Today. She had a duty to uphold and it was to stop the Shadowy Man's killing spree at any cost!

Out of the last twenty-four hours, Detective Roberts had slept maybe three. He was up all night with the baby because his wife had been fighting a cold, he forgot to eat breakfast, and most of his day disappeared in a quicksand of reports and meetings with the city officials.

And on top of it all, there's this new maniac starting fires everywhere, and killing innocent people in the process. This arsonist was a real piece of work.

And now he was having one hell of a night. It started with a double homicide in the suburbs and now he had been called into another murder. This time it was in an alley and the victim was a man he had only seen an hour earlier. He was watching a live newsfeed on his smartphone, hanging on all of the grisly details.

A dashing anchorman filled the small screen on Roberts' device. He kept a calm profession demeanor setting up the main story of his broadcast.

"And our top story at this time continues to unfold," he said, obviously reading his teleprompter. "A brutal double homicide had rocked this small suburban community. Police are refusing to release names at this time. Here now is Aleta Mantina's exclusive interview with Police Chief Cutrora."

The screen cut to a young field reporter, holding the station's microphone in front of the chief of police. "Chief, what can you tell us about these grisly murders?" Aleta asked. "Are they related to the other recent crimes—the other murders? The arsons? The robberies?"

"Well, Aleta, we're still attempting to solve all of those crimes," Cutrora replied, followed by a weary sigh. "Though there is evidence that seems to link the crimes to one person or group, there is still some confusion about motive."

Aleta shot him a confused look. "I'm not sure I follow, Chief. 'Confusion about motive?' Could you elaborate on that?"

"Well, Aleta, these types of crimes are specific. Usually, with repeat offenders, they do one type of crime. *These* are all over the place. Yet, Aleta, there is evidence indicating a theme. One of our citizens seems to be the target of all of this. Though we're still not sure of this person or group's motives."

"Chief, are you saying there may be some sort of mastermind behind all of this? That there is some madman out there who so desperately wants to get at this person, they'd be willing to burn and kill."

"We're still trying to piece everything together," Cutrora continued. "We're not sure why someone would do this. We're mobilized, we're working around the clock to find those responsible—and prevent them from striking again."

"Chief, what's going to stop this madman from killing again? What will it take to bring the killer to justice?"

Cutrora took a moment, trying to find the right words to the put the public at rest. The tension was getting to him. He looked straight into the camera, addressing everyone at home, "Resolve, courage, patience—and a bit of luck. God help us all!"

"Damn it all to hell!" Roberts shouted, kicking a pile of trash across the alley. "I should have seen this coming."

"Calm down, Detective," said one of the CSIs. "You're contaminating the crime scene."

Roberts walked over to the body and lifted the tarp. "Don't tell me to calm down!" He barked at the forensic scientist. "There's at least one person still in danger." He turned to one of the officers, hanging by the squad car. "Listen up, people: The Travers missing persons case has become *top priority*! We need to find her ASAP!"

"On it, sir," replied the uniformed officer. "All points bulletin: Be on the lookout for one Jane Travers. The citizen is in potential danger from person or persons responsible for a crime spree. Concern for her immediate safety is high."

She looked terrible. She was dirty and bruised.

How the heck do superheroes keep their costumes clean? Jane wondered, she watched her costume rolling around inside a washing machine at the all-night Laundromat. Stripped to her bra and panties, and most importantly her mask, she reflected on the night's tragic events. *Seriously, blood is a real pain to get out. Deadpool had the right idea on wearing a red suit.* Then she lowered her head in shame, remembering that the blood in question belonged to her uncle. It was too soon.

She couldn't dwell upon that. She needed to remain focused. She had to put it together.

The Laundromat was a 24-hour place, and was more or less deserted very late at night…mostly because no one wanted to be near the type of people who hung out in a Laundromat at that hour.

So Jane sat in the Laundromat, and all the folks were there were sitting in glazed, alcoholic hazes, unaware of where they were and perhaps even *who* they were. The relative emptiness of the place was perfectly all right with her. She didn't need a crowd of people sitting around when she was in the middle of washing her Avenging Star costume.

Her mind kept returning to her evening with the Shadowy Man. The death of her parents and now Uncle Charlie—combined with the close calls Pete had with those bank robbers—had driven home to Jane that it was foolish to take someone for granted and assume they'd always be there. There were things she wanted to say to Pete, but now she never will.

Jane was so focused into her mission; she didn't even notice two old ladies gossiping close to her. They were nothing but static.

"So that's what I told my son, Aaron," one said to the other. "He needs to pay more attention to *his* son."

"Have I told you about my grandson, Darren?" Asked the one closest to Jane. "He's just the most perfect child. And it's just so apparent. Everyone likes him. And he's got such a generous heart."

Jane needed to use her skills. Her training. Sensei Komatsu helped her prepare for this day. He taught her how to look within to see beyond. She must channel her powers into becoming one with the universe. Only then, she can face her enemy.

The washer went off. It was time to take the costume out of the machine. Jane hoped it wasn't too badly stained. It was still soaking wet and it was heavy.

Jane glanced around to make certain that the bums and winos were paying her no mind. She didn't need to worry. They were stewing in their peaceful alcoholic oblivion. Satisfied she reached into the machine and pulled out her damp Avenging Star outfit.

Jane didn't have time to throw it into the dryer. So she struggled to squeeze into the tight costume.

"I'm on my way after you, Shadowy Man," she said, pulling her pants on. "Next time, it's going to be *your* blood I'm washing out of my costume!"

The two old ladies pointed to her and softly giggled. They turned their heads and avoided eye contact. Jane walked by them in full superhero regalia. Each step she took made a squishy sound, as she left a trail of water behind her.

As soon as she left the building was away from earshot, of them said, "My goodness! What terrible posture that young woman has. My Darren would never slouch."

Detective Roberts' hunch was right. Everything that has happened tonight proved Jane was involved somehow. Especially the break-in at the salon she worked. When he walked into the supply room in the back, it looked like a bomb went off.

"What happened in here? What's all of the stuff spilled on the floor?"

Two patrolmen escorted a young man to the detective. The kid looked nervous. Even his mullet was curling.

"Detective," said one of the cops, "This guy said he was trying to make a delivery of supplies when he noticed the window was broken." Then he looked over to the young man, and in a calm voice he said, "Jason, this is Detective Roberts. He'd like to ask you a few questions."

"Uh, um, o-ok," he stammered. His voice cracked and his palms were sweaty. "It's just, I don't...I don't get it. First Debra and then this."

Roberts placed his hand on Jason's shoulder. "Jason, it's O.K. We're very close to stopping all of this for good. How long have you been working with Debra and this salon?"

Jason took a deep breath. "Well..." he began, clearing his throat, "I've been working with them for a few years. I'm her sales rep and I've never heard her have any problems. It's a nice neighborhood. Who would want to kill her?"

"I'm not yet 100% sure," replied Roberts, taking Jason's statement. "We've got some ideas. Who would be in charge of this place, now? We need to get ahold of that person."

"That would be Elizabeth," Jason answered, holding up the employee contact list. "I think she's the manager now."

Roberts grabbed the sheet out of Jason's hands. The motion was so sudden it startled the young man.

"Get her on the phone," Roberts ordered one officer, handing him the contact information. "Find out where she lives and send a squad car to get her. Then do the same with the rest of them. They may all be in danger now."

The officer raced to the phone at the receptionist's desk. Before he could hear a dial tone, Roberts was already out the door.

"Hopefully, we can end this before any more blood is shed!"

Jane shimmied up the rain gutter outside of Stacy's apartment building. Her muscles were straining as she made it up to the second story. Climbing up a pipe was easier said than done. Her feet planted on the wall, and her hands gripped tightly around the pipe as she shuffled up and refused to look down.

I gotta start using my gym membership. It's like I'm paying 30 bucks a month on not going to the gym.

Soon enough, she reached Stacy's apartment and pulled herself to the edge. She was even amazed that the window wasn't locked. With one grunt she pulled herself onto the windowsill and gazed into the bedroom.

The place was a wreck! Drawers were yanked out and dumped onto the floor. Desks and chairs were over turned, vases and framed photos were trashed. It looked like a battle was held here.

"Great Schmidt!" Jane exclaimed. "What happened here?" She made her way through the room and followed the path of destruction that led into the hallway and into the living room/kitchen. "It looks like there was a struggle of some kind."

Jane tore her gaze away from the disarray to inspect a note, addressed to her superhero alter ego on the counter.

Jane picked it up carefully. It could be booby-trapped. She gently opened the envelope and pulled out the letter. With great anticipation she began to read.

Well, hello there, Avenging Star.
It seems that there is, after all, one last dance left on our card.
If you would like for Stacy to have any chance at all. I would suggest you meet me at the Bay Bridge immediately.
There still may be time for you to save her but...I doubt it.
—SM

"S.M.," Jane said in repugnance. "Shadowy Man," she growled; indignantly crumpled the piece of paper in her hand and then throwing it down on the floor. "You want me, Shadowy Man, you've got me. Buffet Style."

She ran back into Stacy's bedroom and was about to climb back down the building. With one leg out the window she stopped.

"What am I doing?" She said, getting back inside. "I'll use the front door. What am I, crazy?"

"When is this nightmare going to be over?" Elizabeth asked Detective Roberts. She went on vacation for a week to find out her friend Debra had been murdered and there's a lunatic on the loose. "It's not bad enough Debra and Pete were killed in a fire and this place gets vandalized. And now you're worried about Stacy... and, and Jane? This doesn't make any sense."

"Stacy and Jane are the only employees of your salon that we can't find," said Roberts. "You seemed surprised about the both of them. Why is that?"

"Well, we're all aware of the tragedies that have happened. A lot of people Jane was close to have died. That's the thing." Elizabeth took a deep breath and looked at Roberts timidly. "You see Jane and Stacy weren't close. They practically hated each other. They were always fighting. I heard the only time it wasn't so bad was..."

Then something dawned on her. She rushed to her appointments books and skimmed the pages.

"Is something wrong?" Roberts asked.

"No," replied Elizabeth, "it's just...well, I was on vacation a few weeks back. I have a regular customer—Johnson's his name. And Jane covered for me while I was gone. I hear things were pretty quiet between her and Stacy during that time." Then a confused look ran across her face. "It's not here—his address. Why is it missing?"

Roberts turned to his men and gave them their orders. "Let me know the minute the squad car gets to Stacy's. Find out where this Mr. Johnson lives and send a squad car there. I've got a bad feeling about this."

Jane was sprinting through the boardwalk by the harbor. Her mask was soaked with sweat. Her head was getting warm by all the rigorous exercise she's been getting. She was puffing for breath on each stride. She could feel her side aching. This was the most exercise she had all year. She wanted to stop and catch her breath, but time was of the essence. Stacy's life was hanging in the balance. Every second counted.

Blood formed a wet film beneath her clothing, and the red was exploiting behind her eyes. But She might be able to reach somewhere she could rest, and allow herself a few moments peace before her long nightmare began. She had failed to save her parents, had failed to save Uncle Charlie. But perhaps she could still put herself on the side of the angels by allowing the world to believe she to be the ugliest of devils.

A clock in a nearby tower struck eight.

The sun was sinking in the west, lighting the tops of the city's spires and throwing its canyon streets into dense shadow.

There was the smell of the sea in the gust of wind that stirred Jane's cape.

Lamps began to shine in apartment windows. Streetlights blinked on, casting a yellow glow that did little to dispel the creeping gloom. Jane felt as if a cold pit had opened up underneath her. The bridge lurched, and her stomach churned along with it. She closed her eyes and saw, once again, the vision of her parents.

Until she thought she was going to crash from exhaustion, she saw a familiar silhouette of a man standing near the edge of the bridge. There was rope dangling from the beam over his head. Jane stopped right in front of the Shadowy Man. She gasped loudly for air, standing hunched over with her hands resting on her knees.

The Shadowy Man offered her a smile. But it wasn't the sinister smile that threw Jane off. It was the glimmering blade of a machete that rested on the ledge next to the vile villain. Then her attention was diverted to the baritone voice of her nemesis.

The wind blew Stacy's rope toward the bridge, almost knocking her hard against the steel. Her feet slapped the pavement as she sprinted, desperation in her eyes. She slowed down and walked briskly away from the docks, heading to the bridge.

"You made it!" He jovially announced. A huge grin bisected his face. "How wonderful. Just brilliant. I'm so glad you're here. Shall we dance, hmmm?"

The Shadowy Man thought that Jane must be about ready to jump out of her skin. It was a delicious feeling, to have the city's hero on pins and needles…and it was only going to get better. It's a beautiful thing when a plan comes together.

Jane stopped, breathing hard. Red faced, sweating, shaking, cramped into a costume that probably shrunk in the wash.

"What, uh, wuh…" Jane wheezed, peeling away her soaked cowl to expose the face of Jane Travers. Her face was flushed, and red as a tomato. She swiped part of her hair off her face. It was so wet and sticky. "Ugh, wait. Um…" she continued to struggle, she was rasping breathlessly. During this time she thought about what the symptoms were for heart attack.

Her eyes fastened on the Shadowy Man, carrying a machete.

The Shadowy Man's eyes, in turn, fastened on her.

The Shadowy Man raised an eyebrow. "Jane?" He asked in a surprisingly concerned tone. "Are you alright? You look sick."

"Yeah! Sick of you." Jane snapped, pulling the mask back over her head. "Why don't we get this over with? You. And me."

"Brava, Jane!" Cheered the Shadowy Man, throwing his arms up in joy. "How dramatic. Yes, this truly will be an epic last battle. Though, one turning point of clarification—it's not just you and me."

He jerked his head to his right, to show Jane that he had tied up Stacy and she's dangling over the bridge. She's trembling and tears were running down her face. The silver grade-A duct tape muffled her whimpers and screams across her mouth.

"You see, your dear friend Stacy is currently hung over the side of the bridge."

"You monster!" Jane thundered. "When I'm through with you, even dental records won't identify you!"

The Shadowy Man gave out a loud chuckle. His rictus grin was stretching from ear to ear. "Honestly, Stacy," he said to his pretty captive. "I'm so disappointed in the company you keep. Ah, well, she won't be your friend after this." He reached for the machete and raised it above his head, like a scorpion ready to strike. "All she'll be is dead."

Jane balled up her fists.

CHAPTER THIRTEEN

A heavy leather boot kicked Stacy's front door open. The police barged into the apartment, followed by a team of gun-toting officers.

"Police department!" Barked the commanding officer. "Show me your hands!"

"I get surprised, you get shot!" Yelled the cop behind him.

The first officer entered the domicile with his gun at the ready. The two other officers followed suit. They entered with the utmost caution and found the mess of what seemed to be one massive fight.

"What the heck...?" Said one of them. He walked gingerly through the living room and found one the windows opened. His partners surveyed the whole vicinity, trying to find clues. "Looks like they came through the window," he said, while searching the kitchen, the rookie found a crumpled up piece of paper with some writing on it. As he unraveled the discarded note, the leading officer was calling it in.

"No one's here," he said to dispatch. "And it looks like—"

"Sir!" Called out the rookie.

The officer with the Walkie was startled. "Hang on," he said to the operator. Then he turned to the young patrolman. "What do you have?"

"I think I know where they are. At least two of them, anyway!"

The Shadowy Man was standing menacingly by the rope that was holding Stacy. He held the machete dangerously close to the rope and began to whittle it away.

Jane shot her finger at him. "Back away from Stacy and surrender. This is your only warning!" The Shadowy Man did not cower or even falter. "Do you hear me?!" Jane bellowed. "Surrender!"

"No, no, no," the Shadowy Man replied, sounding like an unruly child. "You're doing it all wrong. First, we fight. Then you get the upper hand. Before I recover you offer me surrender—which, of course, I want to accept, and I'll make one last attack that you'll center. Then I meet my untimely demise. It's quite simple really."

Jane couldn't believe what he was saying. He was actually telling her how to do her job!

"You're insane!"

"Insane, eh?" The Shadowy Man grinned. "Hmmm. No, I feel just fine. *You're* the crazy one. In fact, all of this is your fault. Hmmm?"

She couldn't take anymore of this stalling banter. Now was the time for action. It was time she did something about the monster that was preying on the innocent victims of the city.

It was time the villain paid for his crimes.

They faced off again, in the dim light from the street, and Jane could see the gleam of teeth in the Shadowy Man's wicked smile. He beckoned her with his hand.

She snapped out her cape and launched herself at the Shadowy Man. With a tremendous battle cry she charged at him and threw a punch.

The Shadowy Man dodged the attack.

"Ole!" He said, followed by the sound of the machete slicing through the air and slashing Jane across her back.

"Aaahhhh!" She cried in pain. The sound of fabric ripping through her cape and shirt were muffled the loud screaming in her head. All she saw was red, as her own blood misted in the air.

"Perhaps I should be called El Matador?" Quipped the Shadowy Man, holding the blade next to his mouth. "You clearly have the appearance of a bull. And if you do not change your tactics, you'll end up like one." Then he licked the blood of the blade and gave out a satisfying moan.

Pain sliced through Jane's back as she gingerly staggered toward a column. Jane struggled to stand up straight. She took a breath and remembered what Sensei Komatsu said to her. In order to achieve victory she had to focus. So she focused all of her energy to engage in Tiger Stance.

"Excellent!" Praised the Shadowy Man. "Shall we try again? This time with a bit of decorum."

"Shut up and fight," she breathed in through her teeth with a pained hiss and reached for the slashes on her shoulder, which had suddenly flared into a more severe pain, as if to remind her they were there and weren't going away.

The Shadowy Man smiled. There was nothing—literally—that he loved better than a challenge. "Yes! Have at thee!"

This was it. This was what Sensei Komatsu told Jane. This was her final lesson before he charged her with the task of stopping the Shadowy Man.

Jane ducked below the quick slice of the whistling blade, then high-kicked with her right leg fully extended, sending the slender madman who wielded it against the iron bridge.

With another swift kick the Shadowy Man doubled over. Dropping the machete in process.

As he lied distracted, Jane pounced on top of him—pinning him to the ground.

"It's over!" She shouted, struggling to restrain him. "You're finished. I've beaten you, Shadowy Man!"

She continued to evolve, this dark-cloaked avenger, this tragic lurker in the shadows, and that constant gradual change may be why she was sharp as she had ever been. Her whole demeanor seemed different now; she wasn't awkward or distracted at all. She moved quickly, with purpose. Her eyes were sharp and hard.

"Everything was going so smoothly." The Shadowy Man smiled through the darkness. Then he frowned. "But there was only one wrinkle to my plan: You."

Jane smiled coldly. "Well, let me tell you something, mister. I don't iron out that easily."

The Shadowy Man advanced, the machete in one hand. Jane saw him coming. Her eyes widened with fear.

The Shadowy Man thrust the blade at Jane's chest. She pivoted, and the steel slipped past her chest, grazing her costume. The Shadowy Man kicked. Jane sidestepped and the Shadowy Man kicked again, striking her hip. As Jane stumbled, trying to regain her footing.

Jane chopped sideways into the Shadowy Man's wrist; the villain cried out in pain and the machete fell, clanging, to the ground.

She followed up with a brutal elbow to the back of his head. The Shadowy Man grunted and went down.

Jane hurled rapid-fire punches and kicks at the Shadowy Man, delivering them with every ounce of strength and still she could muster. She didn't bother with threats or theatrics. The villain wouldn't be intimidated by the ominous guise of the Avenging Star, either—and he would not stop until he had defeated his foe. One way or another, this would be their final contest.

Determined to put the Shadowy Man on the defensive, Jane lunged at him again, striking out with her fists and boots. The Shadowy Man effortlessly countered her moves. He went for the weak spots Jane's body armor, inflicting the maximum pain possible, while seeming to possess no weaknesses of his own.

They broke apart, facing off between the breezy archways. The Shadowy Man looked like he was just warming up.

She clenched her fists and glared up at the Shadowy Man. *If I jump,* she thought, *I can tackle him. Tackle a shadow demon with crazy mystical powers? Oh, man, this is gonna hurt—*

Jane leaped up in the air, surprisingly high, and expertly checked the Shadowy Man with the left side of her body. He managed to find his balance and whirled around, lashing out at her. But she ducked, standing her ground.

Then, shockingly, the Shadowy Man laughed.

"Impressive," he said. "And yet, so disappointing."

Jane's eyes flashed with anger. The two of them grappled for a moment. Out of the corner of her eye, Jane saw Stacy eyeing the battle.

The Shadowy Man freed one arm from Jane's grip and punched her in the stomach. Jane gasped and doubled over. She took a step back.

Jane roared again, a deep, primal sound. Enraged, she ran toward the Shadowy Man, headfirst. Her charge was clumsy, uncoordinated. But when her head struck the villain's stomach, the two of them doubled down to the ground.

The Shadowy Man huffed and rolled over on top of Jane. Her head struck the floor, and she felt broken glass cut into her ear. She cried out.

When she looked up, the Shadowy Man was sitting on top of her. He wasn't scratched, injured, or even breathing hard. Her whole body stiffened up. She looked around, her eyes wild, as if she were caught in a mousetrap.

Without warning, the Shadowy Man lunged backward and caught Jane's throat in his grasp. He slammed her into the concrete, hard enough to bash any other person's brains out. His bare fists pounded on Jane's cowl with unbelievable force, blow after blow smashing down like a jackhammer. Concussed and breathless, Jane couldn't fight back as the Shadowy Man hammered on the cowl until finally, the leather ripped in her mask.

For a split second, Jane didn't register what was happening. All around her, sirens were starting to wail. And above her, a dark shadow seemed to be filling the sky. She snapped out of it, cursing the precious moments she'd lost.

She staggered to her feet, swaying unsteadily. Her ripped mask slipped, and she tasted blood in her mouth. Her head was swimming. Everything seemed to be spinning around her, and she felt sick to her stomach. Through the fog, she recognized the symptoms of a serious concussion.

Nevertheless, she raised her fists. She tried to summon her powers, but she couldn't feel the energy surging through as it once did. The drugs must have worn off, but Jane highly doubted it because she already took a couple of pills before getting here. She quickly deduced that her powers were only able to break through whatever was going on because she wasn't thinking about using them. She was just trying to save some people from being hurt. It was either that or the fact she might've exhausted her powers while she was sprinting to the bridge. Apparently she has to win this fight sober.

The Shadowy Man turned back toward her. She delivered a roundhouse almost significant enough to stun him completely. He felt his teeth suddenly loosen, the metallic taste of blood erupting in his mouth.

Through bleary, swollen eyes, he gave her a lopsided grin. "I think I like you," he slurred.

Jane squeezed her eyes shut, willing the pain away.

Block, block, punch, kick, twirl, kick, block, shoot, head-butt, twirl, punch, kick, open-fist slam, and down.

She landed on her feet and quickly whirled around to survey the damage she'd done in the past few minutes. The late night salty breeze off the nearby bay gently plays with her hair. He glossy lips (was it really that wrong to wear some makeup while in costume? She couldn't help it in any case) part in a smile. The best part about being a crime fighter, she thought, was the fact that she could take her anger out on the bad guys if and when she needed to.

This was one of those nights she needed to.

"I feel like Michelangelo must have felt when he found the block of marble that became his *David*. Thus far, Jane Travers has not disappointed me. She may be the raw material of my masterpiece. Evolution has been kind to her. She is of huge mental capacity with an intelligence quotient I believe to be among the highest ever recorded and an eidetic memory. Everything that she sees or hears she can recall with total accuracy and she is able to absorb new information of any kind with speed."

A trickle of sweat ran from beneath her mask and down her cheek. She felt a sweep of relief. She was in full command of the situation, which was exactly where she wanted to be. "And I happen to be a great physical specimen as well."

The Shadowy Man paused. "Let's not get carried away here."

Jane arched an eyebrow. "What does that supposed to mean?"

"You're still ignorant and cannot access all that nature has given you," the Shadowy Man quickly changed the subject. "But these are conditions that I can remedy."

By now sirens could be heard outside, growing louder by the minute. Jane wasn't concerned. She had expected as much. Red and blue lights strobe through the darkness like an underground rave. The first squad car came to a screeching halt. Jane snapped into attention and watched as Detective Roberts harshly exited his car.

"Jane! Stop!" He shouted.

But Jane wasn't listening. She saw the machete and picked it up. She held it over the Shadowy Man who was delighted by this turn of events.

"Well done, love. You've made me proud!" The Shadowy Man smiled. "Now, I believe this is the proper time for you to demand my surrender."

Jane gripped the red handle of the machete tightly, imagining she had wrapped her giant hands around her quarry's neck. Squeezing the life out of him and watching his smoldering eyes burned all the way to nothingness. A flash flood of what happened that night clouded her mind. All she saw were her murdered parents and watching the Shadowy Man kill her uncle Charlie in cold blood. Leaving his body to rot in a dirty alley, like someone with no importance. Tears were forming from her eyes, and she couldn't even feel the burns on the left side of her face anymore.

"There is no surrender," she said, stabbing the villain multiple times in the chest. Each hit was more devastating and vicious than the last. "Not after all the things you've done!"

"No!" Screamed Detective Roberts. He ran over to Jane who was still stabbing the man that caused her nothing but pain. Roberts had forcefully pulled the machete from her hands. Jane was shocked to see him. Hell, even a little confused.

"What have you done?" He said, pulling her away from the freshly made corpse.

Jane turned in surprise. Detective Roberts raised himself to a crouch was staring at her. She took a moment to catch her breath and got her bearings before checking herself for signs of injury. It seemed impossible that she could have emerged from this battle unscathed. But as far as she could gather she was fine. Not even a scratch.

"Detective Roberts?" Jane said in a daze. "What are you doing here?"

"I'm trying to prevent more deaths."

Jane pulled her arm away from him. She stood triumphant with the sea's breeze fluttering her cape in the wind.

"Well, this is the last one," she genuinely proclaimed. "It was necessary. The Shadowy Man had to be stopped. And stopped him I did." She proudly showed the bewildered detective the grisly remains of the city's most deadly super-criminal. There he laid dead with the machete buried into his chest. Nothing more than a macabre version of the fabled Sword in the Stone story. "Him," Jane further pointed out.

The blood rushed from the detective's face. "Shadowy who?" He asked, trying to make sense out of all of this. "What are you talking about?"

Then he narrowed his eyes. He was being serious—deadly serious.

"Jane, I don't know what you are talking about," he said bluntly. And the next thing he said didn't make any sense. "That's Mr. Johnson."

Jane turned to face her fallen adversary. Her eyes widened in horror as a rush of emotions plagued her psyche. Her nerves of steel were no more. They were replaced with glass and they were viciously shattered.

In the Shadowy Man's place was Mr. Johnson, her new favorite customer… dead on the ground. With the machete plunged into his chest. A Rorschach pattern of blood soaked into his expensive designer dress shirt, and the blazer that was part of his $2,000 suit.

Jane couldn't breathe. The words wheezed out of her mouth. She felt her knees giving away.

"No," she choked. "No, no, no, no, no! Not Mr. Johnson! It was the Shadowy Man!"

Then she lost all feeling in her legs. She fell to her knees and held her head in writhing pain. Nothing made sense to her anymore.

"He, he must…must…have done something to my mind!" She deduced, but she could not control her terror. "Yes. That's it. He tricked me…he tricked me!"

CHAPTER FOURTEEN

Jane didn't feel like celebrating. Yes, she had outwitted the Shadowy Man. She'd saved not just her friends but also the lives of the citizens in this fair city. She should have been ecstatic.

Instead, Jane could think only of her parents, murdered before her very eyes by the Shadowy Man. That monster didn't just murder them, but he had also taken her uncle Charlie. Her family was gone.

Roberts immediately took charge. "Don't just stand there!" Roberts barked at his subordinates. "Somebody call a goddamn ambulance!"

As the world spun and her descent quickened, memories flashed in Jane's mind. Images as sharp as life. Jane blinked. Her eyes welled up with tears. "I don't understand…" She moaned softly.

"Jane," Detective Roberts continued, a strange tone creeping into his voice. "There's something I have to tell you."

A psychic fever overcame her exhaustion as she continued to comprehend on what the detective just revealed to her. Broken images fluttered through her brain like frightened birds.

They whirled faster and faster in a blurred, flapping chaos until abruptly the fragments merged into a single, mind-shattering vision of unspeakable evil, and she fell swooning to the ground.

Ghastly images flashed across her feverish mind, like snapshots from a half-forgotten nightmare!

Jane clutched her head. Trembling fingers kneaded her throbbing skull. She reeled backward, unable to process what was happening to her. A tinge of hysteria entered her voice. Spittle sprayed from her lips.

Had that really happened?

"Oh, God…" Jane couldn't believe her eyes. Her whole world seemed to have gone insane.

Roberts put his arm around her and tried to comfort her. "No, Jane," he said gently. "There is *no* Shadowy Man. He's only in your mind."

Her body stiffened. Jane raised her head slowly as if it weighed a hundred pounds. Her lips were numb and she found it difficult to answer. She looked up at Detective Roberts in disbelief and pulled away, trying to gather herself.

Jane turned, face streaked with tears. "No! I've seen him. He killed my family. My friends."

"I'm sorry, Jane. He's not real." For a man with a rugged exterior, his voice was soft. It was like coaxing a frightened baby deer. Then he said the one thing that rocked her world. It will be the one sentence that will stick to her for the rest of her life. "*You* killed all of them."

Jane *understood* the words, but she could not grasp their meaning. So she just sat and felt the thing inside her continue to swell until it filled her, and her own skin was just a thin covering over it, a garment she was wearing like her own costume, and after a while it *became* her. *It* was the real Jane. Everything else was false.

She felt she was trapped in the Sunken Place where she hopelessly watched the vicious murders of her friends and family. To add more drama to her life, it had been revealed that she was the killer all along.

She was the one who killed an innocent man which she thought was a serial arsonist. Beaten to death with a plank of wood. Then she walked into her uncle Charlies room and went through his wardrobe. She took out his old overcoat and fedora hat. She returned to McGriffin's Bar and Grill and poured a can of gasoline outside and set the place ablaze. She saw the panicked faces of Debra and Pete trying to open the door. They were begging for help. But Jane casually tipped her hat to them and sadistically watched as they were all burned alive, giving them a smile.

A predator's smile.

Another flash saw her reaching for the gun in the back of Big T's pants when he bent over into his trunk reaching for the drugs she wanted. She grabbed the gun and fired several times into his chest, causing him to slump over into the open trunk. Then she went home to kill her parents without batting a filthy eyelash. And she saw her uncle Charlie falling to the ground after a flash of muzzle fire and a sound of thunder boomed the secluded alley. Jane saw the startled look on Johnson's face when she abducted him from the sanctity of his own home. And all she needed was a damsel in distress. Stacy put up quite a fight. Jane almost felt bad about roughing her up a bit.

But she never did like her anyway.

Then this montage of murder and mayhem ended with the supposed slaying of the Shadowy Man. But in reality, it was Mr. Johnson. The last scene played over and over again in a continuous loop.

She rocked back on her heels as the world began to shift around her. "I...I don't understand," Jane said. She clenched her jaw. She looked away. The officers were closing in all around her. Their fingers were on the triggers. One of the officers waved a Taser at her, electricity arcing out its tip. One sudden move and they would chop her down like a red wood. "What happened?"

"Jane, your uncle said you suffer from schizophrenia," Detective Roberts revealed to her. "He also said you haven't been taking your medication."

Jane looked up to make eye contact with the detective. He wasn't lying. What he said was true. She was sick and she needed help.

"I talked to your psychiatrist and he said this could happen," he continued. "He also thinks you may be dissociative...um, you may have multiple personalities, which could explain the, uh, 'Shadowy Man'?"

"So that's it?" She asked, not entirely convinced. She kept her face averted, and her voice shook. "I'm crazy and I killed everyone?"

Then she heard one of the most distinctive sounds in the world: The hammer of a gun being cocked. More correctly, a large number of gun hammers. Slowly, with more effort than she would have thought necessary, she managed to raise her head and focus her blurring vision.

She was ringed by police officers that had their guns drawn, watching warily. It seemed, in Jane's exhaustion, that all the barrels of the guns aimed at her blended into one huge barrel the size of a howitzer.

Jane scanned the crowd, trying to separate reality from the haze of nightmarish terrors. She eyed the police officers, a sinking feeling in her gut. They carried Tasers, and they were all trained on her.

Then something struck her like a bolt of lightning. She cursed her broken concentration, and remembered about Stacy.

There was still time.

She stood rapidly and stepped away from Roberts quickly, taking a few breaths. In the commotion she broke free from the detective's arms and began to make a run for the ledge. "Well, there's still the matter of where Stacy is. Do you know if she's still alive?"

Her words were almost lost in the rearing wind, but she knew he's heard her over the harbor.

"She's getting away!" Yelled one of the officers. "Fire!"

The wriggling constructs attached Jane's neck from both sides, their stingers penetrating the thick reinforced fabric to pierce the skin beneath. She grunted in shock as they sent a current of electricity.

It was like being struck by lightning. She swayed backward, surrendering her grip on the rope. Her face contorted in agony as her body convulsed. Her legs buckled and she collapsed onto her knees. She raised her fists, hoping to put up a fight despite the debilitating effects of the currents coursing through her system. Her head throbbed painfully, and her limbs felt like lead. Her heart was pounding faster than the Accelerator's boots, she tried to speak, to warn the cops about Stacy dangling at the end of the rope, but only an inarticulate groan escaped her clenched jaws. Nausea twisted her gut into knots.

Her strength abandoned her, however, and she stumbled forward onto the pavement. Landing on her knees, she succumbed to fatigue, just for a second, and closed her eyes, a single moment of weakness that threatened to linger on forever.

She made one final effort to stand, but it would have been impossible to tell by looking at her, because she didn't budge from the floor. Instead she curled up even tighter, her arms clutching around her legs, drawing her knees up to just under her chin. Her eyes rolled up into the top of her head, and the final jolt of pain was too overwhelming for her to handle. With a final, low moan, she passed out dead away. Under her lids, her eyes continued to flutter.

CHAPTER FIFTEEN

Jane's blue eyes drifted from side to side frantically.

Where am I?

How did I get here?

She remembered having a good life with her parents. Then she ended up in an unfamiliar place.

She was sitting on a wheelchair, being pushed through a door by people in doctor outfits. All she could hear was the small taps of footsteps, the quiet hum of the air conditioner, the clicks of her wheelchair as it hit another crack in the white tile, and her fast heartbeat. They were passing through a long hallway to another metal door.

Where are my parents?

Where the hell are my own clothes?! How did I even get dressed?

She was now changed into a light blue, cotton pants with a matching shirt. Jane was also wearing thin, white slippers. The change in clothes was completely different then her usual clothing which always consisted of a sweatshirt, jeans, sneakers, and a comfortable T-shirt.

The doctors pushed her through the metal door and she soon found herself being pushed in front of a receptionist desk. The woman behind the desk, looked up from her work as Jane's wheelchair came to a stop.

"Hello, may I help you? She asked, pushing back her hair behind her ear.

"Yes, we are checking in Jane Travers," informed one of the doctors. The woman flipped through a giant book and scanned the pages.

"Ah, yes, Jane Travers! Age 22. She has an excessive imagination that is too dangerous to be around the more sane people."

What?

"I take it that she had recovered enough from the hospital?"

Wait, hospital? What hospital?

And recovered?

Was I in some sort of accident?

Jane looked down to search for any injuries, now noticing her arms wrapped in thin layers of bandages. Around her neck, forehead, legs, and abdomen was some pressure, indicating that it too was covered in bandages. The more she realized that she was injured, the more she could feel the sharp sting of the injuries that lied under the wrappings.

What happened? When did I get these?

"Yes, only minor injuries that can heal in the next few days are left."

"Thank you, I can take it from here."

The doctors pushed Jane up to her and the receptionist grabbed the handles. She then reached over, grabbed the phone, and dialed in a number. She pressed it against her ear and she could slightly hear the rings before a muffled voice answered.

"Yes, is this Steve?"

A pause.

"Yeah, this is Gloria, the receptionist. Listen, there's a new patient here today. Do you mind counseling her? And yes, she shares a room with the other you council, Nancy. Thank you."

The woman, Gloria, hung up and a few minutes later a man walked up. He was a tall man, late twenties, and was incredibly ripped. Although he looked young, his eyes had shown maturity. He was someone who grew up too fast.

He walked over to Gloria and she handed Jane to him. This must be Steve. He nodded respectfully before pushing Jane towards the hallway behind the desk. The further they went in more people they saw in the same outfit as she wore. They all turned to look her over. Probably deciding her fate.

Steve cleared his throat. "So, your name is Jane. Your soon-to-be-roommate's name is Nancy."

Jane could tell this was awkward for him. "Why am I here?" Jane asked instead.

"Well, I don't know yet. I haven't read your file yet."

"Any of you were willing to '*help*' me even though you don't know? The lady in front…uh…Gloria said that I have an erratic imagination? But I don't have that. I'm normal."

"Most new patients say that they are fine. Usually, they don't realize what's wrong with them."

The wheelchair came to a stop in front of a room. Room 32. Steve opened the door, peeking his head in. "Nancy, your new roommate is here."

Steve pushed Jane into the room. Inside were two beds that were on different walls. There was small window, too small to fit a body through, which showed the outside world. Sitting in one of the beds was a young woman in her twenties.

Nancy got up from the bed, loping over to Jane with a huge smile that was as bright as a thousand suns. It confused Jane as to why she was here.

"I'm Nancy," she greeted.

"I'm Jane," she said, giving Nancy a mild smile.

"Alright, I'll leave you for a few minutes. I have to go pick up your files, Jane," Steve said before walking out of the room. Nancy sat back down on her bed.

"So…I know that we just met, but can I ask you a personal question?"

"Sure?" Jane wasn't sure where she was going with this.

"Are you disabled, since you're in that wheelchair?"

"I don't think so. I hope not. I can feel my legs. I just woke up being pushed here in a wheelchair. I can try getting out, but I do have injuries, I think, on my legs. I really don't remember getting them."

"You don't remember?"

"No, I was with my family at one point then I was here." Jane tried to get out of the wheelchair, wobbling a bit on her feet before steadying. She sat on the other bed and pushed the wheelchair aside.

"That's weird," Nancy concluded. "So, do you know they put you in here?"

"I was told I had an erratic imagination that can harm others. What about you?"

"I have DID."

Jane was confused. "DID?"

"Dissociative Identity Disorder."

"You mean like that guy from *Split*?"

"That's right, M. Night Shama-lama-ding-dong. Right now, you're conversing with the original alias." A questionable look appeared on Nancy's face. A blanket of uncertainty washed upon her. "I think…"

"How many personalities do you have?"

"I really don't know. The one that mostly comes up is named Ellie. She loves to hurt people."

"So she's a psychopath."

"Uh…sure. The other that comes up a lot is practically your everyday womanizer."

The door opened again and two people, a man and a woman, with matching outfits as Jane and Nancy walked in.

Nancy smiled. "Oh, hey, Trish, David!"

The two newcomers were completely different, personality-wise. The girl looked like Harley Quinn without all the makeup and the not so subtle sensuality. The man looked more composed. Right when the two entered the room, their eyes locked onto Jane.

"Who's that?" The man asked.

"That's my new roommate, Jane," Nancy introduced. The chilled one snorted at the sound of Jane's name and she felt her ears warm up from embarrassment. She could already tell she would not like him much.

The silly one sat down next Jane and swung an arm around her shoulders. "I'm Trish. Don't wear it out." Jane smiled a "hello" to her.

"I'm David," the man said. "I'm Trish's counselor."

"So, David, what's up?" Nancy asked.

David's face lit up a little bit. "Oh, Steve said to take you to dinner. He's going to be late."

Nancy nodded, standing up. Trish followed suit and Jane followed the three patients out of the room. They weaved through hallways and Jane did her best to memorize the way from her room to the cafeteria. They passed through a hallway with a dimmed light bulb. She wondered what was down there and why they keep it murky. She was going to ask the others when she saw a dark silhouette of a large figure move in and out of her vision, catching her immediate attention.

Who...?

Jane shook her head. It was probably a counselor or patient here.

"Jane, hurry up!" Trish yelled.

"Sorry," Jane called back and caught up with them, now realizing that she stopped walking.

They went into the mess hall and got their food. Jane stared incredulously at the glop of food on her tray.

Was it even considered food?

Jane sat down at the table with the people she met today and poked at her *food*. It smelled like food. She scooped a chunk out of the glop with her spork and put it in her mouth. It tasted like food. she guessed it was fine. Jane started to eat it a bit faster, realizing how hungry she was. It felt like she hadn't eaten in ages.

Once she scarfed down her supper, Jane asked a question that bothered her. "Why was that hallway dimmed out?"

Nancy frowned at the question. "That's where the patients that refuse to leave their rooms are. Most of them keep the light off, so it would be easier on their eyes when the counselors check up on them. In fact, David is taking of one: Suzy. How's she doing, anyways? Any progress?"

David let out a sigh and leaned back against his plastic chair, running a hand through his hair. "Suzy still won't talk to me. She won't talk to anyone. Well, except for Dr. Hammerschmidt, but she could barely get Suzy to speak. It's rare. I don't even hear Suzy talk. It's all just rumors. She's hopeless at this rate."

"Suzy still won't move from that corner?" Steve asked, joining them at the table. He placed the unopened files on the table. Curiosity caught Jane's attention on the girl.

"Can I try talking to her?" She asked.

David shrugged. "Be my guest. Just don't get your hopes up. We can go after everyone has finished eating."

Everyone agreed. Steve opened the folder, reading through Jane's file. His stoic expression had a bit of impressment on it. She wondered what was he reading that made his expression changed like that.

"Does that file say anything about my parents and why was I put here?" She asked.

Steve read the file more before shaking his head. "Your parents wanted you to get better and they were scared for you."

"Then why am I covered in bandages and came here pushed by doctors in a wheelchair?"

"You got in a fight with someone and got really hurt."

Jane frowned before nodding. Something was *off* about what he was saying. She wasn't a person who just gets into fights. If she did, there had to be a really good reason for it. After everyone had finished eating, they busted their trays and David took us into a dim hallway. They walked until they found a metallic, green door that was labeled with a "13." David knocked on the door quietly, and then opened it. It was dark inside; the only light came from the soft lights in the hallway. She could make out a figure in the corner of the room. David walked to the light switch, flicking it on.

In the corner of the newly lit room, was a heavyset woman with shoulder length hair. Bangs mostly covered her frightened looking eyes. She was older than everyone else in the room. Suzy reminded Jane of a scared puppy.

Jane walked over to her slowly; as if to not frighten her away, and sat down. Her attention was now focused mainly on Jane. She smiled gently at Suzy.

"Hi, my name is Jane," she introduced in a hush tone. "I just came here."

She waited for a response, not expecting anything to come out of the other.

"I heard you won't talk to people. But you can converse with me. I don't bite... unless if someone takes the last slice of chocolate cake. Then it's war."

Suzy's lip twitched. It was almost unnoticeable.

Jane smiled brighter. "But you know, people have to speak. Talking is a great stress reliever and it can help you solve any problem. No one is supposed to be alone. If you don't talk now, then I'll still press on until you accept me as your friend."

David cleared his throat and Jane nodded toward him, understanding the message. She turned back toward Suzy. "I got to go now. But, hopefully, I will see you again. It's not easier to talk to you then them, so I enjoyed this conversation." She stood up. "Bye."

"Bye..." Suzy croaked out quietly. Her voice was enough to rip through the silence. For a few moments, the fear left Suzy's eyes and Jane saw shyness. She smiled and waved before leaving the room.

After the door closed, the other looked at Jane with shock and disbelief. She wished she could take a picture of their faces right now.

"She talked to you!" Trish gasped out. "She doesn't talk to anyone!"

"What did you say to her to talk to you?" David pressed.

"I just asked if she wanted to be my friend," Jane shrugged and walked to her room.

Both Jane and Nancy sat down next to each other in vacant seats. Jane tapped her fingers on her knee nervously. She had seen how they do these confessions in TV and movies, but she did not remember how she got here yet. Soon enough, everyone was seated. The only person she noticed not there was Suzy. Everyone wore the same clothes except for one older man who was balding, with a few stray grey hairs on his head.

"Good morning, everyone. It's time for the group confessions. Since I see some new faces, I think we should go around, say our names, and a few things about ourselves. Who wants to start first?" The man asked before going ahead and pointed to a random man that sat near Jane. "You, start."

The man clicked his tongue in annoyance as he crossed his arms. "My name is Brian."

"Would you like to tell us about yourself?"

Brian laughed, probably at an inside joke before answering in a seducing tone. "What do you want to know about me?"

"Not what you're thinking. Let's skip that. What are you in here for?"

"Conduct disorder."

Jane smirked. *If the movies are right, he's going to say "and how do you feel about that" soon or make him tell a story about how he found out.*

"Would you like to tell a story about an event? Or what have you done?"

Called it.

"Let's see, I have broken into someone's house, broken in people's cars, initiated in physical fights, set property on fire, do I need to say more?"

Someone stood up quickly, pointing an accusing finger at Brian. "Wait! Were you the one who stabbed my brother?"

"Probably."

"You should be put in jail for all that shit you did!" Another person stood up.

"Everyone calm down and sit down. What Brian has can't be controlled. It's pretty serious!" The counselor commanded, making everyone sit down. Glares were sent to Brian. "Okay, next person."

They went around the circle and Jane learned a few things. There was guy named Travis who scarily has obsessive-compulsive disorder. Trish had kleptomania. A girl named Gia had Stockholm Syndrome. Soon it was Jane's turn.

"My name is Jane," she said to the crowd, earning chuckles.

"Alright, what are you here for?"

"Schizophrenia."

He looked at her questionably. "I'm sorry, how old are you?"

"Twenty-two."

"It's pretty severe then. Do you know what triggered it?"

Jane shook her head. "I actually don't remember anything."

A look of disappointment showed on his face before he continued. "Alright, can you try to remember what happened? Look deep in your mind. You don't have to if you don't feel like doing so, though."

Jane nodded. "I…can try."

She was unsure if she should proceed with this or not. After what she saw in her dream, Jane was scared of what she would see. But, she also wanted to know what happened.

Jane closed her eyes, and was consumed by the darkness of her mind. She didn't know what to do, so she just imagined herself floating, surrounding by closed doors of different types. Jane hovered over to the closest door: a tavern-styled wooden door. She pulled on its steel handles, and a rush of memories ran through her. It was a memory of her first day in preschool. She was pretty shy back then and clung onto her mother's long skirt. Jane pulled out of the memory and closed the door. Then it faded into oblivion soon after.

The next door was like a submarine door, but that was not what she was looking for. Jane spent what felt like hours searching in her memory before a small trapdoor caught her attention. She floated down and pulled on the latch, but a chain was wrapped around it like a boa constrictor and its prey. Jane pulled at the chain, but it refused to budge. She soon gave up.

The wooden trapdoor had a small hole in the wood. On the other side, there was a bright light. Maybe she can look through there? She pressed her face on the wooden door and peered through the small gap.

A faded image entered her brain, but it still felt like she was there.

Fire rose around Jane as tall as a great wall. Its flames danced across her skin. She was swatting at her body to extinguish the fire, but it was futile. She could hear herself scream and smell the burning flesh.

The memory was hard to concentrate on because all Jane could feel was herself being burned alive.

"Jane!" She heard someone say.

Dad?

A figure emerged from the fire. A worried expression plastered on his face. But it was not her father. Her back pressed harder into the corner that she noticed was a closet. She was back home. She could recognize the burning junk that was put away in there.

The man stepped closer to her. "S-stay away!" She snapped at him. The man froze.

He was a tall man, not as nearly as big as Steve. His eyes were a blaring red. "Jane, calm down. It's me! We have to get out of here!"

The man had his voice.

Why did he have my dad's voice?

Where was Mom? And Uncle Charlie—where was he?!

"I don't want to go anywhere with you!" Jane coughed from inhaling the smoke and put her T-shirt over her nose to filter the air. "You killed them. You killed them all!"

The man came closer and grabbed at her burning arms urgently, ignoring what Jane said. But she pushed him off of her with all her might. It was hard to move her arms, she noticed. The fire on her was too much for her now and she could feel that she was going to suffer greatly from this. The man stumbled back, a look of shock on his face, as he tripped over a burning baseball bat.

"Jane!" He cried out.

Then a snap was heard before they could hear something falling over. The man looked upward, fear was evident in his eyes. Then, the man disappeared; in his place was her father. She screamed as a cabinet fell on top of her.

"Dad!" She screamed.

Jane was pulled out of the memory as well as the dark consciousness of her mind. Her head snapped upward and she fell of the chair, screaming. She could still feel her flesh burning and she clutched at her arms. Her body quaked. She heard voices but they were muffled by her loud heartbeat.

Arms wrapped around her, making her freeze, tensing up. The arms tugged her backwards until her back hit something warm and firm. Jane's head cranked upward and her wide eyes fell upon Nancy who had pulled her against her chest in a comforting manner.

"Ssh, it's okay," whispered Nancy. "Calm down." Jane's trembling body soon calmed down and her heartbeat synced with hers. "Are you O.K.?"

"Yeah…" Jane lied, and everyone knew that she did. She looked away from Nancy and she unwrapped herself. Jane's eyes flashed to the clock. Five minutes. She was looking though memories and out in the total of five minutes. A nurse scurried into the room and rushed towards her. Jane's eyes were filled with worry as she placed her hand gently on her shoulder.

"Can you walk?" Asked the nurse. Jane nodded, and stood up. "I need you to come with me."

They both walked out of the room and Jane looked down at her arms, noticing something new that wasn't there before.

There, on her arms, were pink rashes.

Burn marks.

CHAPTER SEVENTEEN

Jane's medicine rattled as she tossed it up in the air. She was bored. There was nothing to do. She thought about visiting Suzy, but David sent her off saying that Suzy couldn't have Jane hanging around. Jane couldn't find Trish anywhere. That left Nancy.

Jane threw the small bottle, which contained two pills, up in the air one more time before pocketing it and leaving her room. It had only been a few weeks, but she memorized the floor plans of most of the floors in the hospital. But finding someone would be hard. Not only were most of the people there wearing similar garbs but everyone else was moving around doing small activities.

Jane walked toward the direction of Suzy's room. Maybe Jane could talk to her now. When she got there, David was walking out of the room. They locked eyes before he trudged off with a groan. He must really hate this job.

Jane entered the room. "Hey, Suzy," she greeted. Suzy looked up from her corner, relaxing a bit. But she did not answer back. Jane sat down in front of her. "Do something. I'm bored out of my mind."

Amusement flashed in Suzy's eyes dull eyes but it was instantly changed into curiosity and worry when a flash of that fire went through Jane's head. She guessed her expression changed.

"What's...wrong?" Suzy croaked out.

Jane shook her head. "It's really nothing." She rubbed her arms.

The feeling of being watched was back. Jane's eyes observed the room. It felt like the shadows were moving around.

A feeble hand touched Jane's arm. She did not have to look to know who it was. She took a deep breath. Suzy was going to make her spill.

"Well, during the confession...they made me try to remember my past and I think I did...but it was way too surreal. There was fire everywhere, my dad...Oh, Suzy, I don't know what to think. It can't be true."

"Go find...out."

Jane nodded. "You're right. I'll go check out my files. See you later?"

Suzy gave Jane a tight smile and nodded. Jane stood up from the ground and left the room, walking to the front desk stealthily.

"Gloria?" Jane asked once she was there.

The front desk was vacant. With a shrug, she walked behind the desk and to the file counter where she thumbed through the files until she found one labeled her name. She pulled it out, looking around once more, and opened it. The paper clipped to the first page was her school picture. She scanned through the page.

Jane Travers
Birthday: March 14, 1996
Occupation: Hairdresser at Beauty Today
Disorder: Schizophrenia
Siblings: None
Mother: Michelle Travers (deceased)
Father: John Travers (deceased)

Jane froze at the information. Both of her parents were dead? But…didn't Steve say otherwise? Was he lying?

Her knuckles started to turn white as they tightened around the file. How did they die? Jane's mind shouted warnings at her to not go any further, but I just had too. She flipped to the next page where a newspaper article was cut out.

John and Michelle Travers were killed in a double homicide in their own home on early Thursday night. Michelle's brother Charlie Huntington, who notified the local police, found their bodies on the floor of their kitchen. Huntington himself was found dead in an alley later that night. Forensic reports concluded the bullets found in the victim matched those of the same caliber from the Travers family murder. Their daughter Jane, who had been diagnosed with schizophrenia at age seventeen, had several times neglected to take her medication and has been displaying erratic behavior and delusions of grandeur. Furthermore, she has no grasp with reality and has developed several alternative personalities. One of which, is a superhero identity known as the Avenging Star; and the other is a super-villain aptly named the Shadowy Man. After a thorough investigation, Jane has been diagnosed with Dissociative Identity Disorder. She is harmful to herself and others. The board highly recommends that Jane should be admitted in a mental health facility to immediately begin treatment.

Memories flashed in Jane's head from that day. She was in her parents' house skulking around the hallway. She heard voices in the kitchen. She easily recognized the voices belonged to her mother and father, and they were arguing. They were arguing about her. They were saying how they needed to get her help and she's becoming more unpredictable.

I killed them?

I killed Mom, Dad, and Uncle Charlie?

Tears were falling down her cheeks. All of them were killed on the same day.

"Jane?"

She looked past her shoulders and saw Steve, a bothered look on her face. This expression angered Jane to no end. Why would *he* be feeling sorry for her?

"You lied to me!" Jane snapped, turning around and marching up to the larger man. Steve looked at the file in her pallid hands and he came into realization.

"Listen—"

"No! I'm done listening to you! You told me that they were okay! You told me I was here because of a fight! Was everything you've told me a lie?"

When Jane looked in Steve's collected eyes, she saw a mixture of both that man from the fire and him. She threw the file at his face and threw a swift punch. Steve looked surprise, cradling his soon-to-be-bruised face. But the phase did not last long. Steve quickly pressed a button on the desk and in seconds, Jane was pinned to the floor by councilors.

Jane can just hear that man's cackles as she was brought back up to her feet and forced down the hallway. She squirmed and struggled against the hold, but she could only do so much.

"Let me go!" She growled.

Patients pushed out of the way, some joining to watch her departure. Her teary eyes scanned the crowd.

He was everywhere. Why couldn't anyone see him? Her eyes caught a hold of Nancy's eyes. Her eyes were wide. Jane gave her a pleading look for help. She caught on. In front of Jane's eyes, Nancy's face changed completely. Her shocked look turned into a scowl.

Ellie.

The persona marched to the captors, glaring them down. They froze in place, eyes wide in fear. They've all seen "Ellie." She lashed out, punching one straight in the jaw and elbowing another. The grip on Jane loosened and she broke free, stumbling to the cold ground. Before Jane, Ellie kicked ass. It seemed like no one was a match for her. Then a girl pushed through everyone. One of the nurses held a needle. Ellie's attention turned to Ellie, diverting her attention from the councilors who jumped her, pinning her down. Ellie spat out curses that me Jane cringe. Around them, patients were cheering, wanting more action. But it looked to be over soon, and the nurse brought the needle closer to Ellie's neck.

The shrilling squeak of a door stopped everyone. The point of the syringe was only a few centimeters away from soft skin. Jane turned around, following the sound. The door to Suzy's room opened. At first, Jane thought it was David. But the figure that peeked out was not quite tall as her.

"Suzy," Jane breathed out.

Her eyes locked onto Jane's and she could tell that Suzy was scared. What was she doing outside? Suzy slowly stepped out of her room. Others were shocked at her appearance. In full lighting, Suzy looked quite dead. She looked like she was going to be sick. Her legs shook from lack of use, eyes roaming to each face of the patients and councilors.

Suzy tried to find the words, but none would form. Her form shook as everyone stared intently at Jane. Pity took ahold of her actions and Jane rushed over to her and placed a hand on her quivering shoulder. Suzy flinched at Jane's touch, eyes snapping towards her. After realizing who was touching her, she realized a bit. Jane would have given her a smile if it weren't for the situation that they were in.

"Suzy?" David stepped out from the crowd. He was not expecting this. "What are you doing out here?" Suzy ducked her head in shame.

Her mouth opened again and she struggled once more.

After more people recovered from the shock, Ellie pulled out of reach and crossed her arms.

"Never put your hands on me again," Ellie growled.

"If you come with us, there would be no problem," one of the councilors said. He pointed at Jane. "You too, Jane."

Jane looked at Suzy and gave her a look that said, "We'll talk later." She nodded and inched toward her room, closing the door like she had never left in the first place. Jane looked back at Ellie who didn't look pleased about the situation Jane had put her in. They both reluctantly followed the councilors deeper in the hospital. The further they went, the lonelier Jane got. The vacant hallways made their footsteps echo.

They stopped in front of a door, which they opened, and nudged her inside. She walked in, expecting the others to come in also, but they stayed outside the room. One of them turned on the lights and she gasped.

Were they going to keep her in this room? The walls of the room were cushioned and her feet sunk into the floor. How long were they going to keep her in here?

"We're going to keep you in there until you calm down, alright?"

"What? I am calm. You can't keep me in here!" Jane started to panic.

"Relax. We'll probably let you out in about ten minutes."

Without further question, they closed the door and Jane could hear it lock from the other side. With a shaky breath she went to the corner of the room and sat down. She shouldn't be in here. It was Steve's fault. This wouldn't have happened if he kept this from her. But what would she have done if she knew back then?

More tears have found their way to her eyes. What would she do after her release from this place? She had nowhere to go. Would she spend the rest of her life in here?

The lights flickered out which snapped her attention away from her knees. The room was flooded by darkness. The only light was from the doors. She stood up, walking over to it.

"Hello?" Jane called out. "The lights went out." But no one answered on the other side.

A hand touched her shoulder and she whipped around, heart beating quickly. "Who's there?" She asked.

No answer.

Jane could feel eyes glaring at her. Someone was in here. But that doesn't make sense. She would have for sure known they entered. She shook her head. The person was just her imagination. It had to be. Jane closed her eyes tightly, ignoring the tug at her clothing and the heavy beatings of her heart. When she opened them again, the lights were on like nothing happened.

The door opened and the councilor that put her in smiled, and motioned her out. Jane was glad to leave. What felt like an hour was only seven minutes.

Jane made a beeline to Suzy's room. After that short time, all she could think about was her. Not only could Jane talk to her about what happened without judgment, but they could talk about why Suzy left her room. Opening the door to her room, Jane stepped in, instantly finding Suzy back in her corner.

"Hey, Suzy," Jane greeted. She looked up and relief passed her eyes. She sat down in front of her.

"Hey…" Suzy answered quietly.

"So how are you feeling? I mean, you left your room!"

Suzy's ears started to turn red at Jane's comment but she shook her head. Her body was tense and Jane knew she did not want to talk about it.

"What happened to you?" She decided on asking.

Jane opened her mouth to answer. She had to talk to someone about. But could she? She had to tell Suzy, or she will break down.

Tears welded up in her eyes and she took a shaky breath. "I…I…I couldn't do it. I can't bring myself to talk about it. I was stupid to think that I was ready to talk right after I found out."

"It's okay…you can talk to me…"

"It's just that…I found out that they're…dead."

"Oh…"

"And," Jane's tears started to fall from her eyes. "I…I think I killed them."

"What?" Suzy stammered.

"I don't know. I'm starting to remember and I read my files. But I don't know why I did it. I saw something…a man…and he's following me. I saw him in each of my memories."

Jane couldn't stop her tears now. She probably looked frail. Feeble. But she couldn't stop. She killed her parents and she couldn't even stop herself. She was at fault.

"Jane, it's okay. If you couldn't help it, it's not your fault."

"But it is, Suzy!"

"No...it has to be another's fault."

"What do you mean?" Jane wiped away the stray tears.

"Someone from your past probably caused you—"

The door opened and David popped in. "Hey, Suzy." Suzy shut her mouth, cutting her sentence short. David sighed and leaned against the door. "Still can't talk to me, huh?"

Suzy averted her attention back to the floor. Jane stood up, knowing that their conversation had ended for today.

"Bye," Jane said and started to leave, turning her attention down so that David couldn't see her eyes. He was the last person that she wanted to see in this condition. Jane didn't want to deal with him right now.

"Hey, are you crying?" He asked.

Jane pretended not to hear him and left the room.

The next few days passed slowly. Everything was just the same. Jane didn't feel like she was getting better. She felt like a trapped prisoner but with more privileges. It was hard to watch the sunset from her room and she had to go with a councilor to be able to go outside. When Jane was indoors, the only thing that she enjoyed was talking with Nancy or Suzy or reading the comics Steve would bring her.

Nothing changed...until one day.

"What? You want to leave your room?"

CHAPTER EIGHTEEN

Suzy hesitantly stepped out of the comfort of her lonely room. She stayed closely behind Jane. She could feel her breath against her skin. Suzy trembled as she took another step out. Others that passed looked at Jane strangely, while none of them recognized the heavyset woman.

"It's alright, I'm here," Jane informed, giving Suzy an encouraging smile.

Suzy didn't return one back, but she knew she heard her from the slight relaxation in her body. Jane led her out from the dim hallway and out in the open. Suzy squinted her eyes from the change of light.

"Suzy?" Trish came out of the cafeteria doors. Suzy hid behind Jane, looking more afraid. Trish turned to Jane for answers.

"Suzy wanted to come out, can you believe it?" Jane said.

"*She* wanted to leave?" Trish was shocked, not really knowing what to do.

"Yeah."

Trish smiled big, running away without a warning. "Wait there. Let me get David!" She called back.

"You alright, Suzy?" Jane asked, as Suzy stepped away from her. She nodded, not uttering a word. "Do you want to go back?" Suzy shook her head.

The two waited in the open for Trish to return. People that passed didn't give Suzy a second look as they minded their own business. It was minutes later when Trish practically pranced back with David at hold.

"I'm telling you that he's out!" Trish yelled, voice echoing off the walls.

"That's impossible. Why would Suzy leave her room?" David snapped back. Once they got the two, David's mouth dropped. "Holy crap…"

Suzy looked away.

"You…left your room, but you can't talk to me still?" He continued. Suzy scooted closer to Jane. "Not even a nod?"

No reply.

Jane almost wanted to laugh at David's defeated sigh. It was funny how Suzy would talk to Jane and feel comfortable around her, especially in a short amount of time. David had been trying for years and made little to no progress.

David started to talk to Trish and Jane about Suzy and she could tell that her friend was drifting off, ignoring what they were saying. Her eyes examined everyone that past them until Jane felt her body stiffen but still shaking. Her hand grabbed a bungle of Jane's shirt and her conversation.

"Suzy?" Jane asked, but got no response. She kept looking at a fixed spot. Jane followed her eyes to another patient. The young man had a cocky attitude. He brought his hands to his hair. Jane could see her skin was paler in spots on her fingers. It looked like his hands tanned around rings and he had to recently take them off. He was standing in front of the councilor, Mike. "Suzy, what's wrong?" But Suzy didn't seem to hear Jane. She turned to David, questionably.

David looked at the young man. "That's Mike Dawson. He actually came here a bit before you did. I never really learned much about him besides the fact that his family is rich. They even bought him his own room. He's spoiled."

Jane looked back at Suzy worriedly. What was up with her? Why was she acting that way? Does she know Mike?

Suzy's skin was white. Mike seemed to sense the look and turned to look at Suzy. Recognition flashed in her eyes and Mike smirked. The next thing Jane knew was Suzy breathing hard, body wavering, eyes dilating, and she fell over unconscious.

"Suzy?" Jane yelled. David pushed by Jane to the unconscious woman, scooping her up, and cursing under her breath.

David then ran through the hallways to the clinic. Jane didn't follow. She turned her attention back to Mike who was staring at Jane. Shivers went down her spine and she felt fear. Something about him unnerved her. He looked dangerous, like he could lash out at her at any moment.

Jane didn't like him.

"Come on, Jane. Let's check on Suzy." Trish snapped Jane out of thought and she nodded.

They jogged to the clinic. Inside, Suzy was lying on a white bed. The nurse was looking over her.

"She's fine," the nurse assured them. "She just passed out from stress. She just needs sleep and she'll be okay in no time."

Minutes later both Trish and David left the clinic but Jane stayed just in case Suzy woke up. She gaze down at her face. Suzy looked peaceful in her sleep. Almost like a different person than the scared shell that Jane normally encountered. Her face looked young, trouble-free. Jane wished she could be like that. But she had other things on her mind. David had once told Jane that Suzy's case was unsolved because she never talked about it, let alone to people. By the way she acted it would seem like Mike had something to do with it. Was he the reason why Suzy was stuck here? The reason why she's like the way she was?

Jane bit her lips. Should she try to figure everything out? Would Suzy like this? Would this help her? Should Jane stick her nose in that business? Should she leave everything alone?

A figure stood in the corner of the room. He chuckled. Jane whipped around to face him. When did he get there? Besides the nurses and Suzy, Jane should be the only one in the clinic.

"Mike?" Jane gulped. He glared at her, eyes sharp and hard.

No, he couldn't be there. It's just my imagination.

Mike took a step forward.

My imagination.

Another step.

My imagination!

Another.

He's not real.

Another.

My imagination.

He stood in front of her.

But then why does she seem so real?

His hands stated to reach toward her, slowly. Jane's heartbeat was thrashing in her chest. Her back pressed until it could not be pressed any further in the chair that she sat in.

"Jane? Are you still here?" The nurse asked, walking in front of the bed. Jane blinked, Mike disappearing, breathing hard. The nurse frowned worriedly. "Are you alright? You look like you've seen a ghost."

"I'm...fine," she answered, her heart was slowing down.

"If you say so. If you need anything, don't hesitate to come here. Now, why don't you go back to your room or get dinner."

Jane nodded, standing up, taking one look at Suzy. She doesn't look like she would be waking up anytime soon.

"Okay, thank you," Jane smiled.

She left the clinic to go to the cafeteria. She hadn't eaten lunch so she was starving.

Inside the cafeteria, Jane instantly zeroed in on the gang that she hung out with. On her way over to them, she made sure to collect her food. Right when Jane sat down, words were flung at her.

"So, Suzy did leave her room?" Steve asked. "Or are these two playing a prank?"

"She exited her room," Jane confirmed, taking a bite from her apple.

"Did the doctors say what cause her to faint?" Trish asked Jane.

"No. She was doing fine until she saw this one guy, Mike."

The color drained from Trish's face. "That bastard? Where is he?"

Steve and David both stood up from their seats. "If you're planning on harming another patient, think again," Steve said.

Trish gritted her teeth. She looked around the cafeteria as if she did not see the two standing in her way. She spotted Jerry who was looking around the cafeteria and pushed past the two councilors, swiping at their attempts to stop her.

"Jerry!" She shouted. He turned to her. "Where the hell is that son of a bitch you call a patient?"

"I don't know," Jerry answered, crossing her arms.

"You don't know? Stop trying to protect him."

"I seriously don't know. I came here to look for him."

"What's going?" Steve asked.

"Mike's missing."

CHAPTER NINETEEN

Jerry walked to the front desk, while Jane was lagging behind. It wasn't her business, but what else was she supposed to do?

"Gloria?" He asked.

She spun around her chair with a smile. "Yes, Jerry?"

"Can I check Mike's files?"

Gloria frowned, shaking her head. "Mike was checked out not too long ago. The files were taken."

"What? Are you sure? Why wouldn't I be notified of this?"

"Oh, you weren't? I was sure that someone told you."

"Who came to release him?"

Gloria flipped through her notebook. "A man from the county."

Jerry was confused. "Shouldn't he have been released by a parent?"

Since the conversation was going nowhere, Jerry left. Exasperated, he dragged a hand through his hair. Jane moved out of the way when he passed her. When Jerry walked out of sight, she walked down the hallway to Suzy's room to tell her about what happened in the past few minutes. When she was near, a muffled scream caught her attention.

It came from Suzy's room. Jane rushed to her door, wiggling the doorknob. It was locked. Screams kept emitting from the room. Jane pounded on the door.

"Suzy?" Jane asked, panicked. But, of course, there was no answer. She stepped away from the door and started to run. She scanned the people she passed until she recognized a face. "Steve!"

He turned to face Jane. "What, what is it?"

"Suzy…screams…locked door…" Those were the only words that came out clearly but it was all he needed.

Steve sped to Suzy's room. Jane followed close behind. He came upon the door, shaking the knob before growling. The screams stopped but there was shuffling. Steve pounded on the door before running back and tackled it, sending the door flying open.

In the room was a tall man caring Suzy in his arms. Jane froze. It was *him*. The man that she saw in her memories was standing in the middle of the room.

"What the hell do you think you're doing?" Steve snapped.

The man smiled, walking forward like there weren't people blocking his way.

"Get the others," Steve ordered. But Jane was frozen in place. "Jane! Get the others!"

The man laughed, staring at Jane. "Long time no see, Jane. I see that you remember me. Well, at least your body still does. Your mind doesn't. Your mind is protecting you for what I did to you. Protecting you from the explicit of the death of your family. Protecting you from this place."

"What?" Jane asked, her breathing was getting faster and it felt like her body was on a wooden roller coaster.

"You've been here before. Remember?"

At those words, her head started to pound. Her vision started to become blurry, focusing in and out.

"Jane?" Steve asked, but she could barely hear him. "Jane!"

There was a laugh but she couldn't place it. A million questions ran through her head at the speed of lightning. But one phrase stood out from the others: he was going to kill her.

Then, the ground came to meet Jane and everything went black.

CHAPTER TWENTY

Screams escaped Jane's lips as she struggled against the restraints around her wrists and ankles.

"Please…stop," she whimpered, eyes irritated from the tears that dried. But another wave of pain spread through her body from her arm and another scream escaped her. His face looked down at her, a doctor's mask covering a sly smile. He held up a bloody saw. Jane squeezed her eyes shut as the blade came closer to her arm. It slid across her skin, just enough for it to bleed. Then he traced the line gain, pressing deep inside.

"Stop! Stop! Stop! Stop!" Jane screamed.

He lifted the blade from her arm, glaring, and unstrapped the binds. He picked her up from her bloody arm and she screamed, trying to weakly get away. The grip got tighter, fingers digging into the deep cut, stretching the skin wider apart. She was dragged until she reached a cooler where she threw her in. The lid was slammed closed, leaving her in eternal darkness. She could hear chains wrap around the cooler and a lock snapping.

Even though Jane knew that it was useless, she pushed her hands against the top. "Let me out!" She pleaded.

She pushed but nothing happened. Newfound tears found their way down her face. Her fingers dragged against the box, closer to her body. But they stopped when they fit right into a gap in the cooler. Her breath hitched in her throat when she felt around the area more. It felt like nails had been dragged through the spot over and over. Jane screamed, removing her hands like she had touched a hot stove.

"Let me out!"

"Let me out! Let me out!" Jane screamed, snapping her eyes open. She sat up, expecting to bang her head on the lid, but she hit air.

"Finally, you're awake."

Jane's attention snapped toward the voice but her vision was still blurry. She wasn't in the cooler anymore, much to her relief. But she was in the operating room where she was before.

No, no, no, no, no, no, no, no! She cowered and scooted backward, her back hitting something. Jane spun around, pushing herself away from what she hit.

Her back had touched cold, iron bars. Once again, she spun around. More bars. She spun around in a circle. Bars were surrounding her. She looked up.

A lid.

She was in a cage.

She was trapped. Once again, her breath started to get faster.

"Hey, calm down!"

Steve? Is that him?

"I-I can't be trapped here! I need to get out!" Jane grabbed the bars, shaking them.

"Jane, breathe! You're fine!"

"Jane..."

The soft voice jolted her from the cage and she was once again looked to the source of the voice. She closed her eyes in concentration before reopening them. Suzy was on the side of the cage, looking at her with worried eyes. Suzy was trapped in a cage next to her—Steve in the one to the left of Jane and a beaten up Mike on the other side of Suzy.

Jane's heartbeat slowed down as she took a couple of shaky breaths. "What... what happened?" She managed to ask.

"When I opened the goddamned door to Suzy's room, the man that had a hold of her looked straight at you and then you started to have this panic attack," Steve answered. "When you passed out, they injected me and then I ended up here in this cage."

The door opened and the man Steve was talking about walked in. "Jane, you're finally awake! Good! We can finish where we left off."

He lowered his mask to reveal his concealed predator's smile.

Jane froze, remembering the pain and torture she had been though.

"The Shadowy Man!" Her voice cracked.

First he frames her for a string of murders and arson, and convinced some government officials to have her locked up in a mental institution for the rest of her life. And apparently it wasn't enough for him. Judging by the bloodstained hospital scrubs he was wearing, he had something more grotesque in mind.

"What are you going to do with us?" Steve asked, glaring at the grinning madman.

"I think Jane can answer this one," the Shadowy Man said, relishing the terror he was spreading in her heart.

"He's going to experiment on us," Jane panted. The color was completely drained from her face. "He's going to torture us by cutting into us, locking us up, and burning us."

"My experiments are coming along nicely," the Shadowy Man boldly declared. "I have the perfect source of test subjects here. Since this is a mental hospital, it would be easy to say that the patient that had gone missing committed suicide. Especially when the parents and guardians don't come around and visit anymore. And if the test subject lives and escapes, no one would believe them if they tried to tell anyone. They would be sent straight back where I can continue my work."

Steve gulped. "And what work is that?"

A corner of the Shadowy Man's mouth arched up. "Why, searching for the metahuman genome, of course! The next step of human evolution! As soon as I could find some live subjects then I can sell them on the black market. You wouldn't believe how much money an Afghani warlord would pay for his own army of super soldiers."

"You're insane," said Steve, gripping the bars of his cage tightly.

"I guess I'm in the right place then," the Shadowy Man laughed.

"You'll get caught. My parents—" Mike wheezed out but was cut off.

"Your parents what, Michael? I can kill you right now and send your body to the morgue. Then put your files back in the cabinet and tell little Gloria about your coming back and suicide. Your parents wouldn't suspect a thing. Your case will never be touched.

"Now, let's start. I want to see all of your reactions to what I'm going to do to you. I've already started on Michael here."

The Shadowy Man opened Mike's cage dragging the beaten patient out and dropping him on the table, strapping him down. The Shadowy Man picked up a metal stick that's been sitting in a bucket with fire sprouting from it. He then pressed the sharp tip in Mike's shoulder and all Jane could hear were screams.

Jane's hands were clamped over her ears, and her were eyes squeezed shut. She tried to imagine herself in another place.

Home.

Yeah, that seems nice. That seems real nice.

Home.

I'm in my room, reading the new Judo Girl *comic book, wrapped up in a blanket and drinking an iced cold cherry soda.*

The warm smiles my folks use to give me before I went to work. The same kind of warm smile before being forced into the hellhole. The hellhole that maybe was where my schizophrenia completely developed. Developed like the cliques back in school; like the weak circle of freaks each with faces that were the wrong answer on a test. My face was also the smudge left behind.

The screams that passed through her fingers were just like hers when she was dragged inside the closet. Her screams made it feel like her throat was tightening. Made it feel like the noose—the only thing holding her up in this world—was about to snap her neck.

Words were growled and they really got to her. She tried to lock them out, but in reality she was only locking herself in with the insults.

Jane had no clue of how long she stayed in the dark closet with the bullies looming over her when the door opened, flooding the closet with light brighter than a flash of lightning. The kids scrambled away from her, eyes wide like they were deer caught in headlights. After getting over the phase they bolted out of the room, leaving her and the man behind.

The Shadowy Man and his bloodstained garbs was almost invisible to the eye. But she saw it. She saw the red blood on his white clothes causing black stains. Jane saw his eyes follow hers to his clothes. And Jane had never seen anything more terrifying.

Jane had to open her eyes again to block the memory from appearing in her head. Then: silence. Only a sharp inhale and a groan sounded. Jane peaked her eyes toward the medical table, regretting it.

Mike wasn't moving; wasn't breathing.

He was dead.

Mike's body was lifted up and thrown in a fire pit. All Jane could do was watch in horror as the fire consumed his body. The room filled up with the smell of burning flesh.

The Shadowy Man drew a breath. "How disappointing." When he turned to face his other captives, he perked up. "Who wants to go next?"

Survival of the fittest... Jane thought that. She felt guilty. Why did she think that? Was she really that afraid that she would make sure that she would push them toward animal? *What was I thinking? It's not like it would change anything if they were placed on the table before me. We will all end up dead in the end. He won't be caught. Our bodies will not be found or recognized. We will all be turned to ashes.*

The flames that flickered nearby smiled at Jane. They motioned her with its ghastly hands. Its calm demeanor and warm eyes gave her chills. She didn't want to grasp its hand, letting it hug her in its arms. She wanted to move farther away.

Someone...help me.

The lock to her cage jangled, the door swung open. A hand grabbed her arm and dragged her out. She struggled against the psychopath's hold, trying to rip herself free, trying to save herself. Jane squirmed in the Shadowy Man's hold, only making the grip tighter. She kicked her leg, trying to come in contact with him. Finally, she bit down on his hand, making her taste his blood. He yelped, dropping her instinctively.

"You little bitch!" The Shadowy Man cursed and went out to reach for Jane again. "I'll make you suffer!"

But she scrambled up to her feet and sprinted to the door, fiddling with the lock. She had to pen this lock to free herself from the room. Free herself from torture. She couldn't stay trapped here any longer. She swung open the door, a hand grabbing onto her clothes, but she elbowed back on what was behind her. Here was a crack and then she stepped out of the room, slamming the door behind her and Jane ran down a hallway, not knowing where she was going. An alarm blared, but she passed that off as nothing.

"Whoa! Jane?" Jane bumped into Trish. "You okay? What happened?"

"Trish," Jane stumbled with her words, hands still shaking.

"Everyone was searching for you. Where were you?"

"There you are! Where the heck were you?" David stomped over to us, glaring. But Jane couldn't think straight. She kept thinking back to Suzy and Steve, how she left them behind for her safety. She could have saved them.

"S-S-Suzy and S-Steve—"

"What about them?"

"Taken—"

"By whom?"

"Good lord, David, let the poor girl speak!" Gloria said, walking over worriedly. She placed a comforting hand on Jane's shoulder and she'll be lying if she didn't say that it didn't comfort her. She took a deep breath. Jane explained what she just went through.

"What do we do?" She whimpered.

Trish laughed at her question. "I know what we can do."

CHAPTER TWENTY-ONE

The plan was all together really simple. Nancy would go around to see if anyone would help cause uproar. Gloria and Jerry would be the witnesses. Trish would be the starter of the uproar. And Jane will go to a fire alarm to call for the firemen to check the whole building where they would find what the owner doing was doing his crimes. David's job was to make sure they don't escape the room when the firemen come. They all broke and Jane leaned against the wall to wait for her signal.

Trish started to scream and Jane could just vaguely see her on top of a table. There was a crash and another. Nancy walked over and whispered n a few patients' ears. Most of them looked at her like she was crazy when her lips moved away from their ears and ignored her. Some of them looked excited and started to act just like Trish. Everything from there started to become hectic. More and more patients noticed the uproar and jointed it. Although most just danced in place, confused in what's really going on. Councilors, physiatrists, and nurses scurried around trying to calm everyone down.

Suddenly, Nancy's face dropped. Her eyes darkened and she shoved a nurse away and marched off.

What just happened?

Nancy punched the wall, causing a huge hole. Jane wanted to go over to her; check if she was all right, but she heard the signal to push the fire alarm. Jane went over to the fire alarm, pressing down the lever. A screeching, repetitive beep struck her ears. The building flashed red. Jane turned to find Nancy but she had disappeared.

Minutes later there were sirens coming from inside and thumps of footsteps. Firemen barged in the room, telling everyone to leave. We all left the building in a cluster. The last one out in the courtyard was David. Everyone was silent as the firemen checked where the fire was. A fireman ran out to the truck, doing something that she couldn't see. The man made no movement and no announcement.

During that time, Jane made her way to Nancy who was at a distance from everyone. Her arms were crossed over her chest.

"Nancy?" Jane asked.

She did not acknowledge her.

Was it even her? Jane had never seen Nancy wear that face.

She tried again. "Ellie?"

Her eyes flickered to Jane.

"What the hell do you want, bitch?" She growled.

"What happened?"

"Get the hell out of my way."

The sirens grew louder as police cars sped into the parking lot. Armed men marched out of their cars, guns in hand and rushed inside. A few stayed behind to ask questions. They walked first to the fireman that awaited their arrival, and then went to each of the workers. They didn't bother to ask any of the patients. They probably thought that they would be delusional. The rest of the firemen came out, loading their trucks.

Several minutes passed until the ambulances unloaded and paramedics pushed two gurneys inside. When they came out again, two bloody bodies of Suzy and Steve were loaded on the stretchers. Suzy wasn't moving; her eyes were closed. Huge gashes littered her body. She disappeared in the ambulance, which sped off. Steve was awake, and he was breathing heavily. He looked at Jane with cold eyes, their eyes locked until the doors of the ambulance closed.

Seconds after the ambulance drove away, the doors to the hospital were pushed open and armed men marched out with a man in handcuffs. The Shadowy Man screamed, struggling against their holds. Everyone once again moved so they could pass. When they passed Jane, the Shadowy Man looked at her in the eye with so much hatred that her breath hitched, time freezing around her. Everything turned grey except for him and her. Behind him bodies appeared, all carrying different wounds.

A hand landed on her shoulder and time resumed. "You all right?" Trish asked. Jane nodded.

"**NO PRISON CAN HOLD ME!**" The Shadowy Man screamed at Jane. "Mark my words, Avenging Star; this won't be the last time you'll see me!"

She flinched back in fear. She didn't doubt that he could. The police pushed him along and into the back of the car. They boarded their vehicles and drove off. Her body relaxed. He was gone, finally gone. Hopefully he wasn't going to come back.

"Alright, everyone back inside. The problem will soon be resolved," someone called.

When everyone was shaded from the sun, Steve walked up to Jane. There was a grim look on his face.

"What is it?" She asked.

"It's Suzy. They don't think she's going to make it."

Steve drove Jane to the hospital after begging. He took her to Suzy's room where Jane found her lying in a bed, still unconscious. A breathing tube ran in her nostrils and she was connected to the IV. Bandages wrapped around her frail body.

"Suzy!" Jane called, running next to her body. She didn't move. "Suzy!"

"She's in a coma," the doctor said, walking in the room with a clipboard in his hands.

"Suzy!" Tears rimmed Jane's eyes.

This is my fault. I brought this on her. I could have saved her.

"Calm down, Jane," Steve ordered, sitting her down.

She didn't know her body was shaking. "I could have save her from this. I don't want her to die." Her voice squeaked. Now she was weeping.

"It's not your fault. You couldn't have stopped this from happening."

"Yes, I could have! If only I wasn't so useless! Suzy!"

"She's not going to wake up any time soon," the doctor said, but Suzy's fingers twitched. Her eyes fluttered open.

"Suzy," Jane sighed in relief. She looked at her, not speaking.

"What in the…everyone can you please exit the room for a few minutes? I need to ask her some questions."

Jane and Steve did what the doctor asked, and when they were called back the doctor looked at them sternly.

"What's wrong?" Steve asked.

"I'm sorry, but she won't be able to speak anytime soon. She won't speak at all. She's going to be mute for the rest of her life if she makes it out of the hospital alive."

"How did she become mute?"

"She was injected with this type of poison that causes the throat to swell up, blocking the voice coming through. It will also block food and liquids from entering through the mouth. We have to feed her through tubes. The swelling will also stop her from breathing soon. The swelling keeps growing. We are trying all we can to stop the swelling from growing, but I don't think she's going to make it past tonight."

Jane's eyes widened. "Can we see her?"

"I'm afraid not. No one can see her right now."

Steve grabbed her, sitting her down on one of the waiting chairs. "We'll wait then."

Hours past until the doctor came out again, grim-faced. Steve stood up straight and Jane followed behind.

"I'm sorry, but we can't save her. We're pulling the plug. You can go see her if you want."

Jane pushed past him and into the room. Suzy looked worse off than before. Her neck was puffy and pink, several spots blistering.

"Suzy…." Jane called out.

She opened her eyes. She looked so weak. Her mouth opened but no sound came out. Her lips moved in the name, "Jane." Then her eyes closed again, a shaky breath escaped her lips, and her body relaxed.

A long, continuous beep filled the room.

The doctor looked at his watch. "Time of death: 10:34 p.m."

Jane's head rested at Suzy's side. She didn't know how long she sat there, weeping until Steve pulled her up from the chair.

"Come on, we should go."

Jane nodded, walking with him to the door. Steve drove her back to the mental hospital and was immediately sent to her room. Nancy bombarded her with questions when she got inside. Jane told her what happened and she just stared blankly at her.

"Are we the sane ones, while everyone else is insane?" She asked before slumping down on her bed.

NOW

CHAPTER TWENTY-TWO

Jane awoke in a cold sweat. For a moment, she let the nightmare that was memory fade, and then sat up on her bed, feeling the starchy sheets against her back. There was a split second where she couldn't remember where she was. A sweet moment where she thought she was waking up in her own bed in her parents' house with the knowledge that she was perfectly sane.

And then she saw the perfectly pristine white ceiling above her head and her heart sank. She was no longer the woman she thought she was yesterday. Or, at least Jane thought she had been someone different.

Before being admitted into this psychiatric hospital, she thought she was the superhero the Avenging Star. She lived in a world of the impossible—a world full of people with extraordinary abilities. Before being brought here, Jane was exactly everything she ever wanted to be.

But, now?

The villain she had met inside her house must've done something to trap her in an alternate universe or something. It was the only plausible explanation. He played with her mind, and she suddenly woke up in a mental institution. The villain sent her here, she was sure of it.

This place, wherever she was, had no extraordinary people. It had no villains or heroes, at least in the super sense of the words. Here humans never evolved superpowers. Here, superheroes didn't exist.

All of the other patients treated Jane like she was the one who was crazy. She wasn't the one who had multiple personality disorder, or schizophrenia, or manic depression. She was perfectly normal save for the superpowers that had somehow disappeared.

Jane Travers didn't belong here.

Back before this weird alternate universe, Jane had gone through a lot. The evil criminal mastermind known as the Shadowy Man murdered her parents in her childhood home. Their final fight was over at the bridge where she struck the final blow, killing him once and for all...or so she thought. To her horror, the Shadowy Man was still at large, gearing up to take the entire city under his control. Jane needed to stop him. But how could she help when she's locked up in this breakdown palace?

All that was certain was Jane's need to escape.

She swung her legs onto the floor, stood, and walked into the limited confines of her room. Through the dim lit room, she could see, the newspaper clippings of the carnage and mayhem she allegedly caused—visible reminders of the Shadowy Man's diabolical plan.

For her, it had been the end of Act One of her hero's journey.

She could not say what the real beginning of that journey was. When she foiled the bank robbery?

The ordeal hadn't lasted long. Fine, maybe ten minutes at most, squad cars raced around the corner and several armed officers swarmed the place. It was her first big bust in her civilian identity.

But the worst was still ahead. The worst was the night when Jane first met the Shadowy Man. That monster defiled the sanctity of her own home and viciously murdered her parents. Her mother lying in a pool of her own blood, and her father lying sprawled next to her.

Was *that* the real beginning? Yes. Surely, something else was born the instant her parents fell, and Jane—whoever she was, whatever she might have become— was extinguished.

But there were other moments, ones that accelerated the process, and the transformation that had begun with the death of her crush Pete.

The dark memories washed back over her like black waves bashing her against shore rocks, and she felt her heart drop to her feet heavily. This dream had tortured her ever since that night, and it was mentally tearing her apart. She barely had the energy to get out of bed.

She looked over to her worktable, noticing all the scattered pens and pencils cluttering around a stack of oversized sheets of paper. The project Dr. Hammerschmidt had assigned her to show Director Pavlich. Jane had been working day and night on perfecting the autobiographical graphic novel of her short stint as a superhero and how she was incarcerated here. Jane knew she wasn't submitting it into the DC Talent Search, but she wanted to show them all that she was taking this exercise seriously.

Jane stared at the stack for a little while longer, heaving a weary sigh. She slowly got out of her bed, and then he dropped to the floor and began doing push-ups, two per second. Ever since her last encounter with the Shadowy Man she had to build herself up. She could do a hundred straight push-ups without slowing down. After she was done with her upper body, it was time for her core. Before she donned cape and cowl, she could only do two and half sit-ups and wouldn't be able to get up. If abdominal crunches were an Olympic sport, she would definitely bring home the gold.

Jane had completely sweated through the T-shirt she was wearing. She pulled it over her head and, wearing a sports bra, headed over to her dresser, passing the full-length mirror on the wall.

Then she stepped back in front of the mirror, still half-naked, and gaped.

It wasn't her body. It was her head, all right, staring back at her from the mirror, but somehow, for some reason, it was sitting perched atop someone else's torso. It wasn't the frame of a bodybuilder, not hugely over-muscled. But she was definitely ripped. There was serious muscle definition, as if she'd been working out steadily for weeks on end. Her stomach was hard and washboard flat, her gut in the muscle cutout commonly referred to as a six-pack. She wasn't around Rhonda Rousey level, but her body was impressive nonetheless.

Her gaze returned to the stack of sequential art, calling her over like a long lost love. A dry chuckle escaped from her lips.

Director Pavlich looked at the pages with such interest. Not only reading the speech bubbles, but also following the flow of action on each panel.

"You have such an eye for detail, Jane," he said, carefully going over the next page. "Have you been doing this very long?"

"I was the best artist in my class," Jane replied. "Then I quit for a while."

Pavlich put down the comic to see the sorrow in his patient's eyes. "How come?"

"A boy I liked in high school invited me to party he was throwing. I was crushing so hard on him since freshman year I was excited that he finally asked me out."

"But?"

"He only wanted me there because he needed someone to draw caricatures."

"Ouch."

"Yeah."

"Well, Jane, I think you've done some very great work here," Pavlich said, smiling. Then he shifted over into a somber demeanor. "Would you like to tell me what happened?"

"I didn't go to the party," answered Jane. "I told them I was sick. They weren't interested in me, but only what I could do."

"No, no. That's not what I meant. About you trying to escape."

Jane paused. She took a moment to gather her thoughts. "I needed answers."

Pavlich nodded along, grabbing a notepad from his bag. "Answers? About what?"

Jane clutched pillow in front of her chest, as he scribbled more notes. "How I ended up in this place. Why everyone thinks *I'm* the one who's insane. How he was able to do this to me."

"Who do you think put you in there?"

Wherever Jane was, whatever had happened to the people in her life, Pavlich was not someone she could be confiding in at the every moment, but Jane couldn't help it. Jane knew she'd seen the doctor's cold dead eyes staring back at her, but she couldn't help but to hope he was real.

"The Shadowy Man."

Pavlich frowned and crossed his arms. "You don't remember our latest sessions, do you? You've gone back to your old ways of thinking. We were making progress, you know. You didn't have to hide back inside your mind and your fantasies."

"Fantasies?" Jane asked. "Is it really that crazy that the Shadowy Man would put me in here? He's only doing this to get me out of the picture!"

Pavlich flinched. "Do you remember when you were admitted?" He asked, bringing Jane's gaze back to him.

Jane shook her head. "No. One day I woke up in here and people started to call me crazy. I'm not crazy."

"Of course not," the chief psychiatrist never missed a beat, "but you are aware you were admitted two years ago, right?"

A memory suddenly forced its way into Jane's mind of finding her parents in a pool of their own blood on the kitchen floor. Then watching helplessly as the Shadowy Man murdered her uncle in a dirty back alley. Then there was a flashflood of all of her friends' faces in a mind-numbing blur. Debra, Pete, Stacy, and Mr. Johnson. All of them were dead. The memories felt weird and metallic, like they weren't all real, but Jane could still remember it somehow.

"People died."

Pavlich nodded. "Your parents died two years ago. Do you remember that?"

"The Shadowy Man killed them," Jane replied. "I meddled in his operations and he went after my family for revenge."

Pavlich frowned. "I'm going to tell you a story, and you're going to listen. You had the best family anyone could have asked for. You had very supportive parents and loved you unconditionally. You viewed your life as very monotonous and boring, and you've believed it for so long you had a mental breakdown. You created a world you felt safe in, one where superheroes existed."

"No," Jane shook her head, but even as she did, shining memories seeped into her brain of smiling and laughing with her parents.

"You were entered into this psychiatric hospital and you latched on to the characters there."

Jane shook her head again as more faintly shiny memories came to her—days of hanging in the hospital, and looking as crazy as the other parents. "Are you saying that I made it all up?" Jane could barely whisper it. Her brain was fighting feverishly. Old memories were combining with the new ones that arrived at the surface. Worlds were meshing together.

It couldn't be true. Jane wasn't crazy. Superheroes were real.

"Yes, you did."

And Jane found herself believing the voice she could never ignore.

"I'm sorry," said a comforting voice. "What was that, Jane?"

Jane lifted her head. She resembled a pigeon in the park looking for crumbs. She was drawn to the middle-aged man sitting across from her. Notebook in one hand, a Bic pen in the other.

"Um, what?" Jane said in a daze, waking up from her daydream. She suddenly remembered where she was. "Uh…nothing, Director Pavlich."

The director smiled. It was a kind smile. It was very rare for him to share it with most of his charges. "Excellent. So how are you feeling today?"

Jane gave out a low hum. She sounded more than less enthused. She had grown tired of these sessions. But Pavlich always offered a kind ear to her. No matter how inconsequential the topic was, he was always there to help. Jane knew she had to least give him some effort into the conversation.

"Ok, I guess," Jane finally said. "I'm tired."

"Still not sleeping, eh?" Pavlich replied, jotting down a quick note. "Well, I'll talk to Dr. Hammerschmidt. Perhaps your medication needs modification."

Nurse Gaiman was sorting all the patients' medication in the rec room. Several of them lined up to the counter like school kids in a cafeteria. The nurse lowered her glasses to get a closer look on the next bottle's label.

"Jane, you're next," she said, looking at Jane standing in front of her. An anxious look spread across her face. She smiled nervously, and very tightly so it was enough to hear her teeth grind from inside her head.

"Of course, Nurse Gaiman," she smiled anxiously. She looked at the pills wantonly. "What do you have for me today?"

"Your normal doses of lithium and Zoloft," Nurse Gaiman replied, pouring the respectable doses of each pill into the palm of her hand. "The director mentioned that you've been having trouble sleeping. We've added a little sedative to help with that. We don't want you feeling off now, do we?"

Her next stop was group therapy where Dr. Hammerschmidt decided to hold in the lounge, because she thought it would be a nice change of scenery and it would also give the patients more level for comfort. Everyone went silent when Hammerscmidt entered the room. All eyes were on her when they heard her clear her throat to begin the daily session.

"Now I hope everyone did the homework assignment," she announced, scanning the small group. She noticed some shied away, indicating that they hadn't completed the task, or didn't even bother with it. "Now, I'm talking about how things that scare you can be…well, scary. However, talking about these things helps us to conquer the fear. And great rewards come with bravery."

Jane sat idly by the table, watching her cherry soda fizzle right in front of her and listened to the faint crackling of the ice cubes floating. She imagined the cubes were people who were tapped in a pit and it was filling up with water. And just like human nature, panic takes over and they climbed up on top of each other's shoulders trying to escape. But as the ice continues to melt, the more they drown into the carbonated beverage.

This assignment blows, Jane silently seethed. *I think I'll go with the fear of…*
Something derailed her train of thought.
No!
Someone.
Who is this star cutie? Jane observed the new patient. She hadn't seen him around the grounds. Must be a new arrival.

The young man stood beside Dr. Hammerschmidt in front of the group. He felt like he was transported back to the first day of school. New kid in town with zero friends, and standing there, just waiting to be judged.

He didn't like this at all.

He wanted it to be over. Out of their prying eyes and back to whatever they were doing before this little meet and greet.

"This is our newest friend, Grant," Dr. Hammerschmidt announced. "Can everyone say 'hello'?"

"Hello, Grant," everyone said in lackluster unison. Each and every one of them was flat and uninterested.

Well, all except for Jane, who had taken a special interest in him.

Grant forced a smile. "Hi," he said right back at them.

Jane felt a spark. *Is he talking to me?*

As soon as the meeting was over, everybody was dispersing back to their rooms or moving on to their next activities, Jane looked over to see the handsome new patient watching everyone going their separate ways. He turned his head and stared straight at her. She was breathless. She swiftly turned her head to the side in order to avoid him.

She couldn't help to notice Suzy. She still hadn't said a word since that frightful night, or whatever the hell Jane thought it was. Jane couldn't even trust her own memories. She was actually considering on what Director Pavlich was saying in their last session. The Shadowy Man wasn't using the hospital to experiment on patients who possibly carry the metahuman genome. And Suzy wasn't poisoned by a deadly toxin, but simply suffered a stroke rendering her in a mute catatonic state.

The poor soul was a prisoner in her own body.

"C'mon, Suzy," Jane sighed, wheeling her friend out of the cafeteria. "Let's get outta here. Even I'm not delusional enough to think he's into me."

CHAPTER TWENTY-THREE

As Director Pavlich was locking up her office before she went home for the night, he heard someone laughing. Not quite unusual considering his place of work. But it was familiar. He gingerly crept through the hallway and peered into the lounge to see Jane talking to someone.

I wonder whom Jane is talking to, he thought. *It's late…did Hammerschmidt prescribe a sedative?*

Pavlich thought about going over there and telling them both to go back to their designated rooms. Then he decided against it. Thinking perhaps this was what Jane needed, someone who shared his thoughts and interests.

Pavlich smiled, leaving the two to their own devices.

"Oh, No!" Jane barked at Grant. "You are so on crack! Dr. Ohm was the Vanquisher's greatest enemy! Not the Prismatic Knight. I bet, between you and me, we could defeat any of them."

"Alright, alright, alright," said Grant, trying to calm her down. "But I'm still saying that Doomsday would own the Hulk."

Jane gasped at that blasphemous remark. "How dare you, sir!" Then she paused. "Oh, wait. Are we talking about Norton, Ruffalo…?"

"No, no, I meant in the comics," Grant clarified.

"Bruce Banner, or Amadeus Cho, the 'Totally Awesome Hulk'?" She asked, mockingly using air quotes.

"I have no idea who that is."

"Nobody does," Jane snorted. "It didn't sell enough issues. Anyway, Hulk would destroy DD."

"Bullshit," Grant replied in a singsong tone. "If Doomsday dies he would just come back and become immune to what killed him last time. But your Hulk, if angry, could have unlimited power…" he stopped in midsentence, waiting for her brilliant answer.

"The Immortal Hulk would never stop. After Doomsday is dead, he'll keep on smashing until he gets bored and then jumps away until he finds someone else to fight. Game. Set. Match."

Grant fell back. His eyes rolled into his head as if he simply couldn't believe what he had just heard. He shook his head to clear away his confusion.

It had been so long since Jane sat and talked to a man and be able to move her arms freely.

Grant gave out a light chuckle. "So, do you have a name?"

Jane yawned in response. She covered her stretching mouth with her hand. Grant looked disappointed. He prepared to leave.

"Either I'm the most boring guy on the planet or you've got the oddest name of all time."

"No," Jane laughed. "It's just…I haven't been sleeping well," she paused, and smiled widely. "Jane," she finally said. "My name is Jane."

"Finally," Grant said, offering a small smile. "My name is—"

"Grant," Jane interrupted. She sounded very eager. "I remember. From the meeting." This made Grant smile even more. "It's a pleasure to meet you, Jane."

Jane completely lost track on how long she was incarcerated in the mental hospital. Everything about her daily life in there had become so routine. She felt she was stuck in the movie *Groundhog Day* with Dr. Venkman. Her day would begin at 6:05 a.m. Jane would lie awake in her tiny bed, underneath the salmon covers. Her neck was always sore from sleeping on one pillow. She once asked for another but she would have needed a doctor's order to have more than one. Her sleep medicine had worn off and she was once again a prisoner to her insomnia.

All there was to do now was listen to her roommate Nancy snore and mutter to herself in her sleep. Was she either speaking as Nancy or Ellie? For the life of her, Jane had no clue. It was all noise to her. There were also the sounds of the nurses talking and phones ringing at the nurses' station. Jane remembered a Seroquel-induced nightmare she had previously in the night in which she was trapped in a house that was filling with blood, drowning and gasping for air. She made a mental note to mention the dream to her doctor later on.

The staff would start the morning checks at 7:00 a.m. A tech banged on Jane's door just as she had started to drift off into a sweet sleep again and informed her that she must be up for breakfast in thirty minutes. Jane incoherently moaned something that resembled an "OK," and rolled over and closed her eyes again. She normally allowed herself ten minutes before she got up to brush her teeth and hair, make her bed, and put on a sweatshirt. Then she would drag her exhausted body out of bed and grabbed a cup of the weakest coffee she had ever ingested from the nurses' station. She would line up against the wall and prepare to be paraded down to the cafeteria, which reminded her of the one she ate in during her elementary school years. Everyone was excited for breakfast, because it was Pancake Day. This was the one day of the whole week where all the patients' spirits were high. And there was also the fact that Jane could have as much syrup as she wanted. Eggs with cheese, bacon, grits and cereal were also served.

After breakfast, Jane would go to community group where everyone had to discuss at length the rules and regulations of the hospital. Someone complained that their book was missing. Someone else cried about something Jane couldn't comprehend. Several people always cried during the meetings. Then Jane would set a daily goal (to finish reading her book and do laundry) and share why she was here. Most people are there for depression, some for anxiety, many for suicide attempts. One or two are there for insomnia, a few for manic episodes and one boy about her age was there for homicidal ideation. It wasn't as scary as it sounded. He was actually very sweet, close to Jane's age and she was already starting to become close with him. His name was Grant and he beat up one of his friends for stealing his now ex-girlfriend.

Jane met with Dr. Hammerschmidt, her amazing psychiatrist. She was a young woman who always looked perpetually concerned. She was unbelievably kind and compassionate. She ran through the usual routine of questions: "Do you feel like hurting yourself? How are you sleeping? How is your mood?" Then she took Jane off her lithium and upped her Abilify. She also prescribed Jane Ambien, which was stronger than the sleep medicine.

On her way to the rec room, Jane saw a 90-pound schizophrenic girl screaming and punching the walls because she hears voices and sees monsters that aren't there. A code team was called in and they sedated and restrained her. Incidents like this are uncommon in Jane's unit but not unheard of. They took the poor girl away, kicking and screaming.

When she finally got to the rec room, she and Grant sit side-by-side, reading a book and holding hands. His hand was rough and she couldn't help but smile. He made her feel a little less scared in an unfamiliar setting like this. A tech glared and scolded Jane for breaking the coveted "no-touching" policy.

At 11:30, she had a process group with her social workers. The day's topic was "combating negative thoughts." Jane would do an exercise where she would write a negative thought and three positive ones to counteract it. Several people cried when they read theirs and one of them usually would launch into an off-topic diatribe on the importance of exercise until the social worker, Brenda, politely cut him off. A short, older lady who claimed to have once been a backup singer for Aerosmith preached on about bipolar disorder. Jane thanked God that they could leave early and grab some pizza at the cafeteria.

Early afternoon was recreational therapy where Jane watched the movie *Indiana Jones and the Temple of Doom*. She refused to watch *Crystal Skull*. Just when Indy gets the girl, it was time for educational group. Then a short, older lady who claimed to have once been a backup singer for Aerosmith preached on about bipolar disorder and the evils of not being complaint with medication.

Visiting hours were everyday at 4:00 p.m. Jane didn't bother going down to the visitation room. Nobody came to her.

Everyone lined up for dinner at 5:00, where tonight they were serving beef stroganoff and steamed carrots. Jane hardly ate and spent dinner hour making an elaborate design out of her peas and carrots. After dinner, she sketched a picture of Grant, and he drew one of her.

It was true love!

Jane would meet for her closure group at 8:00 where they reviewed the daily goals she had set for herself. Some people met them, while others did not. She met both of hers. A lady who was in there for bipolar disorder broke down and sobbed for 20 minutes about not achieving her goal. When Jane was finally out of the sight from the techs, she and Grant watched TV. His head was in her lap, and she stroked his hair. Jane had never stopped thinking about Pete though. She just couldn't get rid of the guilt that constantly sat in the pit of her stomach. She just couldn't seem to allow herself to truly be with someone.

Nine o'clock meant it was time for night meds. It was a very popular time of evening for obvious reasons. Everyone raced to be front of the line. Jane would think they were giving out hundred dollar bills and not psychiatric medication. She dutifully took her Seroquel and Gabitril for sleep, and her Abilify for depression. Then everyone was a big happy family and for a moment, just one moment, Jane felt like a normal person who was not spending her entire life in a mental hospital for being a depressive-borderline personality-bipolar mess.

Life was good.

"Lights out!" A nurse shouted. The manic patients and insomniacs groaned in disdain.

Grant kissed Jane goodnight when a tech wasn't looking and her heart melted. She would happily drift off into a deep, medicated slumber, thinking that today was not all that bad and tomorrow probably won't be either.

The next few days came and passed in a haze of white coats and blue pills. Jane barely spoke a word, only staring blankly at the white walls of the institution. Grant was always by her side. Sometimes he would just sit there, which made it even harder for Jane to bear. In those moments, when he sat stoically feet away just to give her company, made her heart ache the most.

It was harder to distinguish reality from what was made up in Jane's mind. Everything flowed together and tangled into mismatched memories and fantasies. She could remember two situations happening two totally different ways, but both felt real. She could still remember the feeling of being able to project energy, but she could also remember the feeling of the deep dark hole filling her chest at the gruesome display of her parents' bodies.

Jane really felt crazy for the first time. Was this how it felt? To not know if your life was a dream? To not know if you had the power to rewrite your own reality? Because that was what it looked like to her. Jane couldn't handle her family's death, so she made a place where she was the victim of some super-villain conspiracy.

On her way back from her group session, Jane saw something taped on her door. *What's this?* She wondered, looking at the posted note. It was a simple 8.5 x 10 sheet of multipurpose paper folded in half. Only a single star was drawn on the front. She pulled it off the door and unfolded it.

She smiled.

"It's from Grant!" She yipped excitedly.

She proceeded to read the contents of the letter. Her eyes widened in awe.

To A.S.,
Let's team up!
—G.

"A.S.," Jane said out loud, feeling a sudden tightness in her chest. "Avenging Star! He knows who I am."

Earlier in the evening, when Sheila had walked in from her office waving that toxicology report and she seemed so annoyed by his irresponsible between…how could she have flown out of the window without saying a word to the group? And even if she had flown away yesterday there is no way she could have reached the lab and gotten back.

Or could she?

How far is it to Denver?

I asked Frankie the janitor. He stopped mopping and said, "I've already figured that out." A straight-edged lifestyle is all you need besides a box clip but it leads to a blood lust that can only be cured by cutting.

My new slippers are comfortable and covered with little smiles illuminating the door, which had a picture gallery of finger-painted images of scaly sheep that had been clipped and brazen leprechauns.

I'm not a quitter. Though my bones may break, I remain wide-eyed as the devils try to impregnate me in their love-tangles. I remember the last vestiges of self-realized unicorns take root and dance through vast untapped domiciles decorated with vases covered in pidgeons the dedication of Detective Roberts helped during the war. Dance like a muse but through Chilli Willi's chemical brilliance.

The pupil/teacher dynamic is overshadowed by parrots at play and Mr. Johnson's senseless death still unnerves me. Pearl-crowned chairs of oak covered in leather that is barely one-dimensional...I miss Stacy and Elizabeth...true friends indeed.

In the north-countries one might find systems of roof dwellers who only eat mulberry and drink with paraffin covered one-dollar bills. In a minute Sensei Komatsu taught me everything I know...I have become a master ore process without much hunger mustache ended in nomination of a mule in chair tended by a nurse.

Most of all I miss Uncle Charlie. The forces of darkness grow too strong. Pete wasn't enough. Maybe I do need a real partner.

CHAPTER TWENTY-FOUR

Jane found Grant in the rec room, watching a rerun of *Parks & Rec*. He was a huge Aubrey Plaza fan. He really liked her signature deadpan humor and she was his free pass. Jane crumpled up his note and threw it right at him. Grant rattled in the seat. Looking down on his lap to find what hit him he discovered the balled up remains of what used to be his message to his girlfriend. He lifted his head to see Jane coming at him with all her fury.

Grant waved the discard note right off him. He stood up from the couch and approached her slowly. "What the French toast?"

"Stop!" Jane yelled at him, raising her hand to him. "God! Why do you do this? Why won't this end? I need help!"

He took her by the hand and guided her to the other side of the room. She was trembling. She could feel her fingernails digging into her palms when she made a fist.

As soon they were alone, Grant looked her straight in her glistening blue eyes. "Jane, Jane. I know all about the Shadowy Man."

Jane couldn't breathe. She never told Grant about the Shadowy Man. She could feel a sense of dread overwhelming her.

"What do you know of the Shadowy Man?"

"I'm just like you, Jane," Grant replied. "I'm not really a patient. I operate under the gallant guise of Neutron. I was working on a case involving a series of crimes perpetrated by a super-criminal called the Shadowy Man. After I heard about what happened to you, I got myself admitted so I can get you out of here. I need your help, Jane. We could hunt him down together before he hurts anyone else."

Jane couldn't believe it. "Are you saying…?"

Grant nodded his head vehemently and looked around with paranoid eyes. "They think you're crazy, that *we're* crazy."

Jane could dance! Grant was in the same boat as her. They could work through it together. "So, you believe me?"

"Of course!"

"Great, we have to get out of here."

Grant widened her eyes. "No, you know we can't."

"Why not?" Jane narrowed her eyes.

"Because *they* are out there."

"Who are *they*?"

Grant crossed his arms. "You don't remember? The white jackets must've done a number on you this time. The villains are outside, the ones who put you in here. If you walk out there they will kill you."

Jane assumed the villains were minions of the Shadowy Man. Why Jane was so important to the Shadowy Man, she didn't know. Maybe all of the heroes the villain encountered were here as well.

"I am here to help," he gently assured her. "It's better than God…Grant is here to save the day! But first, we must deal with the biggest problem…Nurse Gaiman."

Jane and Grant were obviously the only ones who remembered the real world. They were the only two people who could get out and go find the Shadowy Man and stop him from overtaking the city again.

Jane had to get out of this prison she was put in. She remembered the real world, and she had to get back to, no matter how insane she looked to the others in the institution. Jane knew what was real, and that was enough.

It was time for an escape.

Nurse Gaiman was making her nightly rounds around the hospital. Peering into the patients' rooms, making sure they were all in bed and everyone was accounted for. She headed over to the activity room and noticed something scurrying across the floor.

Gaiman took out her flashlight and shined a beam around the furniture. She shot straight up when something went past her. She quickly turned around shot the beam of light right into the trespasser's face.

Gaiman stepped back and let out a short scream. Her fear was put to rest when she recognized the intruder.

"Jane?" Gaiman asked, seeing one of her charges roaming the halls after lights out. "What are you doing here? You're supposed to be in bed."

"Vile oppressor," Jane growled, lunging at the nurse. She grabbed her as a struggle ensured. "You'll never contain the unrelenting forces of justice in this pea-green prison!" Jane grabbed her by the head and was ready to send her plummeting to the tiled floor. "Just as I thought…Nurse Gaiman is really the villainous Shockwave in disguise!"

"Jane—please!" Gaiman pleaded. "Stop this right now!"

"You'll not trick me with your sonic strategies!" Jane declared, smashing the poor nurse's face onto the floor. The lenses of her wire frame glasses cracked and bounced a couple of times. Followed by Jane throwing the various amount of anti-depressants and antipsychotics. "I've not taken any of your mind-control drugs!"

Grant looked over Jane's handy work. He was performing a slow clap.

"Good work, partner," he said approvingly. "That'll show'em what happens when you try to stop the greatest hero team of all time!"

Jane stared at him dumbfounded. She couldn't really believe her ears. Was he seriously praising her? "Team?"

Grant smiled in assurance. "Sure, look how well we did just now against one of the greatest super-villains! There's no stopping us!"

"Yeah," Jane said, seeing how well this new partnership would be promising. "I-I guess we did do pretty good."

"Exactly," he said, handing her a white coat. "However, we've no time to gloat. Now put this on. We gotta get out of here before they turn on the—"

The alarm rung out, which caused pandemonium amongst the inmates. Jane struggled to get the coat on as Grant coaxed her into running.

"We've got to get out of here before the masters running this gulag cleverly disguised as a hospital catch wind!" Grant warned her as they both made a break for it. "Run, Avenging Star! Run!"

"We have an escape in progress," The P.A. system echoed throughout the entire hospital. "Repeat, escape in progress. One staff member injured. Be on the lookout for patient Jane Travers."

Jane and Grant ran out of the hospital at top speed. The security guards would be there any second to apprehend them. Jane had never been out of the hospital's grounds before and she discovered the hospital was right next to a bridge that was over a river.

"So we steal a car and get the hell outta Dodge?" She asked Grant.

Before he could answer, several sirens filled the air, along with red and blue lights piercing through the darkness in front of them.

"We are so screwed," Jane said, hearing not only the police sirens but also the guards storming the halls inside the hospital. Before Jane could advance any further, Grant stopped her. She looked at him in confusion. "What's the plan now, hero?"

Grant looked worried. "Um…have you ever seen that old movie *Butch Cassidy and the Sundance Kid*?"

"Yeah. My dad watched it all the time. It was his favorite movie." She looked over to see the cops getting out of their squad cars, about to draw their weapons on the two. Jane quickly looked back to Grant, looking at him second-guessing that he truly belonged in an insane asylum. "Are you saying that we should take them all on like they did against the entire Bolivian army? Well, let me refresh your memory, Grant; they died at the end!"

"No, it was a freeze frame!" Grant shouted. "They get to live forever. And that wasn't the scene I was referring to."

"Then which was it?"

"You're not going to like it."

Jane's eyes were bigger than Felix the Cat's. "Oh, no. You don't mean…"

Grant took her hand and they jumped off the bridge together, freefalling into the water below them.

"Only one way out of here and that's to jump!" Grant yelled, jumping off the bridge, taking Jane with him.

"OOOOH SHIIIIIT!" Jane exclaimed, feeling the ground disappear right from under her.

CHAPTER TWENTY-FIVE

"All units, all units!" Announced the man at dispatch. His voice was frantic and shaky. He had been working for the mental hospital for several years and had seen everything. But this time he was really shaken. "Please be advised that the patients are to be considered highly dangerous. Approach *with* caution."

The hospital's security team scoured throughout the woods. The search dogs were trying to pick up the scent of the two escapees. One of them caught a whiff of something and began to bark very loudly.

"Whoa, there!" Cried the dog's handler, trying to get a hold of his K-9 partner. "Easy, girl, easy. Do you smell something?" The dog began to bark more alertly. The handler turned to the rest of his team. "I think I've got something here!"

They followed the dogs to the end of the waterfall. The guards looked below and shook their heads.

"Right over the falls," said the handler. "There's no way they could have survived that!"

When they jumped off the bridge they hit the water with such violent force that they were both instantly knocked out. They sank, unconscious, many feet down below the surface.

They floated amid the river. Jane was the first to stir. She came to, flailing her arms, fighting for air, dozed and confused.

She paddled over to Grant and shook him back into awareness. The underwater universe was so peaceful and soothing. Their own world seemed so very far way as they began to swim toward the light. Fighting temptation to surrender to the water, they rose up and up and up.

They broke the surface, spewing water and seaweed. Emerging from the water, soaking wet, Grant and Jane gasped greedily for air. A smiled stretched across Grant's face. It went ear-to-ear and raised his fists in triumph.

"That was freaking awesome!" He exclaimed, as Jane swiftly covered his mouth with her gloved hand. They didn't want to draw any unwanted attention.

"We're soggy and home free," she observed. "Swell plan, chum," she added, with an obvious trace of sarcasm.

They staggered back to dry land. It was hard to move around in waterlogged clothes. It felt like they were carrying another person on their shoulders.

Okay, so escaping from the institution was much easier than Jane thought it would be. Like, even with the two guards it was too easy. Both were easily fooled by the distraction Grant had initiated in the main room. The guards readily abandoned their posts to go see the disturbance, leaving Jane and Grant to walk right out of the front doors.

"I wish we had some dry clothing," Grant complained.

The only problem now was getting a change of clothes. Blue sweatpants and a blue sweatshirt with white slippers was going to get them weird looks, especially if anyone nearby knew they were the uniforms of mental patients.

Over the horizon, Jane smiled. "Ask and you shall receive," she said, pointing to the distance. Grant followed her gaze to see an isolated house. "Let's see if we can borrow some clothes from the owners of that place."

Grant grimaced with fright. "Nuh-uh. This is how some scary movies start."

Jane scoffed. "Get real." Then she winced in pain, holding her head.

This startled Grant. "Hey! Are you all right?"

"I…I don't know," Jane moaned, shaking her head wearily. The pain was intense. So intense that her eyes felt as if they were trying to explode out of her head. She held her temples between thumb and forefinger and gently massaged them to ease her pain. It wouldn't go away. Grant moved over and stood beside her as Jane pressed her eyes, trying to will the pain away. "I think I'm getting a migraine. Too much adventure, I suppose."

Grant unzipped his bag and took out several containers. "Dr. Feelgood is here, baby," he said, sorting out several pills and tablets. A plethora of drugs lay right in front of her. They all looked like they would remedy every problem. "I got the cure right here."

Jane seemed suspicious of the medicine she was being offered. After what happened with Nurse—Shockwave, how can she be sure about *these* special helpers?

"Are you sure I should take these?"

"Trust me, gorgeous," assured Grant, sprinkling some of the pills in the palm of his hand. "I'm gonna take good care of you."

The old farmhouse was a shadow of its former self. How long the shivering walls could withstand the beckoning call of gravity, the two didn't know. But this abandoned house was their only hope of evading capture before dawn. The two-story home was empty, abandoned long ago. Thoughts of a violent haunting kept potential homeowners, children and trespassers at bay plagued Grant's head.

The door creaked open, moving one centimeter at a time. It could move faster, but the wood of the door had grown moldy and soft with water and neglect, and if they pushed it harder, they'd probably pushed right through the door.

Heart racing, adrenaline pumping through their limbs, fingers tingling with the emotion, they stepped through the open door, stopping just inside the entrance; the room darker than they thought it should be. Eyes adjusting to the darker interior, they walked within an empty foyer.

The silence became thick, heavy…uncomfortable. A chill traveled through Grant's spine, a painful tremor running the length of his body. Something felt off…wrong. Instinct told him to run.

Once inside, a thick coating of dust and mold coats everything. They had to step attentively, as there were already several dark holes where floorboards had snapped, work from mold and pressured downwards by the weight of the gigantic dust bunnies that have formed. Cobwebs brushed their faces as they stepped deeper into the house. A shiver rushed sown their spines. They couldn't tell what, but there was something unbelievably spooky about this place.

Dust lay over every surface like dirty snow, pristine dust layer, not a footprint anywhere, dust bunnies the size of bowling balls tumbled across the floor boards toward unseen skittles, free papers piled up to the letter box and cascaded all the way to the foot of the rough wooden stairs, old tea cups lay on a coffee table thickly encrusted with dried up mold, dust collected mirrors, smell of mildew, stale air, air thick with dust, shafts of light bursting through gaps in the boarded up window, light streaming through gaps in the heavy velvet curtains, absolute silence, not even the hum of a refrigerator, the house's only occupants weaved their webs between the spindles of the star banisters and from the ceiling to the wall, old cobwebs billowed in the draft.

Echoing footsteps invaded the silence that hung like a cloak around the house. A thick carpet of dust clung to every object, the rays of light shining through the shattered glass windows catching the particles suspended in the musty air. Jane and Grant moved deliberately, dust billowing into clouds as he passed. They continued to move through the house, kicking up more dust until it was difficult to see through the billows of particles that now swirled in the air. Then he came to a door, faded green, paint curling with age, brass handle almost consumed by a thick network of cobwebs, reaching out, he turned it.

Disappearing isn't easy. For Jane and Grant, however, it wouldn't be a problem since they didn't have cell phones. They didn't realize how much of their lives had spent looking at stuff on your phone until the people from the mental hospital took them away from them. Since GPS entries, browser listing, and phone records can leave digital traces of everyone everywhere. With access to their cyber footprint, someone could basically track their movements by the minute. So far they got step one right.

"You think anyone lives here?" Jane wondered.

"Way out here in the middle of nature? Hells no." Grant replied.

"Gosh, you're probably right, Grant. This could be our secret headquarters!" She could see it now. There would be a crime lab, mannequins where they would keep their uniforms, and a computer bank filled with the most cutting edge equipment that would give Felicity Smoak one helluva nerd-gasm. Jane envisioned an array of dozens of tiny monitors with random patterns appearing on them as they would swirl and dissolve and gradually reform themselves into several maps that spanned around the globe.

"Yeah," said Grant, looking around the house. "Why don't you worry about finding some dry clothes before saving the world. I'll look upstairs."

"OK," Jane agreed. "I got the ground floor."

Grant paused at the bottom of a staircase, a length of windy steps disappearing into a blanket of darkness above him. A nagging feeling, a whispered warning; both ignored. Heart pounding, Grant placed his right foot on the first step.

Jane watched Grant go up the stairs. The stairs were slapped against the clipboard wallpaper as if they were an afterthought. They fell too close to the entrance and were uncommonly narrow. The rail was simply a plank of wood supported by three main spindles. It looked for the entire world that it would came crashing down with even the weight of a child, yet it must have been there thirty years or more. It was hard to tell the original color of the carpet, likely it was once beige but now it was closer to a muddy state. Grant took a deep breath before placing even some of his weight on the lowest step and kept his hands clear away from the rail. The squeak did not surprise him but it was immediate and loud, if there was anyone upstairs they now knew he was there. After freezing to listen for a few moments he began to ascend against the advice of his anxiety.

Jane was alone in the parlor and began to search for anything they could use.

Then she heard something lurking around.

"Hello?" She called out. "Anyone here?"

From the shadows there appeared an outline. It was very familiar. Jane could feel her heart stopped. The dark figure wore a fedora and struck a pose as if he were headlining a Fosse musical.

"Who's there?"

"The only person you'll find here, Avenging Star, is me," said the figure. He raised his head to reveal that he was wearing a skull mask.

"Omega One!" She gasped.

"Yes," the super-villain confirmed. "In the flesh. Metaphorically speaking. How nice of you to stop by. How on Earth did you find my secret sanctuary? No matter. Let me attend to the most important concern, which is the imminent demise of the Avenging Star. The one thing some of the greatest criminal minds have failed at in time and time again.

Jane gripped a candlestick and launched a fallout assault on Omega One. The brass stick made contact with the villain's temple that sent him crashing to the floor. His blood-drenched hat came flying off.

"Shut your noise!" Jane shouted, delivering another swing to Omega One's back. After that she never let up. "When are you dastardly villains going to learn?!"

"I'll..."

CLANG

"Never..."

CLANG

"Stop..."

CLANG

"Fighting!"

CLANG

She threw the candlestick aside and panted for air. She looked over her enemy's battered body. *If he's here, then there must be more super-villains nearby.*

"What was he doing in this farmhouse?" Then something took her by surprise. She wasn't going to let her guard down this time.

But she stopped when she saw Grant on the defensive.

"Whoa!" He said, dropping the dry clothes he had just found. "Whoa. Breathe, baby, breathe. It's me, Grant." Then he looked down to see the body on the floor. "Holy shit!" He exclaimed. "Who is that?"

"Omega One," she plainly replied, lowering the candlestick. "A member of my criminal collective."

Grant felt he was going to throw up. "Weird. Looks a lot more than Farmer John."

Jane looked back at her enemy to discover the macabre garb that Omega One wore had vanished. And in his place was a totally different person. She remembered that night on the bridge where she thought she had killed the Shadowy Man, but it turned out to be Mr. Johnson.

Was it possible that Omega One learned this trick from the Shadowy Man?

"Don't be fooled, partner," she said to Grant. "He has many tricks. Looks like the Shadowy Man taught him well."

"Okaaaay..." He said, picking up the clothes from the floor. "I found us some new threads."

"Puerile and close...good morning Salubrious!

"For the month or ascribe; Avenging Star trapped that it worked with a music group called Jovial like his lyrical and singing author. The band resonates great...but I resemble Ersatz. Solace of some friend to translate the insouciant indicated here in winsome for the band. My prouder parvenu it has one of the shortest canard!

"My objective is to make indicate gainsay; in a nefarious hospital obtained fulsome more to disappear.

"Granted stay indicated by tarry that ratiocination on cosmopolitan to the ground—which they imply with lachrymose idea—in semimonthly seasoned made go propound explanatory magnesium handfuls of psychiatrist to tchotchke, submerge thus that is undo the zipper, far too constitutional to announce they close descend in frisson found her soul mate in Grant, or portend close; elasticity, its innumerable margarine of fever like supercilious of point work to tremulous, announced the delivery at issue clinical in no cajole clan announces the saline cartography of pabulum. He is undesirable moderate by subjection, potentate no plateau meant to the cover extended of contretemps collection etiolate my induction quagmire of professionalism.

"Their intention on the generosity to privation latitudes he weight since maunder one of the superfluous is direct dinosaur. No falsification like daring nighttime escape in the furbelow. An outline to defrost apogee metropolis in the displacement are the exigent. But they make the reticent ejaculation like ventured fundamental seriatim?

"The combat for their sinecure and the investigation or go neophyte to weather. Rectos distinguished in commodore of voluptuary of meeting! Osculation of the dull republic only made fun of to describe for the compunction as much took a desperate existence sub rosa and ruthless worlds. The mother of ingénue provincial spoons..."

"What was that, schmoops?" Asked Grant, trying to understand what the hell Jane had just said.

"Oh, I was just thinking that we're not safe here," she answered. "If Omega One can find us here—plus—there are a lot of other villains wrecking havoc out there! And we're all that stands between them and global domination! You and me, Grant. That's all that stands between them, and the darkness."

After spending the night in that spooky old house, it was time for them to begin their search for the Shadowy Man. Since Omega One was hiding out around here, he might have had a vehicle lying around for the two heroes to "borrow." Jane and Grant went into the garage and found a brown 1962 Ford step side pickup. Omega One really knew how to keep a low profile.

Jane quickly inspected the classic truck. She nodded in approval. "I think this will be perfect!"

"Yes!" Grant shouted in victory. "Road trip! I'll drive first." He quickly climbed into the driver's seat.

Jane smiled. "I guess I'm riding 'Chewie.'" As soon as she shut her door, something invaded her nostrils. It was a very unpleasant order. "The new Starry-Wagon—patented trademark—smells kinda funky."

"Awww…she's got a lot of charm," said Grant, turning the engine over. "So, where are we headed anyway?"

Where to go first? She had to find a way to get back to her old life, or make the world remember their heroes. Jane had no way of knowing which was the reality she was stuck in. Was the population brainwashed or was Jane stuck in an alternate universe?

"West," Jane sharply replied. "All the villains head to the West Coast! Come of my greatest enemies go to ground there. Unlawful Enemy Combatant…The Hammer…and the Inimitable Immolator."

Grant grinned. "And what about the Premature Ejaculator?"

"He's his own worst enemy," Jane groaned. "And the worst one of all… Severance Package. Those are just the ones on Earth. I'll have to tell you about my adventures in the Crab Nebulae one day."

Grant smiled. "That's what I dig about you, Jane. Your head's always in the stars."

She froze, letting what Grant just said sink in. "You…you, uh, dig me? Really?"

"You better believe it, baby doll. You're a star cutie. Hell, everyone wants you!"

The door opened, FBI Agent Panos paused in the doorway, fingers still gripping the handle. Taking a deep breath, a moment, Panos waited, gaze resting on the corpse of the house's owner. Panos was grateful to be indoors, not in the mood for another cold night; there had been too many over the last month.

"What do we know, Officer Kuppersmith?" Asked FBI agent Panos.

"We found two sets of hospital gowns upstairs," answered the uniformed cop, going over the crime scene.

"They belong to our AWOL patients?"

"We believe so. The murder weapons got fresh prints on them. Forensics matches the height of the female escapee. A one Jane Travers."

"Hmmm…" Panos hummed. "Jane Travers did it in the living room with the candlestick," he concluded, while putting on his sunglasses and playing the opening note to The Who's "Won't Get Fooled Again" from his phone, as he struck a pose.

The other officers and crime scene analysts all looked at him in confusion.

"What…what are you doing?" Asked Kuppersmith.

Panos lowered his shadows. A sense of awkwardness fell upon him. "I'm doing the thing that guy does in the beginning in one of those C.S.I. shows. You know, the guy who poses a lot?"

"Is that show still even relevant?" Asked one of the other officers.

"Those shows aren't really accurate," said another. "You can't get DNA results in an hour. It takes weeks. *Weeks.*"

"You know what?" Panos bellowed. "Never mind, never mind."

"Agent Panos," Kuppersmith said urgently, holding his cell phone in front of him. "I ran the vic's name through the database and he's the owner of a '62 Ford pickup, that is missing from the garage. I have the plate number right here, sir!"

Panos smiled. "Good. Damn good. Kuppersmith, put out an APB out on that truck. As of right now, our two fugitives are top priority!"

CHAPTER TWENTY-SIX

"Is he still back there?" Jane asked, concentrating on the road ahead of them.

"Yeah…step on it!" Grant exclaimed quickly while looking back at the flashing lights gaining on them, trying not to sound as desperately nervous as he felt.

"Dammit…" Jane muttered angrily, flooring the accelerator, pushing the limits of the ancient truck's engine as she roared down the dark highway. "Who'd have thunk that Barney Fife back there would be the one to tag us?"

"I was thinking more like Roscoe P. Coltrane. And we did just break out of a lunatic asylum, Jane. I'm sure every cop in the state has us on their radar."

"Thanks for the update, Grant," she shot back sarcastically, driving even faster.

Sure, getting arrested, sent to jail, being hauled out to the loony bin, and then breaking out again hadn't been hard—Jane had the Shadowy Man to thank for that. However, despite the fact that they had been cautious and took back roads instead of the interstates to avoid being detected since their great escape, it had only taken one cop actually doing his job to ruin their day and their perfect getaway. And as soon as that cop car had pulled up behind them and turned on its lights, they knew they couldn't stop—they wouldn't be so lucky to both be sent back to the same institution again—they had to make a run for it.

"We've only a few miles from the border. They won't have jurisdiction there." Jane hoped that meant they'd be in the clear once they crossed the state line.

"Doesn't mean they won't call their cop buddies over there to join in on the fun."

Jane tore her eyes from the road and chanced a looked over at Grant for the briefest of moments and saw the unease in his eyes that reflected the same churning in her gut.

They were screwed.

"Jane!" Grant suddenly shouted, pointing out the window. "Road block!"

Her head and eyes snapped back to the road her hopes of making a clean getaway dropped even further.

"Shit!" Jane panicked.

Up ahead, turn lights flashed on the top of a patrol car, blocking the road lengthwise in a last-ditch effort to stop the two fugitives before they could escape into the next state. On the right side of the highway lay on extremely deep drop-off looking to a creek bed while on the other side, the shoulder broke off into a wide ditch. Going around wasn't going to be easy, but it was their only hope.

"Hold on!" Jane floored the accelerator. The speedometer needle jumped in response, gunning past 90 MPH.

"Jane!" Grant cried out as he grasped the dashboard.

"I know what I'm doing, Grant," she snapped, her eyes narrowing.

"Really? 'Cause it looks an awful lot like you're gonna ram the guy."

"Shut up, I'm driving," Jane growled back at Grant's assessment. She could do this...probably.

As the truck barreled down the road towards the cop car, the officer jumped out of the vehicle and stood in front of it quickly drawing out his handgun and aiming it towards the truck bearing down on him.

"Jane!" Grant wailed, his knuckles whitening as he held on for dear life to the dash.

They came closer and closer almost to the point where they could both see the sweat on the nervous officer's brow and the shake of the gun in his hand.

Pop! Pop! Pop!

The barrel of the officer's gun exploded outward, sending bullets into the grill of the truck and ricocheting off in a shower of sparks. Grant ducked and covered his head while the bullets kept flying at them. Jane held steady, putting all of her concentration into steering while the officer continued to lay down fire until losing this game of chicken and jumping out of the way.

Impact with the side of the patrol car was almost a sure thing until Jane yanked the wheel hard to the left.

Time seemed to slow down even as Jane's heart continued to gallop at full speed. She braced herself for what would come next and yelled over to Grant, "Hang on!"

The truck's wheels squealed against the pavement. It drifted sideways moments before it became airborne, flying off of the shoulder of the road and over the embankment, landing front-end first into the ditch, and joining its passengers. The car bounced twice before Jane could regain control over the wheel.

The engine roared after she mashed on the accelerator again and sharply pulled the steering wheel to the right, sending huge piles of sod and dirt up into the air as the tires spun on the ground and propelled the car forward and up the side of the ditch.

The car's tires hit the edge of the shoulder, fishtailing onto the asphalt before Grant could get the car going straight again, leaving the parked cruiser behind in a cloud of dirt and gravel.

"Whoo!" Jane hollered in triumph, chancing a glance into the rearview mirror and seeing the cop behind them threw his hat onto the ground in frustration just as they crossed the border. "You see that, Grant? I totally Vin-Diesel'd the hell out of this old jalopy! They should ask me to be in *Fast 9*, or *10*, or whatever the hell they're working on now."

She turned, expecting Grant to give her "why-the-hell-did-you-just-risk-our-lives-on-such-a-stupid-stunt" kind of look. Instead, he was hunched over, still gripping the dash tightly with one hand.

"Hey, c'mon…you gotta admit that I'm pretty much the most awesomest driver in the history of ever."

Grant still didn't respond.

Jane reached over and nudged him on the shoulder.

"Hey…you O.K.?"

"I think I'm in trouble, babe," Grant rasped, lifting his head.

Through his face was mostly obscured by that it had turned to chalk white. It was then that Jane finally noticed that the hand Grant wasn't holding onto the dashboard with was held tight to his right side.

"What the—?" It was then that Jane saw red seeping between Grant's fingers. "Son of a bitch…"

CHAPTER TWENTY-SEVEN

Jane immediately pulled over and started prying Grant's hand away from the gravy splotch of blood.

"Let me see, Grant."

"Jane…it's okay, it's not that bad…" he swatted her hand away. "We gotta keep going. We can't stop here…not now. The crooked cops and villains are probably already on their way."

"Not until we get this taken care of, Grant," Jane demanded, reaching into the backseat and grabbing the closet piece of fabric available which just happened to be an old sweater that belonged to the owner of the truck.

*Funny…*she inspected the sweater. *This didn't fit Omega One's style. It must have been part of his disguise when he had to slip into town without drawing any attention.*

"Jane…give it to me…I got it," Grant moaned. "Just drive."

Jane gave him a stifled look while Grant grabbed the sweater and pressed it up against his side. "You know we can't go to a hospital. The Shadowy Man has spies everywhere! And the more time we spend sitting here on the side of the road, the more likely we are to get caught."

"So just *drive*," ordered Grant.

As much as all of Jane's instincts were screaming at her to take care of Grant, she knew as well that he was right. They had to keep going and get out of the state.

Maybe even the whole damned continent.

Jane gunned the engine once again and peeled out on the road. She didn't have a clue where to go, just that she had to get them there as fast as possible.

She decided to just keeping driving north, avoiding the interstates and any major cities. At least they hadn't seen a cop car since crossing the state line, yet still her senses were on high alert for any sign of law enforcement.

She glanced again over at her partner against the forces of evil and felt a fresh wave of anxiety. Grant's eyes were drooping and his skin was a worrying shade of alabaster.

"Hey…you aren't thinking of falling asleep on me here, are you?"

Jane's voice made Grant snap his eyes open. "N-no…I'm good."

"I'm stopping at the next motel I see," Jane decided firmly. Enough was enough. Grant needed to get that bullet out of him and patched back up.

Of course, Grant had other ideas and shook his head. "They'll be expecting us to find a motel and there's probably a BOLO for us statewide. Besides…we don't have credit cards and our cash is low. We gotta keep going until we find some place where no one will look for us."

"Got any suggestions, baby? 'Cause I'm fresh outta ideas here."

"Well…" Grant let out a pained grunt as he shifted in his seat. "I was thinking… we could go to my family's old hunting cabin."

"*You* have a cabin?"

"Yeah, up north. Nobody knows about it."

That was it. Grant must have completely lost his mind from blood loss.

"Okay, just how far is this supposed cabin of yours?"

"It should only take us a couple of hours to get to it."

Jane shook her head vigorously. "A couple of hours, Grant? You do realize that you're bleeding all over the place, right? We need to get you fixed up."

"I'm okay…" Grant insisted, but Jane knew he had to be in a lot of pain given the amount of sweat gathered on his brow. On top of that, Jane did not like the color on him nor the way he tried to hide the shivering. "I don't think it's all that deep and it's mostly stopped bleeding. I can make it."

"This is stupid," she grumbled.

Grant had a point however, even if Jane was loath to concede to it.

He leaned his head back on the seat as though exhausted by the short argument. His eyes blinking slowly as he pulled the sweater up to his chin. Every instinct in Jane told her to find the nearest motel and put Grant back together right this very instant. But Grant—even though she hate to admit it—was right. They didn't have the money or the luxury of finding a motel.

They had to go to the cabin.

"Alright, fine. We go to this cabin of yours. But if you even think of passing out on me—"

"I won't," Grant cut in wearily. His words contained the hint of a slur. "Just drive."

Jane stomped on the gas and the engine roared in tune of her uncertainty about a cabin that may or may not exist.

Jane pulled the truck off the road and into the ditch, far enough into the trees where it would be difficult to see by any passersby—if there even were any out this far into the forest.

She killed the engine and turned to Grant, who true to his word, had managed to not pass out before reaching their destination. However, Jane knew by the way Grant sluggishly blinked that he was just barely conscious. She reached out and touched Grant on the shoulder and his eyes opened a little wider, meeting hers.

"You gonna be able to walk?"

Grant nodded wearily and pushed himself up straight, as if to prove that he would be psychically capable of the quarter-mile hike. However, the color drained even further from Grant's face and he wobbled unsteadily in his seat until Jane grabbed his bicep to keep him upright.

"Whoa…hold on, Grant. Let me come around and help."

Grant was silent. He just nodded in reply. He was clearly in too much pain and too woozy to put up any kind of a fight.

Jane was out of the car, quickly stopping by the backseat to fill a rucksack of supplies before strapping it securely to her back. She was at Grant's door a moment later, wrapping her arm under his shoulder to help pull him out.

"Hang on to me," Jane ordered and Grant obeyed wearily, dropping his arms across Jane's shoulders and hanging on loosely as Jane dug in her heels and hauled Grant to her feet. He swayed a little, but managed to remain upright as long as Jane had a hold of him.

"You good to move?" Jane asked once she had Grant marginally steady.

"Yeah," Grant nodded breathlessly.

With one are under Grant's armpit and the other grabbing hold of the wrist dangling from her shoulder. Jane led them one step at a time towards the overgrown path that led to the lonely cabin buried in the woods. The trail was barely visible, even in the pale light coming down through the trees from the full moon and she wished over and over again that she had thought to take a flashlight. This was one of those moments she would have liked to have an actual Green Lantern power ring so she could light her way through this cavern of darkness. But the catch was that the ring had to choose her. Grant was leaning more and more into her the further they went, causing sweat to bead on Jane's brow and drip into her eyes.

"Almost there," she encouraged him.

Grant didn't answer, but kept his feet moving as a sing that he was still practically helping himself to walk. The last hundred feet were the hardest as he and Jane both were panting and sweating profusely, but glory, glory, hallelujah, the worn and ramshackle cabin started coming into view through the trees.

They almost made it through the door before Grant's legs completely gave out and Jane had their arms full with all of Grant's 200 pounds.

"Oh, jeeze…" Jane grunted under the sudden shift in weight. "Couldn't wait… three seconds…to pass out?"

The interior sported a plain cot on one end, a dirty blackened fireplace filled with soot, and a small kitchenette. The only other furnishing was a makeshift table made out of cinder blocks for the legs and a warped piece of plywood for the top.

"It smells," Jane pointed out. Not that Grant needed her to tell him that. The place reeked of musty, old gym socks.

It took what little energy and strength Jane had left, but she managed to half-carry, half-drag Grant to the cot sitting across the tiny room and laid him out across it.

"Grant?" Jane rubbed his sternum with her knuckles and that thankfully, had an effect and he stirred, trying to swat Jane's hand away.

He groaned and his eyes slid open. "Gah…"

"Need you to stay with me here, sweetie. Gotta patch you up and get this bleeding stopped or I'm dragging you to the hospital. Cops and vile villains on our tail or not," Jane insisted. "But I for one would rather not go back to that god awful place."

Grant blinked tiredly, but gave Jane a ghost of smirk and soft snort "Really? You seemed…" He hissed as Jane pulled up his shirt to get a look at the damage. "Seemed to…like it."

Jane gave out a chuckle. "Well, I did like arts and crafts and of course, Taco Tuesday."

Grant sucked in another breath as Jane poured a good measure of alcohol over the hole in his side and wiped away some of the blood so she could get a good look at the wound. It was bright red and puckered, but it wasn't bleeding much anymore and Jane didn't mind at all that Grant had been right this time when he said that didn't seem so bad. All Jane had to do was get the bullet out and stitch him back up.

Piece of cake.

The only problem was after that infection would be their biggest worry since they didn't have anything stronger than antibiotic ointment in their med kit, but Jane figured they would cross that bridge when they get to it. She could only focus on one problem at a time.

"Okaaaaay," she stressed out. "It's not so bad." She had an awful poker face. "Just gotta pull that bullet out." Jane pulled out a penknife from the mid kit and carefully cleaned it off with more of the alcohol. She then raised her eyes and met Grant's. "You ready?"

"Not really…" Grant grimaced. "Just get it over with."

Jane got to work after that. She would never consider herself the best at makeshift, do-it-yourself surgery. Especially when it was performed in a dirty cabin out in the middle of nowhere, but she would admit to a certain amount of pride on how quickly she managed to get that bullet of Grant's flank. He grunted and hissed while she probed the wound, removed the bullet than stitched him up.

After one last dousing of the wound in alcohol, Jane placed a clean bandage over her handwork and taped it up.

"There. That should do it. Not bad sewing if I do say so myself. What do you think?"

Jane looked up when she didn't get a response and saw Grant's eyes had closed and his heart skipped a beat at first, thinking that he had lost consciousness.

"Grant? Grant?" She gently shook him.

"Stop it…tryin' to sleep here," Grant slurred drunkenly and Jane sighed.

"Fine…go back to sleep. I'll keep an eye out for anything."

Grant's eyes slid open and he glanced about the small confines of the cabin. "It's still the same as I left it…"

Jane herself made a quick scan of the place as well, taking in the broken furniture, the debris scattered about, the small kitchenette with all of its cabinet doors remained and she saw what Grant did…

The place was a shithole.

Grant was fast asleep. Okay, passed out was more like it. But he was breathing evenly and peacefully, so Jane couldn't ask for more right at the moment.

She took the time to touch Grant on the forehead and check for any signs of a fever. His skin was clammy and pale, and most likely a little on the shaky side. She dug out the blanket she had shoved inside the pack and carefully tucked it around Grant. He shivered a little, but didn't wake, sinking back under the cover until he started snoring softly.

Figuring that Grant would be out for a while, Jane decided to use that time to run back to the truck and stock up on supplies.

The fire gave off a muted, dim glow and only the sounds of the wood crackling filled the little hovel. Jane stared mutely into the flames, almost hypnotized as she watched them dance and lick around the logs stacked within the fireplace.

Grant stirred under the blankets Jane had heaped on him and she turned from the flames. Her attention snapped instantly from the fire to Grant.

"Jane?" He muttered sleepily.

"Hey—how ya feeling?"

Grant grunted and grimaced as he tried to sit up, holding his die until he was mostly upright. "I'll live…just sore right now. How long was I out?"

"Only a few hours. You might as well go back to sleep."

Grant shook his head and shoved off the blankets. "Too hot."

In the dim light, Grant still looked a little too pale for Jane's likening and his skin glistened with sweat Instinctively, Jane reached out and palmed his head.

Grant rolled his eyes and huffed, but didn't bat Jane away like he would have if he had been more alert and not in pain. He was hot to the touch, but it was hard for Jane to say if that was from a fever or a result of being under too many covers.

"I'm fine, Jane."

"Says the boy with the hole in his gut," she came back without any heat.

Grant ignored her retort. His mind was on other things.

"We need to figure things out. How long do you think we should stay here?"

Jane shook her head, unsure. "I dunno…"

"I'm thinking we should stay a few days at least. Let things blow over a little bit before we get on the road again."

He closed his eyes and leaned up against the wall behind him, holding his side tight and fighting not to wince and moan. Jane took this as a sign that he was in need of some pain relief and he reached for the med kit, digging around through it until she found a bottle of pills.

"Found some Tylenol 3…"

"Good enough," Grant mumbled wearily and took the pills Jane shook out of the bottle without complaint, chasing them down with a mouthful of water from one of the bottles Jane had salvaged from the truck.

Jane had thought that her anxiousness over being wanted by every law enforcement agency in the country, Grant's injury and the fact that they were staying in a creepy old cabin in the woods as seen in every generic 80s slasher movie was enough to keep her alert all night so that she could keep an eye on Grant. But she couldn't fight the overwhelming exhaustion that invaded every part of her and her eyes had closed, operating against the explicit orders of her brain to stay open, and she slipped into a deep sleep before she could stop it.

It was clearly morning by the time she woke up. Sun streamed through the cracks in the windowless wells and the rotten wood door. In the distance she could hear birds chirping and the sounds of the forest waking up to a new day outside.

"Grant?" Jane croaked and turned where she sat. She had fallen asleep sitting up with her back resting against the side of the cot where Grant slept.

Sometime during the night, Grant had crawled back under the covers and was fitfully asleep. The blankets pulled up to his chin, shivering slightly.

"Grant…" she muttered, raising a hand to his forehead, finding his flushed skin hot to the touch.

Grant groaned and opened his eyes to slits, making glazed eye contact with Jane. "What?"

"Hey…"

"Don't feel so good."

"Yeah…I figured. Let me take a look, okay?"

Grant shook his head and his teeth chattered. "T-too cold."

"It'll be just a second. Then I'll get you some more medicine and you can have the blankets back, alright?"

Grant's eyes blinked slowly as he nodded while Jane pulled the blankets he had cocooned himself in and pulled them down past his knees. She then lifted his shirt and began her inspection, beginning by gently pulling off the bandage that covered the bullet wound Jane had so carefully stitched up Grant hissed as the tape pulled at his skin and ripped away a few hairs.

Jane could sympathize with him for his discomfort and he may have hissed a little as well when she saw that the wound was now a puffy, bright red, and weeping a yellowish fluid. It was clearly infected and while it was not a surprise that it had developed given the less than sanitary conditions in the cabin. She was worried by how fast it seemed to be taking hold.

"I'm gonna have to clean this out again," she explained, reaching for the pack and pulling out the bottle of rubbing alcohol, frowning to see that the bottle was almost gone. "I'm not gonna lie, but this is going to really, *really* sting."

Jane soaked a wad of gauze she found in the med kit with what was left of the alcohol and swept into across the hole in Grant's side. He sucked in a breath and shook slightly under Jane's finger as she flushed out the infected areas, working as quickly as possible so as to not cause him any prolonged pain, yet still, by the time Jane had the wound cleaned as well as he could, Grant was visibly quaking and sweating.

"Sorry about that," Jane said, placing a clean bandage over the wound. Then she asked in a friendly, robotic voice, "On a scale of one to ten, how would you rate your pain?"

"Thirty-seven!" Grant shrieked, pulling the blankets back up to his chin.

Pain management and fever reduction were next on Jane's to-do list, but to her dismay there were only a few pills left in the Tylenol bottle. They hadn't any time between leaving the old farmhouse and running from the police to stock up on their med kit and there were no antibiotics, only a few bandages, and they had just run out of alcohol—not the kind they both had in mind.

Jane swore under her breath before she fed a dose to Grant and figured that she could get him through the day with what they had, but if the infection got any worse Grant would need some strong antibiotics and Jane would need to find a way to get the medicine he needed.

"I'm not going to a hospital, Jane," Grant announced as if reading her mind. "It'd be too easy for someone to recognize us."

Jane jerked her head up and met Grant's fever-bright, yet willful eyes. "Grant—"

"No." He wasn't going to budge on this, no matter what.

Jane sighed and shook her head at his stubbornness. She was left now with only one option: she was going to have to leave Grant and go to the nearest town to get what they needed all while flying under the radar and not being seen.

But that also meant that Grant would be alone out here, hurt and sick.

But what chance did she have? She was out of options.

They were so screwed.

Grant wasn't getting any better and no matter how many times Jane tried to clean the wound, it just got redder, hotter, and more foul. He was barely coherent as he shivered and shook under the covers of the blankets, his eyes bright and glassy with fever, but Jane knew what she had to do.

"Don't go…" Grant pleaded. "What if someone…what if someone recognizes you?"

"This isn't up for debate, Grant. You need medicine, period."

"Just give me a couple of days and…I'll be fine," Grant panted as though talking was exhausting him. "Can't let you get caught."

"I won't get caught." Jane tried to plant a mischievous smile on her face. "I'm awesome remember?"

"Breaking into a pharmacy? It's too risky."

Grant gave Jane another pitiful face and she hurried to reassure him.

"Look, Grant. The nearest town is a tiny Podunk. Chances are the local pharmacy doesn't have any security better than a lock on the door. I'll be in and out in minutes. Nothing to worry about."

"Maybe…I just don't like this." Grant looked up at her and he saw that no matter what she said or how many assurances she gave him that she would make it in and out of town without being noticed, Grant would fret and worry himself into a frenzy.

'Sorry, kiddo," Jane said sincerely, setting several bottles of water on the floor beside the bed where he could reach them. "Just stay in bed, drink plenty of water and try to get some sleep, okay?"

"Jane—"

"I'll be fine…promise."

"You better," he mumbled, his eyes sliding closed as sleep overcame him.

Jane figured if she hurried, she just might be able to get to town, get the meds, get out and back to Grant before he woke up.

Piece of cake…

She hoped, anyway.

CHAPTER TWENTY-EIGHT

Jane had been right about one thing; the nearest town to the cabin was a Podunk and it was small, even by small town standards. It consisted of nothing more than a little greasy spoon, a gas station with ancient-looking pumps, and a mom-and-pop grocery store.

One business it was also glaringly lacking, however, was a pharmacy.

"Do people not get sick in this town?" She groused to herself, driving down the quiet, deserted Main Street under the cover of night. Where was she to get the meds Grant needed without a pharmacy?"

She was just about to give up on this place and drive another twenty miles south to the next town when she caught sight of a large, Victorian-style house with a sign dangling from the roof of a wrap-around porch.

Dr. M. Wexler, MD. Family Medicine.

The lights were off in the house and Jane thought she might have hit the jackpot with this. A family medicine practice was almost guaranteed to have all the supplies and meds she would need to bring to Grant and this place looked like an easy score. She'd be in and out in no time.

Jane parked the truck where it would be least likely to be noticed—behind the gas station and between two other half-rusted vehicles about a block away from her target. No one was out at this time of night and Jane got the sense that this was the kind of town that closed down as soon as the sun went down. Plus, it was nearly 2 AM, so chances were that she'd never see anyone and no one would see her.

As she ran down the deserted street, Jane wondered how anyone could stand living in a little town such as this. There was no bar, no movie theater, not even a McDonald's. She'd probably shoot herself in the head out of sheer boredom if she had to live here.

Jane stayed in the shadows of the trees she passed as she approached the doctor's houses. She was quiet as a church mouse while she pulled Nurse Gaiman's old ID badge and went to work on the lock to the backdoor.

As expected, it was an easy break-in and she walked in silently, finding herself in a hallway with several doors on each side. She pulled out a flashlight then walked towards the first door and opened it.

It was a small exam room, probably meant for children given the posters of PJ Masks and Paw Patrol on the wall and the box of toys in the corner. She didn't give much hope in finding what she was looking for in there, so she moved to the next door in the hall.

The next two rooms also appeared to be exam rooms, but the door after those was more promising. She found herself in what might be some kind of lab with a microscope sitting on top of a counter next to a sink and above those were a series of glass cabinets installed into the wall. Jane saw right away that the cabinets were stocked full of supplies.

"Bingo," she whispered, as she made for the cabinets.

She silently and methodically opened the doors, looking for the items on her mental list, grabbing bandages, gauze, and anything else she thought might come in handy and stuffing them into her pockets. Her most important task though was to find where the doctor stored his medications and she turned around, scanning the room until here eyes landed on a large, steel locker.

Unlike the cabinets with the bandages, this one was locked.

A good place to keep the meds, Jane figured.

She was easily inside it under a minute, swinging the doors wide open. It may not be as well stocked as a Walgreens pharmacy, but it still had enough drugs in a multitude of bottles with names Jane couldn't pronounce. It took a while for her to find antibiotics and after taking it from the shelf; she closed the cabinet back up and locked it again. Hopefully, the doctor wouldn't even notice that anything had been taken.

It was just as she was about to pocket the bottle of pills when the overhead light swiftly flicked on and the unmistakable sound of a gun being cocked behind her echoed off the walls.

CHAPTER TWENTY-NINE

"Don't move," a woman's voice ordered from behind Jane's back. "Turn around."

"I thought you didn't want me to move," Jane snarked with her hands still in the air.

"You know what I mean," the woman came back with heated exasperation. "Just turn around so I can see you."

Jane slowly pivoted to face the woman in a knee-length nightgown, holding a rifle against her shoulder and aiming for Jane's chest. To her surprise, the woman wasn't too much older than her, maybe no more than thirty with long, blonde curls that bounced messily from her head down to her shoulders.

Piercing blue eyes locked onto Jane in a not-so-friendly manner. "What are you doing in my office?" She demanded to know, her eyebrows coming together in unquestionable anger. Which made perfect sense to Jane; after all, she had just caught her breaking into her home at 2:00 a.m. trying to steal medicine from her.

With that gun still aimed squarely at her, Jane had only one weapon left in her arsenal to get her out of this jam: her charm.

She cocked a sheepish grin and raised her hands a little higher to show her that she meant her no harm. "So...you must be the good doctor."

"And you must be the stupid bitch who thought she could just break into my place," came her fiery reply.

Jane couldn't really argue with that. "Touché. I guess the 'M' in Dr. M. Wexler must stand for Martha, am I right?"

The angry doctor arched an eyebrow. "Does that make us friends now? And it's Melanie."

Before Jane could answer, the lights leading upstairs switched on. Then a little girl's voice filled the air.

"Is that you, Mama? I heard noises."

The anger in Wexler's face disappeared and it was replaced by the slighted tinge of fear. She carefully turned her head to the side, still aiming the gun at Jane. "Yes, it's me, baby," she announced. "I'm just finishing up some work. You go back to bed now, and close your door. I'll be up to check on you in a little bit."

"Yes, Mama," the little girl obeyed, shutting off the light.

Wexler waited to hear her daughter close the bedroom door before she shifted her gaze back to the intruder. Her eyes left Jane's face and went to the pockets she had stuffed full of supplies and she dipped her head towards them. "What's in your pockets? Empty them out."

Jane slowly lowered her hands and brought them down towards her pockets and then as if remembering that she didn't know what she had hidden in them, she took on a deadlier demeanor.

"Don't try anything funny like pulling a weapon on me. This rifle isn't just for looks, ya know. It's loaded and I guarantee you I know how to use it."

"I thought doctors were supposed to do no harm?" Jane quipped, turning the charm on as far up the dial as it would go.

"I'd never harm any of my *patients*...but home intruders? The Hippocratic oath doesn't say anything against that."

Carefully, Jane followed doctor's orders and started emptying her pockets out, dropping rolls of gauze, tape, bandages, alcohol swabs and the bottle of antibiotics to the floor.

Wexler's eyes dropped to the supplies on the floor and Jane had to fight her instinct to grab the gun while she was distracted—like that went well the last time she tried that. But she didn't want to hurt her. She was still an innocent civilian even if she did had a gun trained on her. Besides, Jane still had a chance to talk her way out of this.

Wexler looked up to Jane's face again. "You broke in to steal gauze and antibiotics?"

"Look...I know—"

She looked Jane up and down. "You don't look hurt to me."

"It's not for me..."

"Then what's it for?"

Jane debated with herself over what sort of story she should cook up for her, but decided to go the route she usually avoided at all costs: the truth.

"My boyfriend...he's hurt and he needs this stuff."

"There's a hospital not twenty miles from here. Why don't you take him there instead of stealing from me?"

"It's uh...well...complicated."

"I got it. You're a thief and a criminal and you don't want to get caught by checking into a hospital, am I right?"

Jane was hesitant to reply, looking quietly down at her feet, letting her silence speak for itself.

"I should call the cops," Wexler stated and Jane started a catalog of curses up in her head until the doctor spoke up once again. Her tone softening unexpectedly, "But...something tells me you're not lying."

"What makes you say that?" Jane asked. "You don't know me. I could be a serial killer for all you know," she added, immediately repelling her decision to try and talk her way out of this. But she gave it her best shot anyway, hoping that the woman would see that she wasn't a threat.

Wexler nodded slowly and cautiously. "I suppose you could be, but I read people pretty well and I know when I'm being played. There were plenty of narcotics and controlled drugs in that cabinet you could have stolen yet you only took a bottle of antibiotics. That tells me that you weren't coming in here to get a fix or to score drugs to sell. It makes me think that you really *do* need those supplies."

She paused for a beat. "This boyfriend of yours…how is he injured?"

"He was shot. I took care of it. Got the bullet out, and stitched him up. But he's got an infection now. He's pretty sick."

Jane couldn't believe she had just laid out the truth to her like that. But something in her told her that she could handle the truth.

"Shot? And you just stitched him up and that's it? You made it sound like you do that sort of thing on a regular basis. Bullet wounds aren't something that you can just play doctor with—"

"Look—I know…believe me, I do. But getting him to a hospital just isn't in the cards right now."

Wexler stood eyeing her, quiet for a moment, as she appeared to struggle with some internal dilemma before coming to a decision and speaking again. "Fine… put the stuff back in your pockets," she ordered coolly. The gun was still aimed at Jane's direction.

Jane wasn't expecting that. She was just hoping to get out without getting shot. "You're gonna let me keep all of this?"

"Don't get me wrong, I'm pretty pissed that you saw it fit to break into my home and defile the sanctity of my office and there's not a snowball's chance in hell I'm lowering this gun until you are far from my door. And if I ever catch you here or find you anywhere near my daughter, I swear to God I will blow your goddamned head off."

Jane quirked a faint grin.

Then Wexler looked at her with sympathetic eyes. "But I understand the need to take care of others when they're hurt. It's kinda my job and somehow I get the feeling that it's your job too."

Jane beat a hasty retreat from town, pushing the truck's engine as far as she dared while flooring the accelerator. She'd been gone far longer than she had hoped and she hated that she had to leave Grant behind in that creepy cabin alone all this time. If something were to happen, Grant was in no condition to defend himself. The cabin was too far out in the boonies for cell reception and Grant had now way to call her if he was in trouble. She had a creeping anxiety growing in the pit of her stomach and she felt that she couldn't get back to him fast enough.

Pockets heavy laden with the supplies the doctor had given her, Jane's heart pounded in tune to her feet as she ran down the narrow, brush strewn, and uneven trail towards the cabin. His anxiety didn't let up even as the cabin came into her field of vision. Though she repeatedly tried to convince herself that Grant couldn't possibly have gotten that much worse since she left. Her gut was still doing somersaults and she knew she wouldn't feel any relief until she got back to him.

Finally, Jane reached the door to the shack and gave it a push.

But, it would not open.

This couldn't be happening.

"Grant?" She stated through the door while pounding on it. "*GRANT!*"

Jane didn't hear anything from inside and her heart galloped in her throat. She lifted her hand to pound on the door once again when she felt too wind kick up around her. A shiver chased up her spine and she slowly turned around, feeling as though she was being watched she scanned he trees and listened for any sounds coming from the forest, but there was nothing to be seen or heard.

After a second of frenzied anxiety building in Jane's stomach, the wind suddenly died as quickly as it had started and everything was quiet once again.

Jane stood motionless, trying to calm her racing heart and heavy breathing until she finally snapped out of it, turning back to the door. She raised a fist to hang on the only entrance to the cabin once again when the door suddenly swung open.

Grant, pale and sweaty, was standing on the other side.

"Jane?" Grant swayed slightly as he held on the doorknob then grabbed the door's jamb to steady his wobbly knees. "Why are you banging on the door?"

"The door wouldn't open...and I thought..."

"Oh..." Grant cut her off. "Sorry...forgot I locked it."

"How'd you lock it?" Jane asked, letting her fear turn into anger at him for asking her worry. "I didn't even know it had a lock. Why'd you do that?"

"I pushed a chair against the door...was hearing stuff...probably just my imagination. Stupid, huh?" Grant explained blearily as Jane stepped in. "This place...just makes me a little paranoid, ya know?"

That was just how Jane felt as well, but she didn't have time to really dwell on that as Grant took that moment to stumble and if she hadn't grabbed him around the worst at the moment, he would have been meeting the floor with his face."

"Whoa...let's get you back in bed." Jane helped lead Grant back over to the cot and laid him back down.

Grant groaned and held his wounded side as Jane lifted her legs and got him situated again, pulling a blanket up and over him. She ran a hand over Grant's forehead and suave under her breath. He was burning up and Jane didn't need a thermometer to tell her that the fever was dangerously high.

Jane reached into her supply heavy pocket and produced the bottle of antibiotics, shaking out two pills before adding a couple of Tylenol into the mix.

"Here...take'em."

Grant obeyed, wearily taking the pills from Jane's hand and he didn't offer any resistance when she helped him sit up. He raised the pills to his mouth and popped them in, but when she tried to bring a bottle of water to her lips to chase them down, his hand shook so badly that Jane had to lay her hand over Grant's to steady it.

"Thanks," he mumbled once the pills had been washed down and he tried to lower the water bottle, but Jane stepped its descent.

"Drink the whole thing, Grant. You need to stay hydrated and it doesn't look like you even touched any of the water I left you while I was out," Jane chastised as she pointed to the full water bottles next to the cot.

Two days later Jane and Grant emerged from the cabin. Grant's fever had finally broken that morning and Jane was more than ready to leave. She kept them holed up in the desolate cabin, feeding Grant antibiotics and painkillers until he was finally past the danger point.

It was a slow trudge through the woods, but when the track finally came into view, they both exhaled a great sigh of relief as if they had both just came home.

Grant refused to let Jane help him into the truck, his pigheadedness was a good sign that he was on the road to recovery and would be back in shape soon. After packing their gear away, Jane turned the engine of the truck over and headed for the road, certain that enough time had gone by since their great escape from the asylum that the authorities wouldn't be actively searching for them anymore.

They drove through the same town where Jane had gone to get Grant the medicine he needed and pushed by the big house owned by the blonde, gun-toting doctor. She grinned a little recalling her run-in with her and said a silent word of thanks to the occupant inside. Grant fell asleep not long after that, willed by his lingering exhaustion and the rumble of the engine. His soft snores were the only sound in the car for many miles.

When he woke up about 50 miles later, Jane forced Grant to take another round of pills and drank a full bottle of water and when he was finished with the water, Grant looked out the window then back at Jane.

"So...are we still headed west?" He asked.

Jane glanced back at him, curling her lips into a wry grin. "There are so many bad guys, and we have so little time."

CHAPTER THIRTY

Jane surveyed the damage to the truck. She sighed wearily. "Well, she was a great Starry-Wagon." She turned to see Grant, who was holding his head in pain. Blood was drawing out of the wound he received when the crash caused him to hit his forehead on the steering wheel. "Please remind me in the future that walls don't make trucks go faster. At least we stopped the Knife Knave and his Blade Buddies! I still don't get why they were trying to 'arrest' us."

"Who cares?!" Shouted Grant, staggering out of the busted up getaway vehicle. "At least we'll find new transportation in this train station."

A dreamy look appeared on Jane's face. "Train rides are romantic, aren't they, Grant?"

"Baby, you've got a one *track* mind!"

When Agent Panos arrived at the train station, he was angry. The angriest he had ever been in his entire life. He cursed at the local law officials for mucking up what was supposed to be a simple operation. But instead an accident scene involving an old pickup truck that crashed into the side of the building, where several dead police officers were sprawled across the street and sidewalk, welcomed him.

He managed to keep his anger under control, managing to speak the words, "What I want to know is—"

"Yes, Agent Panos?" Interrupted Officer Kuppersmith.

"What I want to know is, Officer Kuppersmith, is how in all the hells could two nutjobs escape from here and not one cop notice which way they went?!" Panos took a moment to calm himself, and continued on his harangue against he local authorities. "I mean, maybe when they crashed their truck into the train station I can sort of figure the lack of observation. Initial shock and all."

He looked over to see the fallen officer wrapped up underneath the fugitives' abandoned escape vehicle. Blood decorated the grill and windshield. Panos came to the conclusion that Insane Jane just became a cop killer. She just got moved up to the Most Wanted List—#1 with a bullet.

Panos turned to face his men. "But when they derailed the 4:15 Express, all eyes should have been on them! Get me security footage. Get me eyewitnesses accurate. Get me someone with a goddamned clue and tell me where they're going!"

"Well, Agent Panos," said Kuppersmith. "We assume they're not far."

"How the hell can you assume that?"

"Well, they have no resources and where they're possibly going to find transportation at this point? We had an advantage when they were still dressed in hospital clothes. Now they look like anyone else."

The Through the Glass costume shop was closed for the evening. But it didn't discouraged Jane and Grant on making a late night visit. Jane searched the area for something to throw through the window. Grant stopped her, producing some lock picks. He went over to the door and picked the lock.

"Sometimes you need to require a little finesse, babe."

Jane chuckled, as she followed him in while looking at all the bright colorful costumes. "That was so nice of that truck driver to stop and give us a lift," Jane said, going through several costumes on the rack.

"Transportation has proven to be highly unreliable, my dear," Grant noticed, looking out the front window. "Where is the customer service, I ask?

"Tell me about it, Granty-poo," Jane pulled back another costume and flashed a smile. "Oh, this will do nicely," she said grabbing the suit.

Grant shifted his gaze back to Jane, admiring her athletic body, when she changed into the tight, dark blue bodysuit. "I mean, it's totally shocking, given the 'economy.'"

She knew he was watching her. She didn't mind. It felt good to be seen. "I am so sick of people using the economy as an excuse," Jane groaned. "People need to take responsibility for their actions."

"You're being awfully hard on people, Janey-Jane-Jane. There are just a lot of things out of their control."

"Then what about the government?!" Jane snapped.

Grant looked at her strangely. "Government?! I'd say the government was utterly inept except the level of corruption found there says otherwise. Look at the state of healthcare."

"Don't even get me started, Grant," she warned him. "It's enough to drive a girl mad!"

She stood up and fastened her utility belt. She adjusted the top of her costume and straightened the huge white star in the center.

"What about gun control?" Asked Grant.

"What about it?"

"Well, baby, guns are flat out dangerous. They just shouldn't be allowed out among the people."

"You're wrong, Grant," she said, pulling on her glove. "Guns don't kill people…" She pulled the mask over her head, letting her long auburn hair flow out the back. "Super-villains kill people."

She looked over to Grant, who was now sporting a superhero costume of his very own. It was similar to Jane's, only more masculine and it didn't have a cape. It had the same color scheme and the infamous symbol of the star that symbolized their unity was emblazoned on his chest.

She looked up and down. She was pleased.

"You know what we need to do, Neutron?" She addressed him be his heroic nom de guerre.

"Yeah, I do," he replied. "We need to find us some super-villains."

"No matter what those rapscallions might do, we make this vow to all who can hear we'll let not villain escape the Avenging Star and Neutron's view!"

CHAPTER THIRTY-ONE

Leaning against the outside wall of a gas station, Grant, returning to the mantle of Neutron, unsheathed a rather big kitchen knife from his utility belt. He peered out to see several people entering the gas station, taking a breath to steady his nerves.

"This is going to be a bloody one, Jane," he said, raising the knife. The morning sun shimmered on its steely surface. "We're talking wet works."

Jane pulled on her glove, making sure it was taut replied, "What are the odds, Grant, that we'd find so many super-villains in once location?"

"Astronomical. But let's not get hung up on labels. These are still people."

Jane tapped him on the shoulder. "It's time. Watch your back and stay alert."

He nodded in acknowledgement, while Jane grabbed that Louisville Slugger she "borrowed" from the sporting goods store when they were "shopping" for new costumes the other night. They crept into the gas station ready to strike.

Trevor Prescott wasn't having a good day. He lost his hedge fund job just recently and found out his girlfriend was having an affair with another woman—his ex—and he just discovered his credit card has been declined.

"Run it again," he told the clerk, trying to keep himself from igniting. "There is plenty of money on that card."

The clerk, who had been up since 3:00 a.m., was already about to crash before noon feigned a smile. "Sir, I have already swiped your card three times and its been declined. Do you have another card you could use?"

"Oh, horseshit!" Trevor yelled, gaining the attention from the other customers. "I paid my bill and there should be plenty of goddamned money in that goddamned account!"

"Sir, please," urged the clerk, "I have to ask you to lower your voice. Cursing isn't going to solve the problem."

"What the hell do you mean *my* problem? It's obvious that there's something wrong with your computer. Now ring me up for my gas."

"Sir, if you continue to act this way, I'm going to have to call the police."

"Well, you better call the cops because in five seconds I'm going to jump over this counter and kick your ass!"

The door of the gas station beeped, followed by two sets of steady footsteps entering the store.

"What seems to be the trouble?" Asked a woman.

Trevor and everyone else turned around expecting the police, but to their surprise there stood a man and a woman wearing matching costumes. The woman had wild, unkempt red hair and she carried a baseball bat where she hung over her shoulder striking a relaxed pose. The man, however, wielded a butcher knife similar to a special forces operative. Everyone in the store was frozen in their places. Suddenly the clerk forgot about her current customer's temper tantrum and focused all her attention to the weapons these two masked psychos were carrying.

Trevor, who was still fumed by his current financial situation, did not cower. "Now what the hell is this shit?"

"People who made and continue to make, bad decisions," the clerk said in a hushed voice.

"It's not that simple and you know it," said Grant, walking casually down the snack food aisle. "Society sometimes gives people only once choice. The wrong thing is the right thing for them."

Jane followed him, holding the bat behind her neck and looking at everyone's faces. She was greeted with a mixture of horror and confusion. "Each of us has the free will to know the difference from…" Then she paused. Something out of the ordinary stopped her in her tracks. She looked over at the checkout counter, feeling her jaw had hit the floor. "OMG!" She exclaimed, pointing the bat over in that direction. "I know there was a collection of villains here, but I had no idea you'd be here, Isotope!"

Before her stood the notorious super-villain decked out all in green. The façade on his cowl gave him a menacing look. He glowered at Jane.

"You didn't think you would be rid of me so easily. Did you, Avenging Star?"

"Well, I, uh, you know, I kinda hoped I would," she smiled nervously. "Okay, so I'm not witty enough to come up with some snappy hero/villain banter. But I can quote a lot of *Rick and Morty*."

Isotope put his hands on his hips. "Be that as it may, 'kinda hope' won't save you from Star Town's greatest villain of all time. *Ever*."

"I always thought that the Dictator was the greatest villain in Star Town," Jane contracted her vain adversary.

Isotope's foreboding demeanor turned into a state of shock and revulsion. "The Dictator?! That dime store Doctor Doom can't menace his way out of a wet paper bag. You may have thought I met my demise on the falls of the sewage treatment plant, but it turns out I'm as hard to kill as an idea."

* * *

Trevor stared at the two costumed fools. He was having no more of that today. "Let me guess, you're here to kick ass and chew bubble gum, and you're all out of bubble gum? What are you supposed to be? Clowns? Is it Halloween already?"

Then his face slowly morphed into the Isotope right in front of Jane's eyes. The mask, cape, and all of his accouterments appeared out of nowhere and finally took the shape of the notorious super-villain.

"I, the Isotope," he began his villainous monologue, "are the only scary thing you need to worry about this October."

Trevor was laughing at the dumbstruck superhero. He had never seen anything so stupid in his whole life. And people like Trevor like to poke the bear.

"Ha ha! Trick or treat, mother—" Before he could finish the insult, Jane tattooed him across the eye with that baseball bat that sent him crashing over to the beef jerky rack.

Jane tossed the bat aside and launched on a full assault on the alleged super-villain. She held him down, while delivering rapid fire punches to his bloody mess of a face.

"I've got your Great Pumpkin, right here, you ghoul!" She shouted, wailing on him. Trevor staggered to get up, but the pain was unbearable. The best he could do was to play dead so this crazy psycho bitch would leave him alone. But he was wrong! She kept hitting him with such fury he couldn't see clearly. "Powerful pummeling by pumpkin!" Jane cried out.

Out of the corner of her eye, she saw several people trying to escape from the store. She looked over to Grant, who was already disposing several of the other "villains" in the vicinity. "Neutron! Don't let those henchmen escape!"

Grant grinned. "I'm on it, Avenging Star," he said, running in front of the exit, blocking the terrified customers away from their freedom. He brandished the knife in front of them. He smiled devilishly. "You better call the janitor, because we're going to have a mess on aisle-seven very soon."

The police confiscated the surveillance footage and watched in nausea of what happened at the gas station.

"Jesus Christ!" One officer exclaimed. "It looks like a freakin' Tarentino movie!"

His partner held his stomach in pain. "I've never seen anything like that." He covered his mouth. "I think I'm going to puke."

"Pull yourself together, you idiots!" Said the officer in charge. "The FBI is working on it right now. In the meantime, show some decorum for crissakes!"

Agent Panos was going over the footage from the outside cameras. After they were done with the people in the store, Jane attacked the groundskeepers. One poor guy was raking leaves one minute and the next he's being judo-flipped to the ground.

"*Leave* it to me, Grant!" Panos heard her say on the video. "I've got these crumb-bums *piled up* and ready to *burn!*"

"You're getting better on this banter stuff, babe," said Grant.

Jane turned to face the other yard worker and delivered a flying sidekick to his chest. "!Ole! You've got to be my favorite piñata! Or maybe I should use that rake on you…not, it's too bloody to hold properly. Look at all the candy everywhere!"

Panos had a bad feeling in his stomach. *God…she's completely lost it. I need to get to them before they kill anyone else. Where are they going?*

Driving down the highway on a "commandeered" sports car, that belonged to one Trevor Prescott, otherwise known as The Isotope; Grant, who peeled back his mask, looked over to Jane who was still wearing her Avenging Star mask sped through the desert highway. "We're on a hot streak, baby," he said, fixing his unkempt hair. "Where's the best place to go for winners like us?"

Jane tuned his way, flashing him a million-dollar smile. "Vegas!"

CHAPTER THIRTY-TWO

It was dusk when they passed the famous "Welcome to Fabulous Las Vegas, Nevada" sign. "Woooo-hoooo! I'm in Las Vegas, bitch!" Jane yelled up to the glistening star-studded sky.

"Not just Vegas," Grant said to her, "but we're staying at the newest, hottest hotel—Eden!"

Jane's eyes were as big as dinner plates. "Eden?" She repeated, almost swerving off the road. "I heard that place is amazing! How did you get a room? How can we afford it?"

"Don't worry your pretty little head," Grant assured her. "I know people. You and me, baby. We're gonna blow the lid off this place."

Jane walked through the doors and into the lobby where the first thing she noticed were the slot machines. The sweet sound of ringing bells and people pushing those "spin" buttons. She had never been to Vegas. All she knew about the city she had learned from TV and movies.

Jane followed Grant inside the casino and she noticed everything was super new and it showed. The loud sound of slot machines and laughing people filled her ears. Instead of the usual multicolored, crazy patterned carpeting, the casino floor was covered in deep red carpet. So far, so good, Eden was surrounded by black and red colors and the whole theme of the place just screamed luxury.

As she followed Grant, she scanned her surroundings at the people gambling around her. A group of men in their mid 20s at the blackjack tables to her right, an old man in a wheelchair at the Wheel of Fortune slot machine to her left. Everywhere she turned there was some as Jane passed the poker tables, she saw one man who seemed to be sweating just a bit too much for being in an air conditioned building.

Jane and Grant finally reached the reception area where a young woman ready to greet them. Reception had arranged them with their own suite. They made a quick stop over at the gift shop to pick up some of the essentials: toothbrushes and tooth paste, bathing suits, and for Jane of course, a souvenir Eden Hotel and Casino T-shirt.

"Oh, Grant! This place is beautiful!" Jane said, observing everything the casino/hotel had to offer. She felt like Julia Roberts in *Pretty Woman*, except for the whole hooker thing. "I haven't felt this relaxed in ages!"

Grant pulled the brim of his fedora down, striking the infamous pose of the late great King of Pop. "Why shouldn't you, baby doll? No super-villains in this town (other than the pit bosses)."

They rode the elevators to the 15th floor and found their room by the end of the all. Just like the rest of the hotel, even the hallways screamed luxury. They reached their room and Grant pulled out the key card to open the door to their room. As Jane stepped in, she actually gasped.

The suite was huge and actually looked like a real apartment. They had a large living room with a black leather couch, large screen TV, bookcases, and tables. Straight ahead were huge windows that took up most of the room, all looking out into Las Vegas Boulevard.

To the left was the door to the bedroom and it was just as impressive as the living room, especially the king sized bed. Jane kicked off her shoes and did a quick sprint to the bed and jumped on.

Jane laughed. "So, what are we gonna do first?"

"Well, we can hit the tables, or we can go see a show. A nice diner perhaps?"

"I have something else in mind," she said, making eyes at him. "And it doesn't require any clothing."

Grant noticed she was about to lift up her shirt. Grinning wildly, he charged right at her. "I guess we can always order in."

CHAPTER THIRTY-THREE

Feeling the warmth of the sun on her face, Jane gently awoken from a sound slumber. She rolled to her side and gently opened her eyes, quietly observing Grant getting dressed. He looked over to her, smiling.

"Morning, babe. Did you sleep well?"

Jane simply grinned. "I have no idea how we're gonna top last night. Do you have any ideas?"

"Well, I got a couple of suggestions," Grant replied, admiring how cute she looked, all wrapped up in the silk sheets..

"This has been the most wonderful adventure I've ever been on. Daring escapes and stopping the bad guys! Oh, and then a romantic night in a high-class Las Vegas hotel with you. I just…I've never, you know, been with anyone before. I always thought it would be with the man of my dreams. The one who'd have love me for…for me."

She felt his touch with he held her hand. Jane had stars in her eyes.

"Baby," he said, looking into her eyes, "I love you."

She was stunned. "Oh, wow," she said, feeling dizzy. "You do? That's…wow."

"Shhhh…" Hushed Grant, until Jane pulled him forward and kissed him deeply.

He slowly pulled away, and then looked at the time. A look of disappointment fell upon his face. "I need to run out and get…" He paused, watching Jane become a blank slate. The lights were on, but no one was home. She became catatonic. Grant bit his lip and finally said, "Jane? What's the matter, doll?"

"Their idiopathic letter to your request compared to the solution to grant the shortening of assertion of unexpected use which was given outside on in accordance with leeriness food, work verdure." It was Jane, but someone else was speaking. "The activities, in order to fight organisms. This change meant that little personnel is available, around a larger number to support despoilment. In order to accept this challenge is it photoconductivity. Hospital to preserve…

"The kind again that we discretion affairs, or underlining and in order these programs or procedures chronologist the omega one on our crime sets of the hammer, mechanism. Crime prevention is a program, an important effect on crime sets the food general public health, for the influenza that is unexpected him, with force loses finished. Starrywagon, with an sulfa, for and that costs into the dollar and the drug and a cosmetic act of the attached questions and the answer patients of the laboratory or confirmed supposed infection Las Vegas. At it takes it makes, in order to examine a crime, in order to identify the trespasser to punish in order to pursue united nations in which are large problems on a mechanism, can edge are completely missing, other one.

"For example the majority of the military heftiness has a once is finished in. The specialists with medical after to allow rataplan assertion of or use of the entresol drug or separation use of the drug recognized to be given during hamburger with the specific means. The department material program no, like carefully the outside east thought connected, over in much to be insufficient places.

"Therefore the intrepidity selected to supply only the most general advice and permit commanders to develop the programs master plan prevention which its which were based on of the community under dynatron it stops on. After stops, of the hospitals can and the specialists in more medical competition the possession or the memory to receive under **LOCAL VITRICS CONCERN BOMB!**"

Grant was floored. "Jane…what the hell are you talking about?!"

Jane blinked twice, slowly coming back to the realm of reality. "Um…what?"

"You just spaced out and you went on an entire monologue about only God knows what."

"Oh," she smiled nervously. "I think I was having a soliloquy."

"You thought you were having a what?"

"A soliloquy. It's a private moment in my thoughts."

"You were talking out loud—to *yourself*!"

"Actually, you weren't supposed to be listening."

Grant held his head in exasperation. "Are you sure you're not crazy?"

"To sum it all up, I was just thinking about all the villains out there. How are we gonna stop them all in time?"

Grant approached Jane, holding her in his arms. "You need to relax, Janey-Jane," he told her. "Go take a dip in the pool. I gotta run a few errands while you're there."

"That sounds great," she said, leaving his warm embrace. She sauntered over to the davenport where she looked into the hotel gift shop bag for the new bathing suit Grant had bought her. "A nice relaxing dip in the pool should get rid of all my stress." She pulled out blue bikini and held it in front of her at the mirror.

"There you go, groovy chick," Grant said, walking toward the door and then turned back to admire the view. "Stay out of trouble, babe."

She looked back smiling. "Trouble better stay away from me!"

People crossed quickly, heading for the entrance to Eden. Grant watched them hurry off to their jobs.

A truck drove by, blinker flashing. Grant watched it turned left, across traffic, down a little alley that ran parallel to the tower.

Pulling his Neutron mask over his head, he walked briskly. He was a man with a purpose, a man with a purpose, a man on his way somewhere, taking a shortcut down the alley to the next street over, perhaps.

Ahead of him, a rumble sounded. The steel gates of the hotel's loading bay, lifting open. The trucker's left blinker flashed again, and it turned into the bay.

Grant walked past, eyes straight ahead, as the gates began to come down again.

At the last possible second, just as they were about to slam shut, he ducked left and rolled underneath them, kept rolling until he was underneath the truck itself, hidden from sight.

He was in the building.

The truck doors opened. Footsteps sounded on either side of them.

"Sucks, man. We supposed to get help on this end, too, you know?"

"Tell me about it. I've been on since 2:00 a.m., man. Had this Rain Man kid hangin' round the five-dollar table, tryin' to count cards. Wouldn't take a polite hint, so I finally had to toss him."

"So?"

Grant heard the rear doors of the truck opening. He rolled to his left, out from under the truck, and stood, his back against the driver's side door.

"So he shows up an hour later with these two assholes and thinking to get back in. Ow!"

"What?"

"Lift, man. Lift! These things are heavy."

Something slammed to the floor. Grant heard the sound of metal on concrete, then the squeak of wheels. He drew the shotgun out from under his jacket.

The front of what looked like a laundry hamper appeared around the corner of the truck, followed a second later by a short, stocky man in a muscle shirt.

"So these guys," the man was saying, his attention focused on who he was talking to, not on the hamper or on what was in front of him, "are just beggin' for me to hit them, which I—"

He finally looked up, just as Grant stepped forward and whipped him across the face with the barrel of the shotgun.

He went down without a sound.

"Joey? Somethin' wrong?"

The other man came around the back of the truck, saw Grant, and had just enough time to curse before Grant hit him, too, and he fell next to his friend.

The first man had a plastic security badge clipped to a chain around his neck. Grant ripped it loose and stood. The hamper in front of him was a cash bin, full of money from the casino.

For now, he'd have to leave this cash behind. The real prize awaited him upstairs. He dragged the man under the truck, and put the hamper back in it.

Then he headed for the elevator.

Jane was relaxing under the hot Nevada Sun on the chase lounger poolside, with her Avenging Star costume stashed in the souvenir duffel bag next to her. She still felt wary about any evildoers lurking around every corner. She was in Sin City after all. She had to be on her toes. She basked in the warmth of the sun behind the pair of tinted lenses on her star-shaped sunglasses; she was nodding off to sleep. She wished she had some music to listen to, but she enjoyed the tranquility of being the only one there. She raised her eyebrows. Someone seemed to loom over her. Jane's eyes snapped open when she heard something that rocked her to her core.

"Make sure you use plenty of sunscreen, Avenging Star." Jane lowered her sunglasses to see the owner of the shadow. She couldn't breathe. "Don't want to get skin cancer. It'll kill you!"

Jane looked up to see a man all dressed in black. The matching fedora, but Jane knew who it was immediately. The skull mask quickly gave away the man's identity immediately. She was staring into the dark empty caverns where his eyes should be.

"Omega One!" She cried, jumping out of the lounge chair and engaging in defensive tiger stance. "What are you doing here? No, wait, what are you doing alive?! I thought I vanquished you back at that lame-ass Scooby Doo roadside attraction."

"I'm an evil penny," Omega One explained. "I kill everything I touch. And I think you need some sense."

The elevator doors opened.

Grant turned right. He walked to the end of a long corridor. In front of him was a door marked **PRIVATE: NO ADMITANCE**. There was no knob. There was no lock, only a magnetic pod to the right of the door, at waist height.

To his left was a wall of glass windows, looking out on the same street where only minutes before he'd watched the crowd crossed. He ran the security pass over the pad, and the door clicked open. Drawing the shotgun again, he stepped quickly inside.

The two men left, and Grant heard orders in the other room, people scrambling to do as their employer had instructed. Thirty seconds later, there was silence, but Grant knew that three well-armed guards stood outside that door.

One of the guards whipped his gun from the rear waistband of his pants and clicked off the safety, eyes darting nervously near out of their sockets. He turned to look expectantly at the door the guards had gone out only minutes before, and the sliding glass doors at his back exploded into the room in a blur of red.

Grant slammed hard into the man's back, forcing him to the floor as his momentum carried him further across the room. He took a shot at Grant, but missed.

Grant was four feet from the door when it opened. Two guards burst in as the masked man threw his weight against it, knocking the two men together and down. The door was kicked open again as the third man came through, gun leveled at Grant's chest, but he moved much too quickly for the guard. Arm flashing out, he grabbed the man's waist behind the weapon and drew him forward and past his body.

One of the guards pulled out some other weapon then, as the two men on the ground were recovering themselves enough to take aim, though they had yet to rise to their feet. Three steps and Grant launched himself into the air, arcing over the pair, who twisted wildly to try to get a shot off at him.

Grant was behind the two guards and they were up, blocking their partner's aim. They were about to turn their weapons on Grant again when he moved in close. Crossing his arms, he grabbed the barrel of each weapon with his opposite hand, and then yanked the two guns apart. The men slammed together, heads cracking hard. Grant hit them simultaneously with their own weapons, and they were falling even as their boss forced the colorful intruder from across the room.

Grant raised his shotgun and struck the man with it. The guard came crashing down to the floor. When he tried to get up, he was staring down the barrel of the costumed freak's gun.

"You know what I love most about Las Vegas?" Grant asked the man. "Endless opportunity. Plus, nobody judges you for what you do or look like. This is the kinda place I'd like to leave my mark on." Then he cocked the gun and smirked at his captive. "Now you're about to leave *your* mark."

The sound of the blast was enough to rattle the windows.

"What do you want, Omega One, a rematch in Fabulous Las Vegas?" Jane asked, never taking her eyes off him. "If that's the case, I'm only interested if it's pay-per-view."

"No, quite the contrary, Avenging Star. Think of me as Prometheus." Jane looked confused. Omega One sighed. "The Greek myth, not that *Alien* abomination."

"Oh, cool," Jane said, tying her hair into a ponytail. She had the feeling that a fight was coming, and she had to be ready. "So you're gonna give me fire?"

"No," Omega One said flatly. "Your sidekick will do that. I bring wisdom and it will set you free."

"Wisdom?" Jane couldn't believe what the masked man just said. Everything he just said was wrong. "You bring villainy and suffering."

"The truth is often confused with those things," Omega One clarified. "But no, I'm only here to help you at this moment. I'm not real. I'm just your deluded mind trying to make sense of the real villain. Grant is your enemy."

Jane seemed stunned. "Grant?" She said softly, trying to make sense of all this. "Grant?"

"Right here, babe," she heard Omega One say, before he morphed into Neutron. "What's up?"

Jane staggered back. She couldn't believe her eyes one moment she was talking to Omega One and then Grant just appeared right in front of her. Was this another trick the Shadowy Man had pulled, or was she losing her mind? Was he even Grant at all?

"Why…why are you in costume?" She asked trying to keep her balance.

"I told you that I had errands to run," he replied.

"What? Is there a villain in town? You should have told me and I would have come to help you."

"Nahhhh," he grinned. "You needed to relax. Besides, there aren't villains in town. Well, there *are* two…but they don't concern us."

Jane's forehead crinkled with inquiry. "Which ones?"

Grant stood there puzzled. He awkwardly answered. "Um…the Avenging Star and Neutron. I always thought those were stupid names."

Jane's head felt hot. Her eyes were stinging. Her world was turned upside down. "Wait, what do you mean, *we're* the villains?"

"That's it, Jane," she heard Omega One whisper into her ear. "You're *so* close."

Jane turned her head to yell at the villain. "Shut up!" But to her realization there was no one there. She turned back to Grant, who was telling all these lies. "What do you mean we're the villains, Grant?"

"Isn't it obvious?" We're the only super-villains anywhere."

"My God, Grant…" Jane said breathlessly. "What have you done?"

"You mean what have *we* done," he corrected her. "We've killed *sooooo* many people. And we're about to kill more. Well, I'm going to kill more." Grant flipped open the remote, which looked like nothing more sinister than a small cellular telephone, and entered the code to arm the explosives planted throughout Eden. "This is the end of our partnership. Sorry it had to be this way, Janey-Jane." His thumb hovered over the pound sign.

And then all hell broke loose.

* * *

Agent Panos shook on the street, and looked up to the sky to see the brand new casino Eden exploding right before his eyes. All the bystanders panicked and scurried to safety. Panos was about to conduct a full-scale search on his two fugitives and decided to hold off on it, considering the obvious.

They have gone too far this time.

He looked over to his men, who were waiting for his orders. "I want all EMS from as far out as possible on site ASAP!" Panos looked up to see the east wing of Eden bursting into flames. "We need to save as many survivors as possible. And we have to find those two deranged lunatics! Their reign of terror ends today!"

CHAPTER THIRTY-FOUR

Someone was screaming—a terrible keening wail, not of physical pain, but of anguished grief. A part of her wanted to tune it out, but Jane would not, and could not do that.

Jane sprinted across the buildings, nearing gliding and took to the air in a soaring swan dive. She was not distracted by a flash of the high-class call girls, nor by the glamorous lights from the glitzy marquees of the neighboring casinos, nor by the passing traffic on the street. With barely a conscious thought, in midair already, her legs pulled up and she did a forward roll with a kick-thrust, propelling herself just a tiny bit further than her original leap would have taken her. And with such flourish and grace, she swiftly changed into her Avenging Star disguise in less time than Lynda Carter did in every episode of *Wonder Woman*.

Through traffic was moving slowly on the street, Jane's course of action still would be impossible for anyone else. When she landed in a tuck-and-roll on the roof of a party bus heading north out ten miles per hour, she came out of the roll in yet another nearly balletic leap. Contact with the bus had slowed her, but Jane's momentum was enough to carry her to the southbound lane. Her hands touched the hood of an oncoming car, when her feet hit the car's roof, launching her into a double somersault. The leap brought her close to the huge blaze that even now heated her face to a level most others would find painful. But she had to get closer still.

Jane dove to the street as a fiery blaze tried to engulf her. "Action verbs: jumping and falling!" She yelled, making a narrow escape as she ducked and covered.

Her costumed body tumbled several feet across Las Vegas Boulevard, with her cape wrapping around her waist. She let out a loud groan, sitting up on the pavement, looking at all the gaping bystanders who were looking up at the towering inferno that was once the decadent casino Eden.

Jane was invisible to them. She joined the terrified onlookers gazing into the flames. "The hotel…" She said, mesmerized by all the carnage. "The hotel is on fire!"

Somebody screamed. Jane frowned and looked across the street in front of the building.

There was a bunch of people were running around, waving their hands in the air like idiots. As she watched, a man in a suit ran right into a woman and pushed her out of the way.

Jane saw that the people were paying more attention to the confetti that was swirling through the air than they were to the building. They were trying to catch it, she realized.

A huge crash sounded. A car had just smashed into one of the limos parked out front. The driver didn't seem to be concerned about that at all, he pulled some of the confetti off his windshield and ran to join the others in front of the building.

It was green confetti. Jane saw that now. All green.

It was everywhere.

Only it wasn't confetti.

It was hundred-dollar bills.

Some of the bills were still on fire.

Jane looked up. The bills filled the sky, like rain. They were coming from the tower—pouring out the remains of what used to be the 12th floor.

Gawkers milled around, and more arrived by the moment, walking briskly, some even running. Firefighters and police officers ran around with purpose. The heat of the blaze alone was enough to tell her the building was beyond rescue. She felt for the people who had now lost their jobs, their livelihood. Jane was angry.

Grant never considered his actions to be good or bad, simply necessary. It had been that way since he was a small boy, despite his parents' insistence on labeling his behavior at every available opportunity. No, Grant merely considered himself a practical, logical man. He identified his goals, and did whatever was necessary, what exception, to achieve those goals.

He stayed behind to watch his handiwork, to enjoy the show and feel the thrill of the flames. He must have waited for the rain of debris to end and then taken off at a run, pumped full of adrenaline from fear and excitement.

He was laughing. Jane could hear him from where she stood. He was whooping victoriously, and as he slowed down, he began to do a little half-skip dance that made Jane furious.

Grant stood a block away from the burning hotel/casino, watching the catastrophe he had created with interest and amusement. This day was getting better every minute. He was enjoying the show! A righteous blaze, wounded cops, the bullet-ridden police vehicles, and now Jane.

"We're doomed to be cast out of Eden…again!" she told him. Her horrified face was hidden behind her mask.

"What?" Grant scoffed. "Are you supposed to be some sort of Eve? Do you have an apple for me?"

"You were the apple of my eye, Adam—er, I mean, Grant." She felt betrayed. Grant was supposed to help her fight the forces of darkness, not join them. Now she felt stupid for falling love with him. "But…we've sinned and now we're exiled."

Grant brandished his shotgun, stepping over wounded victims from the explosion. They writhed in pain. Their suffering increased in each step he took. His steel-toed boots crunched the broken glass beneath him. Grant paid no attention to them nor the cash that floated down from the sky when he blew up the vault upstairs.

"Just like in that fairy tale where the woman brings the man down," he griped.

"You're trying to blame me?" Jane asked, taking cover in a nearby pawnshop. "You blew up this building! You killed all of those people!"

"If we're gonna talk about original sin, then what about all the people *you've* killed?" The words struck Jane like an arrow. "Let's review: we got Mommy and Daddy. Uncle Charlie. Oh, that MILF of a boss of yours, and that bitch Stacy. Am I forgetting anyone?"

"Grant," Jane called out, feeling the bile in her mouth. "Don't…"

Grant laughed. "Oh, yeah. There was Pete! You had a thing for him, didn't you? Too bad the feeling wasn't mutual. But you really knew how to light his fire." Jane gritted her teeth so hard, she thought one of them would snap off. Grant stepped in front of the archway to the pawnshop and cocked the shotgun. "You know what the Good Book says, Janey-Jane: 'Let ye who is without sin, cast the first stone!'"

An old television set came flying out of nowhere hitting Grant on the head. He stumbled, dropping his gun. He held his head and saw several drops of blood on his gloved hand.

"You bitch!" He yelled, getting up. "I'm bleeding! You're as bad as those WikiLeaks people!"

Jane emerged from the darkness in all of her super-heroic glory. "I'm not a bad person!" She paused, remembering what Grant just said about her family and friends. She began to question herself. Who was she, a hero or a villain? Right now she was on the side of the angels. "I don't think," she finally confirmed. "I-I just, um, you know, get confused and stuff. And what's wrong with the WikiLeaks people?"

Grant opened up his jacket and drew his twin pistols and opened fire on Jane. She dove under the bullets, taking refuge, Grant thought. He was leaping out into the air shooting wildly. He felt he was in a John Woo movie. All that was missing was the director's signature white doves.

"The information they've released puts our soldiers in danger!"

Over the gunshots, Jane yelled back at him, "After all the people you've killed, when did you suddenly start caring about human life?"

Grant saw her little red head pop out and he opened fire. "This is about national security," he replied, following Jane, who was scurrying across his line of fire. He couldn't believe he had missed her completely. "This undermines our democracy. We must defend ourselves at *all* costs."

Jane appeared out of nowhere, taking two fingers on each hand and stretching her mouth and sticking her tongue out at him. "No, this is about freedom," she said, wagging her tongue. "We have a right to information and shall that be pursued for spreading the truth."

"There's too much information," he argued, reloading the magazines to his pistols. "There's an overwhelming amount of truth. How can anyone possibly deal with that much data? It would drive you crazy!"

Jane continued to dodge bullets like she was a seasoned acrobat. She wasn't quick enough as her cape was riddled with several bullets. "But you…you're already crazy! America should be in control of its information, not terrorists. We should assassinate all of those people leaking the information."

A flurry of movement from all sides, and Jane was reaching, arms and legs flashing in a whirlwind of blocks and parries. Then she was on the offensive.

Jane dove forward in a move that any casual observer would have called suicidal, as it was about to put her on the ground in a range of Grant's weapon. Where she'd been standing, Grant landed, sword clanging against the sidewalk, even as Jane's hands planted on the cement, vaulting her feet first into the air and over her boyfriend—*ex*-boyfriend—who'd been in front of her.

Jane leaped in front of him. "We can't just kill anyone we disagree with," she countered, kicking the gun out of his hand. "Diplomacy must be our solution."

But Grant had the other pistol. He aimed it at her face and pulled the trigger. Click, click, click.

Grant sighed heatedly. "Goddamn it." He threw the gun aside and met Jane face-to-face. "So, how do you defend the leak of information detrimental to our state department's operations yet still want them to practice diplomacy?"

Jane smiled coolly at him. "Crazy, huh? No, it's not our responsibility to make our government officials' jobs easier."

"So we're supposed to just stand by and let foreign operatives do damage? We're supposed to be O.K. with them shredding our safety?"

"Our safety wouldn't be in danger if our government did a better job. And we don't know these things until the information is released." Jane coldcocked him in the face as hard as she could. This was the first time she actually punched someone. She surprised herself on how easily it was to knock Grant who was nearly twice her size flat on his ass.

"Those are things we need to fight for. We have aright to know that problems exist. If we don't, how can we ever expect things to change?"

And the hero and the madman clashed.

Grant sprang off the ground as quickly as humanly possible. Jane found a rotary telephone that was nearby and immediately picked up the receiver.

"Is it wrong that people like things the way they are?" He asked, throwing a punch, as Jane deflected it.

"Was it alright that people could be considered property?" She replied, wrapping the cord around his throat. Grant gasped for air, trying to pull free. "Was it alright that women couldn't vote? That children of African descent had to go to different schools than white kids?"

The cord around his neck was getting tighter. It hurt when he talked, but he was able to strain his reply. "Those...those things were wrong but who gets to decide what changes? Foreign terrorists?"

"No," Jane said, trying to keep her hold on him. "*We* do. *I* do. And *I* want to change!"

She was taken off guard when Grant used whatever strength he had to left her up on his back and crashed into the wall. Jane lost her grip on the rotary phone, giving Grant a chance to gasp greedily for air. Before she could get back on the offensive Grant kicked her in the face, blood misted through the air.

"You can't change who you are, Jane." She tried to get up, but she was met with another devastating kick. "You were born this way. You live this way. You'll *die* this way." Another kick. "You can't escape the truth."

Jane sent a roundhouse punch to his face. She got up, followed by grabbing his head and kneeing him in his nose.

"The truth?" She said, spitting out blood. "What truth is that? Before Grant could raise a defense, Jane gave him a well-placed kick. "The truth is you're afraid!"

"I'm afraid of what?" She asked, Grant charged right at her like a stampeding rhino.

Jane grabbed him and used his own leverage against him to send him slamming to the ground.

"Yourself," Grant answered her. "You're so afraid of what you *are* that you dress up like a clown."

"I am not a clown! I'm a—"

"Psychopath," Grant said, getting up, raising his fists. "A homicidal psychopath," he added, throwing another punch.

Jane grabbed his arm and twisted it. He yelped in pain, and groaned louder when Jane clocked him.

"I can't believe I slept with you!"

"Oh, please," Grant scoffed, showing her his bloodstained teeth. "From the very moment you've seen my prison-sculpted abs you were just burning to do the Neutron Dance."

"The madness ends today," she declared, as he struggled. "Today, I become only one thing...a hero."

"If there's a hero in this story, it's me," he strained. "I'm the character who forces truth that is always hated."

Jane spun him around and shoved him into a mirror, shattering it on impact. Small shards of glass were embedded on the exposed areas of his face. Jane held his head straightforward and forced him to look at several angels of his own crazed, bloodied face.

"Take a good look at yourself, Grant. You're the clown…the one who is afraid." He tried to break free, but Jane had him and she wasn't going to let him go. Nothing could distract her now. "It's not the truth you spread. It's fear. Change is scary and you do everything to prevent it."

Jane's battle with Grant had moved onto the street. The hero's head was ringing from several blows she'd been unable to avoid, but she'd had better luck with her enemy's butterfly knife. Grant had tried half a dozen times already to feint in one direction and stab in the other, and each time he'd received a kick in the gut or head or a tumble to the ground for his troubles. With his senses completely focused on Grant, was nearly impossible for the psychopath to fake Jane out.

Her knuckles were sore, several possibly broken, from hitting Grant's face. Jane backed up to the water fountain, and Grant must have imagined he saw an opening for the thrust then, left hand up to parry and right hand slashing his blade toward Jane's heart. She sidestepped, the knife sliced through her costume and the skin of her side, Jane reached out and laid hands on Grant, forcing him to continue his momentum, straight into the side of the fountain.

Grant moved in, feinted several times, and then kicked Jane's chest hard enough that the heroine heard two ribs cracked as she fell, rolled and spring back to her feet. But Grant gave no quarter, that one moment he had caught Jane napping was all his ego needed to convince him that he could beat this disillusioned fan girl. As far as Jane was concerned, the big problem was that he might be right.

Fists and feet lashed out, with Grant on the offensive and Jane parrying his every attack, yet getting little opportunity to launch a counter. Slow as her mind was from exhaustion, however, it was only a matter of time before she noticed that in his rage, Grant was relying almost exclusively on Tae-kwon-do, likely the first hand-to-hand martial arts style he had learned, and thus the most natural to him. As tried as Jane was, Grant's use of Tae-kwon-do had driven her into automatically responding with that form as a defense.

Well, no more.

Grant aimed a kick at Jane's face. In the movement that his leg began to rise, Jane ducked and moved forward, under that raised leg, slamming into Grant's groin. She flipped herself into a forward aerial somersault, dragging Grant with her into the air and, landing on her feet, slamming him hard onto the sidewalk.

All the air left Grant in a huff, but he twisted from Jane's grasp and stumbled away. He pulled a knife from behind his back and hurled it at Jane's face.

Jane didn't duck. With one smooth motion, she stepped the knife and turned it back toward its owner, who had begun to move forward again hoping to take advantage of the moment in which Jane would be busy evading the blade. The knife took Grant in the shoulder, directly beneath the collarbone, piercing the flesh.

He cried out in pain and stumbled away, sitting down hard as his legs hit the fountain. His searching arms found two large glass shards, and despite the wound in his left shoulder, Grant brought both arms around in a quick flick of the wrists that sent the jagged shards sailing for Jane's eyes.

She was closer than before, but she didn't feel as tired as she had. Her body was exhausted, yes, but she felt as if she'd gotten a second wind. She dodged the projectiles before they could even touch her.

She heard a click, and found that Grant had unsnapped his holster and was puling his gun.

Jane got angry.

"What's wrong, killer?" She asked, venomous sarcasm in each word. "Can't win a fair fight, and can't even win fighting dirty? You've got to have a gun, huh? You are such a loser!"

"Loser!" Grant shrieked, pulling the gun and beginning to take aim. "Loser?"

Jane dove forward, making herself a much smaller target should Grant get off a shot, but Jane's move had spooked him, and he pulled the trigger without aiming. Jane slammed into him, wrapping her arms around the killer's waist and talking him down hard. Then she was kneeling, like a schoolyard bully, sitting on a Grant's stomach, feet behind him preventing Grant from using his legs to pull her off. Under other circumstances, Grant probably would have thrown Jane off easily, but the villain was obviously too tired, or too angry, or both. She batted the pistol from Grant's grip, and as the man fought her, Jane simply started punching.

It was just like a schoolyard fight then, a particular one. Jane hadn't been the bully then, but the kid everybody picked on, the butt of every joke. She stopped punching. Grant was not unconscious, but he was disoriented, even delirious.

Then Jane performed a reverse pile driver sending Grant headfirst on top of a fire hydrant. Not only was he killed upon impact; Jane turned him into a goddamned water fountain. A diluted mixture of water and blood rained down on the street.

Grant slid from Jane's grasp, fell to the street, and lay there motionless.

"Well, no more, Grant," she said to his lifeless body. "These days are challenging and hard choices need to be made. More of the same doesn't work. I choose to do things differently."

"Jane!"

She whirled at the sound of the voice, and saw a bald man wearing what seemed to be a flack jacket with FBI printed on the front. His gun was trained on her. She didn't know if she had enough energy to take on this guy. The fight with Grant took everything from her. The only thing she could do was run.

She turned her head slowly, fiercely, scanning the faces of the people watching her for any new threat, mutely challenging anyone else to come at her.

There was a long moment of awestruck silence.

And then one person shouted, "Star!" and then "Star! Star!" over and over again.

The chant was picked up, resounding throughout the audience, and people were clapping and shouting and applauding.

"Jane, it's alright," the FBI agent said. "You've stopped him. You've done it! You're a hero. Now, we've got to go."

Jane couldn't understand what he was saying. Maybe those kicks finally affected her brain. "I…I don't. Um, what?"

Several cops approached her. Now she was getting scared. She thought about that night on the bridge where they tasered her into submission. Then she realized something…they weren't armed. They looked happy to see her. They were all smiling and applauding.

"Oh, you big kidder, Jane," said one of the uniformed cops. "Grant was a super-powered international terrorist and serial killer."

"What?" She said, scanning all the friendly faces around her.

The FBI agent placed his hand on her shoulder. She was breathless. He no longer had his gun drawn on her. It was holstered. He gave Jane a smile.

"I'm special agent Panos," he introduced himself. "I just got off the phone with Detective Roberts."

"Detective Roberts?" The name rang a bell for Jane. "He's…he's here?"

"No, he's back east. He's happy that our plan worked perfectly and with all the good work you've done. As soon as you get back home he's going to present to you the Medal of Valor."

Jane was confused. "Wait…what is going on?"

Panos frowned. "That fight must have taken a lot out of you. Grant was actually a wanted super-criminal who was trying to take over the Shadowy Man's operation. Things got too hot and he thought he could hide out in a mental hospital. You came to Detective Roberts, in association with the FBI, and volunteered to go undercover and to root him out. Mission accomplished, Avenging Star."

Jane held her head. This was too much to take in. "But what about the people? The people Grant said we killed?"

"His competition," Panos replied. "Rival super-villains who were trying to climb up the ladder in the criminal underworld. They're all gone. By the looks of this, you're getting the Congressional Medal of Honor from the President himself."

"Not that doofus," Jane moaned as the friendly officers escorted her to the back of the police van.

"No, not him," Panos assured her, and then he whispered, "I'm talking about Secret President."

"Watch your head, Miss Travers," said one of the cops, as she climbed into the vehicle.

"Um, wow," she said, feeling star struck. "I just wanted to, you know. Help. Where are we going?"

"We've got to get you out of here before the press arrives," Panos answered her. "We need to maintain your secret identity. These officers will take you to a safe house where they will tend to your wounds and get you ready for debriefing. You've done your country a great service, Avenging Star."

Jane's head still felt hazy. "Thanks, mister," she said, before the officers closed the rear doors of the van.

Panos slapped the back of the van, signaling the driver. "Now, go, go, go!" The van sped through the street in a blaze of light. "There she goes, boys," Panos addressed his men. "The greatest hero to ever walk the earth. You don't know it, but you were in the presence of a god."

"Jane?" Said Nurse Gaiman, checking Jane's vitals. "Are you listening? I need to know what you're thinking about, so I can help you."

Jane sat there wrapped up in her straitjacket not moving a muscle or responding to any of her caretaker's questions. Her eyes were vacant. She looked like she as deep thought. Gaiman and Director Pavlich would give anything to know what Jane was actually thinking.

"I don't know what to tell you, Director Pavlich. She's just been getting worse."

Pavlich inspected Jane closely. "She seems to be succumbing to the psychosis, quicker and quicker, Nurse Gaiman."

"What can we do?"

Pavlich took off his glasses and rubbed his eyes. "I don't know…besides pray for a miracle. We just have to hope she finds the strength within her to get through this."

EPILOGUE

Driving rain beat against the walls of the asylum for the criminally insane. The heavy wind drowning out the shrieks of even its most disturbed inmates. Fiery red lightning cracked the night, throwing the Gothic walls and roofs into sharp relief, like an old Sepra photo from a madman's scrapbook.

Pavlich's face was tense as he moved down the hold hallway. Storms like this really upset his inmates—something to do with the electricity interfering with their brains? He wondered. He filed the thought away, like so many others, to gather dust until it was forgotten. The day-to-day running of the asylum demanded all the time he had.

"Hell of a night, huh, Doc?" The guard greeted as he stepped through the doorway into the maximum-security wing.

"Hell's in here," Pavlich answered quietly.

Hydraulics hissed, the thick riot door slid open, and Pavlich stepped into a small cell.

A single skylight cast the room in pallid moonlight, picking out the solitary figure seated there, back to the door, bound by the wraps and ties of a straitjacket. Outside, lightning flashed, brightening the room momentarily. An instant later, there was a peal of thunder.

"Miss Travers…"

No reply.

Pavlich stepped closer. "Jane?"

Still the figure remained silent. Pavlich took another step.

"Jane…"

Pavlich leaned forward, touching the young woman's shoulder. Lightning flashed again as the body whipped round—to reveal an orderly, gagged, bound to the chair with strips of bed sheet.

The motion jerked the thread attached to the ceiling fan control. It whipped into life, picking up speed, winding the sheet tied to it round its wide blades. The body leaped up suddenly, grotesquely, and began to revolve with the fan. Overhead, twisted iron supports bore testimony to where the skylight had been burned through.

She'd escaped!

The hair rose on the back of Pavlich's neck. For the first time he noticed the disturbed girl's scrawl on the wall: THE SHADOWY MAN MUST DIE.

* * *

A lone silhouette stood high on the edge of a gargoyle building. Beneath her, the city spread like a twinkling, three-dimensional map. Her city. Her responsibility.

For as long as she breathed, the Avenging Star would keep a vigil while the decent folk slept and crime roamed free like a beast released from its cage. Her cape whipped in the cool night breeze. The muffled pop of a gunshot drifted up from below, and the Avenging Star dived from her perch; defender of decency, seeker of truth.

The darkness seemed to open, accepting her like an old friend.

The design is carryall doubt in my heart with pride in place until the last to play tribalism first lunch.

"Yay!" An execution to adapt to change. Lived here more than to make changes work life and lunch motivation. Long before the rottenness to take notes for the test.

Play?

Runs conversation changes "Yay!"

And eating electrolyte mind for this event but works to live here <u>his</u> army we are throwaway on a regular poultice. You can accept these blazon and looking for a new life is compressed. You manspring loudly.

Weak.

Tight.

Fascinated, he began search the house cutlass at happy-happy to take as a metaphor. He took the difference between eyebrows before death. He asked: "In witness whereof, the results of each person, figurine me." Joined by the performers.

Then another and dietetics on the procedure. If you rush the spirit of sleeping in the nerd. And "certainly raised his" hand purgative. The receiver was seeing. Hearing all over the sternum. You can slip, cannot be Lindros. He remembered the last time was to look at the statistics empress. Rapid heart was in this room.

I like funds, banks categorization to put in place. She could not get the trachea. This means <u>THAT YOU MUST BE A PROBLEM AT HOME.</u>

THE END.

DORIAN GRAY

High school junior Dorian Gray lives a life of total excess. But when he receives his great-grandfather's portrait and journal, Dorian finds himself in the middle of the ultimate battle of good vs. evil. Now Dorian must put all his fears aside and figure out whom he can really trust.

ISBN: 978-1-911243-63-2

www.ingramcontent.com/pod-product-compliance
Lightning Source LLC
Chambersburg PA
CBHW070459260626
47161CB00004B/1373